Tyson's han

It was the slighte

how to breathe as his lips brushed against hers.

She pressed her mouth to his, fully, sweetly and not so gently. He curled his large hand beneath her hair, angling her head so he might sample her lips fully.

He tasted like warmth, crackling fire and butterscotch schnapps. She couldn't stop tasting him.

A dam broke inside her, flooding her body so that the woods faded around them. All that existed was this man, this incredible man who did incredible things.

She'd never felt anything like it. Ever. And that was the most dangerous sensation of all.

Dear Reader,

I love second-chance stories—or in my heroine's case, third chance. Something about weary, beaten people finding love when they least expect it restores my faith in romance all over again. I've always believed when people stop wanting love badly or planning for love, it's sure to sneak up on them and grab them by the heart.

Dawn and Tyson are like so many couples in the world today. They each emerge scarred from divorce, so their conflicts with falling in love come from family, bad experiences and self-doubt. And let's be honest, is anything easy when teenagers are involved? But in the end love triumphs. Of course.

I hope you enjoy a trip back to Oak Stand, Texas. It's such a wonderful little town, and in this story I've got some octogenarians who will make you laugh. And, of course, you'll see Nellie and Jack again.

I would love to hear from my readers either by post at P.O. Box 5418, Bossier City, LA 71171 or through my website, www.liztalleybooks.com.

Happy reading!

Liz Talley

The Way to Texas
Liz Talley

HARLEQUIN®

TORONTO • NEW YORK • LONDON
AMSTERDAM • PARIS • SYDNEY • HAMBURG
STOCKHOLM • ATHENS • TOKYO • MILAN • MADRID
PRAGUE • WARSAW • BUDAPEST • AUCKLAND

Recycling programs
for this product may
not exist in your area.

ISBN-13: 978-0-373-71675-3

THE WAY TO TEXAS

ABOUT THE AUTHOR

From devouring the Harlequin Superromance books on the shelf of her aunt's used bookstore to swiping her grandmother's medical romances, Liz Talley has always loved a good romance novel. So it was no surprise to anyone when she started writing a book one day while her infant napped. She soon found writing more exciting than scrubbing hardened cereal off the love seat. Underneath her baby-food-stained clothes a dream stirred. Liz followed that dream and, after a foray into historical romance and a Golden Heart final, she started her contemporary romance on the same day she met her editor. Coincidence? She prefers to call it fate.

Currently Liz lives in north Louisiana with her high school sweetheart, two beautiful children and a menagerie of animals. Liz loves strawberries, fishing and retail therapy, and is always game for a spa day. When not writing contemporary romances for Harlequin Superromance, she can be found working in the flower bed, doing laundry or driving carpool.

Books by Liz Talley

HARLEQUIN SUPERROMANCE

This book is for my brothers, Matt and Blake.
Two guys who believe in happy endings and
always see the glass as half-full...just like Tyson.

It's also for my grandparents,
whose warm humor trickled down into all of us
and made hard times a bit softer.

And I can't forget my husband and boys—
you are my world.

CHAPTER ONE

IT'S A KNOWN FACT THAT when a woman can't find her day planner, all hell *will* break loose.

But as Dawn Taggart stamped the last of her paper work, she gave herself a mental pat on the back. No day planner. No problem.

Hell had been firmly contained.

"Here you go, busy bee. Have some homemade pound cake," her sister-in-law Nellie said, entering the small office off the kitchen. She placed a pretty filigree plate holding several pieces of cake on the desk.

"Nell, you really need to rest before the baby gets here." Dawn gave Nellie a firm look—the same look she'd given her very pregnant sister-in-law over the past several days. Of course, her stomach growled, ruining the reprimand.

Nellie shrugged. "Can't seem to rest. Guess I'm nesting."

"You think?" Dawn said, recalling the cranberry muffins Nellie had made earlier, not to mention all the polishing she'd done on the silver pieces displayed around the center.

Nellie dropped into the chair next to the desk, groaning as she supported her distended belly from underneath. "I'm just worried about the center. I know you can handle everything. It's been important to me, you know?"

Dawn picked up a piece of the still-warm cake. It would go straight to her thighs but was worth it. "We're going to be fine."

And they would. The huge Victorian Tucker House had belonged to Nellie's family for generations. When Nellie had married Dawn's brother, Jack, and moved out to the ranch, she'd converted the home into a much-needed senior center, designed to help families by caring for their elderly family members during the workday. The whole concept had been wildly successful.

When Nellie had learned she was pregnant, she'd asked Dawn to serve as temporary director for Tucker House. The situation proved fortuitous because Dawn not only needed a job, she also needed a break from life in Houston. A life that had made her vulnerable—a feeling she hated beyond all others.

"Ow!" Nellie said, rubbing her back.

"You okay?"

She shifted on the chair. "Yeah, just a backache I've been fighting all afternoon. It's killing me."

She had probably overdone it today. Jack had dropped her off early this morning and she'd worked steadily around the center, only stopping to play one game of canasta with a few clients. Way too much activity this close to her due date.

A thready voice interrupted from the open doorway. "Homer's not here yet."

The last client of the day, Aggie Richards, stood there, her bent form casting a long shadow on the polished wood floor of the hallway. Late-afternoon sun somersaulted through the leaded glass window and fell onto her housedress in whimsical patterns.

"Miss Aggie, I'm sure he'll be here soon," Nellie said, rubbing her back again.

"He had to go to Longview to get a part for that truck of his that's always breakin' down." The elderly lady's voice wavered as she fiddled with the buttons at her throat.

"He's running late," Dawn said, rising from her swivel chair and patting the elderly woman's shoulder. "Don't worry. We'll give him a call. If he got tied up, Nellie and I will run you by the salon on our way home."

"Pish," said Miss Aggie, waving a blue-veined hand in her direction. "I guess I can see myself home. Did it all my life, didn't I? Don't need to hassle with Judy. She's an imbecile."

Dawn bit her lip. She had to agree with Aggie. The elderly woman's daughter-in-law *was* an imbecile. "Why don't you sit and have a piece of Nellie's pound cake? I'll go call Homer."

Dawn slipped into the kitchen to use the phone, leaving the other two chatting about the merits of planting shrubs in the fall. She wanted another cup of coffee though her nerves still felt raw from an afternoon of wading through a mound of applications and permits, not to mention a surprise call from Larry the Snake, her ex. He'd miscalculated on his taxes the year before and wanted her advice. As always. The man wouldn't allow her to break all the ties between them, not that she could, since they shared a son. Still, his constant intrusion really got old.

So as soon as Miss Aggie left, she had a date with a glass of chardonnay and the bathtub.

As she grabbed the cordless phone, the color-coded calendar she kept on the bulletin board next to the butler's pantry caught her eye.

And that's when she saw it.

Highlighted in orange.

Tyson Hart. Tuesday: 5:30.

Nellie must have penciled the appointment in on the backup calendar. It hadn't been in the day planner Dawn had set on the counter but couldn't find that morning.

Damn.

Tyson Hart was the contractor Nellie insisted they hire to finish the upstairs of the center. She'd raved about Tyson all week. About the success of his business in Dallas. About his knowledge. His skill. His broad shoulders and whiskey-colored eyes. The last two attributes had Dawn worried. She didn't need Nellie trying to match her up with random guys no matter what color their eyes were. Presently the romantic part of her life was closed for reconstruction. C-L-O-S-E-D. As in the last thing she needed was another guy to deal with. Between her brother, son, ex-husband and the elderly men at the center, she had plenty of testosterone to juggle, thank you very much.

Still, another one was about to invade whether she wanted him to or not. And he'd do it, according to the microwave clock, in fifteen minutes.

No bath. No wine. No rest for the weary. Double damn.

She shut down her whiny thoughts as a knock sounded on the back door. Big Bubba Malone poked his head in.

"Hey, I smell somethin' good."

Though Bubba was another man to deal with, Dawn couldn't stop the smile that crept to her lips. After all, very few people could resist smiling at Bubba. "Hey, Bubba. Nellie baked a pound cake."

"So I smelled from the drive," he said, stepping into the roomy kitchen. His affable smile offset the hulking shoulders, unlaced work boots and meaty paws. He was a mountain of a redneck with a heaping side of good ol' boy.

"Well, help yourself. Coffee, too, if you want," Dawn said, tapping the schedule with one of the highlighters attached by a brightly colored ribbon, wishing the appointment would magically vanish from the box in which it had been written. "Nellie's in the office with Miss Aggie if you want to say hello."

"Actually, I come to fetch Miss Aggie. Homer called me and he's runnin' late. I'm gonna run her over to Judy, whose doin' something to Betty Monk's hair though I can't imagine what—she ain't got as much as me," he said, cramming a piece of pound cake in his mouth. Crumbs fell onto the tiled floor. Like a typical man, Bubba didn't see them. Or he pretended he didn't see them.

"Well, she's not going to want to go to the Curlique, but I can't worry about that now. I have an appointment with a contractor." Dawn set the cordless phone in the cradle.

"Tyson Hart, huh? Knew him back in the day. He's solid." Bubba poured a cup of coffee and gulped it down like mother's milk. He drank his Budweiser the same way. Cold. Hot. Didn't seem to matter to Bubba.

"Yeah, well at least it's not Brent Hamilton."

Bubba laughed. The sound reminded her of rusty stovepipes. "Yeah, Ol' Brent's good at his job, but he's a horn dog. Tyson ain't thick-headed like that."

Horn dog was right. Brent Hamilton, the contractor who'd added safety rails and ramps to the lower floor a few months ago, figured himself to be Oak Stand's answer to stud muffin extraordinaire. Good looking enough to qualify, the man romanced everything in a skirt. Or shorts. Or jeans. And if Dawn hadn't vowed to stay away from all men, she might have been tempted. But, the past year had proven what she'd suspected all along. She was bad at picking men. And she wasn't ready to sacrifice herself upon that painful altar again. At least not until she found direction in her life.

So Tyson Hart had better not follow in Brent's footsteps.

Bubba stomped off toward the office, and even though she didn't need another cup of coffee, Dawn refilled her mug. After adding some flavored creamer and a package of pink artificial sweetener that she knew probably caused brain cancer, she took a sip and sighed. Mmm. Good. She propped one hip on the gleaming granite countertop and drank almost the whole cup.

Bubba lumbered into the kitchen with Miss Aggie on his arm. "Alrighty, I'm takin' this pretty lady home with me," he said winking at Dawn. "Don't wait up on her."

Miss Aggie beamed and punched Bubba on his beefy biceps. "You do know how to make a girl feel special."

"It's what my momma always said." Bubba's smile held firm, but his eyes flashed with pain. Bubba had lost his mother to cancer only four months before. Wilma "Willie" Malone had been the inspiration for Tucker House. The idea for a senior care center had bloomed after Nellie had cared for Miss Willie while Bubba worked. All of Oak Stand seemed to feel the absence of the courageous woman who'd made them laugh with her wry sense of humor and lightning-quick wit.

"And Willie was a smart woman," Miss Aggie said, patting Bubba's arm this time. She unclasped her purse, pulled a wadded pink tissue from the depths and wiped her eyes. "I do miss her."

"We all do," Nellie said from the doorway of the kitchen.

Nellie's eyes met Bubba's, and they both smiled. The small-town oil heiress and the backwater redneck. Go figure. There couldn't have been a more unlikely pair of friends in all of Howard County, Texas.

"Later, ladies," Bubba called, opening the door for Miss Aggie and helping her down the back steps.

"Bye, Bubba," Dawn said, finishing off the last of her coffee. She eyed the carafe, wondering if she should have a third cup or not. Something more to fortify her for a late afternoon appointment with a contractor who would want to show her blueprints and codes and whatever else contractors liked to talk about. But she didn't need more, so she dropped the mug into the empty sink.

"Ready to meet with Tyson?" Nellie said, as she sank into one of the overstuffed chairs in the sitting area of the kitchen.

"I guess." Dawn sighed, pressing a hand over the yawn that appeared from nowhere. "I still think we should put off construction. With the baby due in a couple of weeks, there's too much going on."

"The center can still function with ongoing construction. We need the room so we can meet the demand. We have a waiting list."

"I hate you're going through all this trouble. The rooms above us are perfectly functional. They need some refurbishment, that's all."

Nellie shifted in her chair. "We need a kitchen upstairs and an up-to-code bathroom. The rooms need to be gutted and converted to smaller rooms for resting. Now is the time. I know this is temporary for you, but eventually someone else will step in as the director and I want Tucker House to be fully operational."

Dawn's heart trembled at those words. She'd taken this job when she'd been forced to close the doors of her antiques redesign shop in Houston last spring. The damn economy had stomped her dream to dust, and with her son, Andrew, on partial baseball scholarship at the University of Houston, she needed money. Tucker House had opened for business a mere two months ago under her direction. She'd told Nellie she'd stay for a year, no more.

But she had no idea what she would do when the year was up. She'd leased her house in Houston to an oil and gas consultant whose rent covered her mortgage. But she had no leads on a job, no idea what she wanted to do. Didn't know if she even wanted to go back to Houston. Currently she floated with no tangible future to grab on to. And she couldn't stand not knowing what direction she should take. She needed a plan.

Nellie bit her lip. "Ouch."

Dawn dropped all thoughts of her own problems. "You're not in labor, are you?"

Nellie shook her head, causing a chunk of caramel-colored hair to fall from her hair clip. Her emerald eyes held unease. "I've still got two weeks left. Just a back-ache. I think."

"Maybe we'd better call Jack." Dawn reached for the cordless phone.

Her sister-in-law waved a hand. "Don't bother him. I saw my OB yesterday. He said I'm on schedule for October 23."

"I don't know, Nell. Babies set their own schedule." The doorbell rang interrupting her lecture.

Dawn's gaze skittered to the clock. 5:25 p.m.

Tyson Hart wasn't just prompt. He was early.

Nellie waved a hand at her. "Tyson's here. Go let him in. I'll be okay."

Dawn wasn't so sure, but the bell sounded again. "Fine. You sit and I'll handle this. We'll call Jack after I cancel the appointment with Mr. Hart."

"Don't cancel," Nellie called as Dawn left the kitchen.

She walked through the living area, which was neat except for a deck of cards left on one of the small tables and a sudoku puzzle book on the other. In the media room someone had left the Wii on. Dawn made a mental list to make sure everything was turned off and put away before they left for the evening.

The doorbell sounded once more.

Dawn released a pent-up breath and pulled open the door.

No one was there.

For a minute, she was confused. Then she looked down.

Hunter Todd.

"Hey, is Nellie here? She said she bought me some of those ice cream bars with sprinkles."

"Ice cream with sprinkles?" Normally Dawn loved having the irascible six-year-old who lived next door visit, but she didn't feel like entertaining him today. "I don't know, Hunter Todd. Nellie's not feeling well, and I'm waiting on someone, so—"

"That's okay. I know where she keeps 'em." Hunter Todd shoved his pudgy little body between her and the door, slipping inside quicker than a cat with a dog on its paws.

"Hunter Todd, please, honey. It's not a good day for a visit." Her plea went unanswered. She leaned her head against the door and closed her eyes.

"Bad day?"

Dawn jumped about a foot. "Oh, my God!"

She turned and met another dancing pair of eyes. These were the color of amber glass. Or sparkling brown topaz. Or aged honey. And they were attached to the most compelling man Dawn had seen in ages.

He filled the doorway and everything about him reminded her of warmth. From his ruffled sun-streaked brown hair to his lime-green-and-black running shoes. A smile curved his lips, lips that made her think of things she was supposed to have put behind her. At once it struck her—this man was dangerous in that golden retriever, scratch behind the ears sort of way. He looked affable and harmless. Like a woman could take him home. But Dawn had been bitten not once, but twice. She wasn't picking up his leash.

"Sorry. I didn't mean to scare you," he said, stretching out an arm. "I'm Tyson Hart, and I think this is where I am supposed to be."

Dawn met his hand with hers. His grip warmed her to her toes and made her feel like a gangly teenager. "Hi. Dawn Taggart, the director. Nellie's sister-in-law."

"Nice to meet you, Dawn."

For a moment, she stood there stupidly, her hand still in his. Then she came to her senses and pulled it away. "Well, come on in."

Tyson stepped inside the foyer as Nellie waddled around the corner with Hunter Todd on her heels. The six-year-old held a huge ice cream bar, which didn't prevent him from lifting the cover of the antique piano in the parlor and plinking a few keys. Sprinkles from the treat fell to the polished floor.

"Tyson," Nellie said, a warm smile curving her lips.

"Nellie," Tyson replied, his voice as smooth as Scotch and likely just as addictive. "So good to see you again. It's been ages."

Dawn tore her eyes from Hunter Todd and his shedding ice cream and looked at Tyson, which in itself was a treat. The man was abnormally good looking in a not so obvious way. More of a rugged, cigarette ad way. *Careful,* her mind said, crushing what her libido said, which was something like, *wrap your legs around that.*

Nellie rubbed her back. Another grimace moved across her face. "I'm so glad you're back in Oak Stand. And you're perfect for this job. Quick. Good. And available."

Tyson grinned and little crinkles appeared at the corners of his incredible eyes. "I bet you say that to all the contractors you meet."

He winked at Dawn and she couldn't stop the silly blush she felt burn her cheeks. Damn. He was everything she needed to stay away from. Good-looking men were like her personal crack—a dangerous addiction that left her strung out and broken.

Nellie laughed then winced. "Sorry, guys, but I'm going to have to sit this construction talk out. Go on up and check out the space. Hunter Todd said he'd swing me on the porch swing."

At the sound of his name, Hunter Todd banged the lid on the piano and took off, circling Nellie and making weird noises. She bit her bottom lip and closed her eyes.

Even Tyson looked concerned.

"I don't think I better leave you right now." Dawn ran her damp palms down the sides of her khaki crop pants. A strange sense of foreboding welled within her, and Hunter Todd pretending to be a screeching jumbo jet wasn't helping matters. She pushed her hair over her shoulders and turned to Tyson.

"Mr. Hart, I know you drove all this way, but I'm not sure this is a good time to meet."

Tyson opened his mouth to speak, but Hunter Todd took that moment to shove past them. A trail of ice cream followed him as he circled her and Tyson.

Dawn let out an exasperated breath. She didn't want to have this stupid meeting in the first place. And now she looked totally unprofessional with chaos prevailing all around her. The man probably thought he'd stepped into a care center for the insane rather than the elderly. She had to get control of the situation. "Hunter Todd, enough! Go sit on the swing and stop yelling."

She propped her hands on her hips and tried to look as though the noise the child made had not accelerated the throbbing in her temples. A whopper of a headache was coming on. No doubt about it.

The boy skidded to a halt and turned an injured expression upon her. "I'm just playing Transformers. I'm Megatron. He's a Decepticon."

Dawn tempered her reprimand with a small smile. "I appreciate your ability to sound like a real…robot machine airplane, but Nellie doesn't feel well. You need to be a good boy. Go sit and finish your ice cream."

"Megatron's not an airplane," Hunter Todd said, licking the dripping bar. "He's a— Hey, Nellie, you're peeing on yourself."

"What?" Nellie said, looking down, her eyes growing wide as reality set in. "Oh, crap! My water broke!"

Hunter Todd took another lick of his ice cream bar. "*Crap* is a bad word."

And that was when it hit Dawn.

Hell had broken loose after all.

CHAPTER TWO

TYSON TOOK TWO STEPS back and hit the doorjamb. Pregnant women made him uncomfortable. Pregnant women who sprang leaks made him want to run and forget about the contracting job.

And he needed this job. Not so much for the money, but for what it would do for him. Re-establish him within the community. Give him ties to Oak Stand. Give him a home for his daughter, Laurel.

So he didn't run. Besides that would be pretty chicken shit of him. He'd faced armored tanks and grenade-tossing insurgents in Iraq. Surely, he could deal with a woman in labor.

He stepped forward and attempted a calming smile. He'd been through this before. Kinda. "No big deal, Nellie. Women have babies every day."

"Have babies?" Her voice sounded panicky. She looked at her sister-in-law. "Today?"

Dawn nodded. He got the feeling Nellie's sister-in-law was the right person to handle a crisis. That impression likely had something to do with the lift of her chin and the squaring of her slim shoulders. "Just let me call Jack and we'll head to the hospital."

Dawn turned and ushered the boy from the house. "Okay, Hunter Todd, go finish your treat on your own porch. We've got to get Nellie to the hospital."

"You mean, she's havin' the baby today?" he asked, not missing a lick.

Dawn sounded agitated as she placed her hand between his shoulder blades and steered him toward the open door. "Maybe. Probably. But you have to go home now."

Once the child disappeared, Dawn spun around and walked toward the kitchen. Nellie still seemed freaked out, so he smiled again and tried not to let his discomfort show.

Dawn returned in less than five seconds with several towels which she handed to him.

"Do me a favor and wipe up the floor." She didn't wait for an answer, just pulled her cell phone from her pocket.

Tyson looked at the floral towels which had seen better days but smelled April fresh. Then he glanced at Nellie's feet. He'd cleaned up worse. Surely.

Poor Nellie stood frozen, her eyes misty and wide. "Today?" she said again.

"Don't worry, Nellie." He grasped her elbow and helped her step from the puddle.

She took a small step then clutched her stomach. *"Ow!"*

Something in the air felt wrong. He'd always had a sixth sense about calamity. In fact, such a premonition had saved his life in Baghdad. He looked over at Dawn, but the only visible sign of distress she showed was one slender foot tapping on the floor. After a moment, she pulled the phone from her ear and glared at it. "Not answering. That figures. The most important day of his life, and the dumb a—" Her mouth snapped shut, and she seemed to regroup.

"No problem," Dawn said, as he dropped a towel on

the floor and moved it around with his foot. "I'll get my car. We'll call him on the way. The doctor, too."

Nellie clutched her stomach again. "Ow. This really hurts."

"Oh, no." A horrified expression appeared on Dawn's face. "My car's at the garage getting new brakes. It won't be ready till tomorrow. Jack was going to pick us up today."

Nellie groaned again calling his attention to where she was holding on to the arm of the old-fashioned-looking sofa.

"Maybe you better sit down, Nellie," he said, pausing in his cleaning.

Nellie lowered herself onto the couch before popping up again. "Wait, give me a towel. I don't want to ruin the couch. Dawn just reupholstered it."

Dawn's head snapped up. "Are you serious? You think I care about the stupid couch? Because I don't. You're in freaking labor. You don't have a bag packed and I haven't finished the quilt for the nursery. And my stupid brother isn't answering his phone. And we have no way to get to the hospital, which is not exactly down the road. So, please, sit on the couch."

Time to do something more than play cleaning lady. Even if it meant he'd be too late to catch a movie with Laurel. "No problem. Let me pull my truck into the drive and then we'll be on our way."

"But the hospital's almost thirty miles away," Dawn said, abandoning her irritation and pushing her long dark hair from her face. She moistened her bottom lip, a very sensual movement he didn't fail to notice even though they were in full-on crisis mode.

"I've been known to drive such distances before." He smiled at Nellie, trying to do his best to reassure his longtime friend. Mild terror had taken its place upon her face.

"What about Bubba? Maybe he can take us," Nellie said, crossing her feet ladylike as she perched on the edge of the couch. "I mean, I hate to put you out, Tyson. You came for a meeting not a...birth."

"Are you kidding?" Dawn said, her brown sandals clacking on the floor as she approached her sister-in-law. She pushed Nellie's hair off her forehead and patted her shoulder. "Mr. Hart doesn't care about the meeting right now. We've got a baby on the way, and even if the first one usually takes a while, we need to get you to the hospital now. So, on your feet. We're taking Mr. Hart up on his offer."

"Tyson," he said.

Her gaze found his. "What?"

"Call me Tyson," he said, taking Nellie's elbow and helping her toward the entrance. The bevel-paned door was still ajar from Hunter Todd's hasty departure. As they passed it, Nellie grabbed it, bent over and groaned.

Tyson mouthed one word at Dawn. "Hurry."

TYSON TRIED TO FOCUS on Highway 80, but it was hard to do with Dawn's light floral scent filling his nose and her nicely rounded butt sliding against his thigh. Which should not have mattered since Nellie was in full-blown labor. But he couldn't help noticing. After all, he was a man.

He also couldn't stop himself from glancing at the clock on the console. Nellie's contractions were coming too fast to still be ten miles from the hospital.

Every few seconds or so, Dawn's chocolaty brown eyes would meet his and a clear message was sent.

Something was wrong. Tyson felt it in his gut as certain as Sunday. He was afraid he'd have to pull the ten-year-old pickup truck to the side of the highway so Dawn could catch her new nephew as he made his debut into the world.

And that would suck.

Not just for obvious reasons, but because they hadn't been able to get in touch with Nellie's husband. Tyson believed every man deserved to witness the miracle of his child being born. It had been the best memory of his life—one of those moments that could not be re-created in any way. So precious was the first breath his daughter took. So treasured the initial high-pitched cry. And Tyson wasn't the sentimental type of guy. Okay, he was. His hands were calloused, his shoulders broad enough for burdens, but his heart was s'more-worthy. As in a big ol' marshmallow.

He wanted Jack to be there to see his son seize life—not the glorified handyman.

"It's okay, Nellie. Don't push. Whatever you do, don't push," Dawn said squeezing her sister-in-law's hand while shoving several tendrils of hair out of her own eyes. Tyson noticed her hair seemed to get in the way a lot. He wished he had a rubber band. At least he would be doing something helpful, something more than keeping the truck between the mustard and the mayonnaise.

"I…can't…help…it," Nellie panted, "I want to get it out of me."

Tyson risked a glance at the two women. Dawn had Nellie's chin in her hand, trying to direct Nellie's eyes to hers. "Look at me. Don't push. Deep breaths only. Focus."

He directed his attention to the patched highway as

Nellie panted like a wounded animal. About fifty yards ahead was a green sign listing mileage. Longview was only five miles away. He knew firsthand the hospital was in the middle of town. He'd been stitched up there several times during his dirt-bike-racing days as a teen. He'd have to navigate late-afternoon traffic.

"Oh, God, something's wrong, Dawn. Something's wrong," Nellie moaned. Her arms locked against the dash of his truck and her frantic breaths sounded louder than any he'd ever heard. It scared him shitless, but he didn't want her to know.

"Just a few more miles, Nellie," he said, angling the air-conditioner vent toward her. Sweat streamed down her face.

Dawn cajoled, murmuring encouraging words as she wiped Nellie's brow with some napkins from McDonald's she'd found in his glove box.

After minutes of passing hilly Texas countryside, Tyson saw the first smattering of Longview businesses—a gas station, a place with shiny tractors out front and a fast-food restaurant. Reaching the edge of town didn't help his anxiety level because as they passed the city-limit sign, his passenger screamed, "Oh, my God! It's ripping me apart."

Tyson pressed the accelerator all the way to the floorboard when he saw Nellie's knees spring into the air. The old truck leaped forward as the cell phone sitting on the dashboard rang.

Dawn looked busy. He didn't really want to know what she was doing, since all he could see was Nellie's white thigh. He heard Dawn chant "Oh, shit…oh, shit… oh, shit," so he grabbed the phone and flipped it open.

"Hey, sis, what's going on? You sounded weird."

"Uh, Jack, this is—"

"Who's this?" the voice erupted from the phone.

"Listen. This is Tyson Hart—"

"Who? Where's my sister?"

"Shut up," Tyson growled into the phone, as Nellie let out another screech. "I'm driving your wife to the hospital. Get in your vehicle and get your ass to Longview. Now."

Tyson clicked the phone shut because a red light was about fifty yards in front of him. The truck swerved over the center lane as Dawn's round butt connected with his arm, and he threw the phone onto the dashboard then applied the brakes.

"Almost there. Jack's on his way."

"Hear that, Nellie?" Dawn's voice sounded soothing, "Jack is on his way and we're here. You're doing great, honey. Just hold on a little longer."

The litany of her voice calmed him. And he felt as twitchy as a man who'd been in lockdown for a month. He searched for a hospital sign, but all he saw were blinking signs advertising pawnshops and Laundromats. Finally he found the blue H symbol and followed the arrow toward 259 North.

More panting, more cursing and more sweating ensued before the three-story white rectangle emerged on the horizon like the Holy Grail of hospitals. Tyson hit the emergency-room drive like a race car driver hit the pit. He likely left two long tire marks when he skidded to a halt.

"Go get somebody," Dawn said, sliding herself nearly across his lap as she turned around in the seat toward Nellie. She didn't have to tell him twice. Nellie's knees were bent and her skirt hiked high.

A woman in scrubs met him at the swooshing doors.

Her face held a mixture of annoyance and concern. She held an unsmoked cigarette in her hand.

"I need a stretcher or wheelchair," he said, looking over her head at the open entrance. "If you don't hurry, she's going to have that baby in my pickup."

The woman sprang into action, first pocketing her cigarette, next calling into the doorway, "Cheryl!"

For a moment, Tyson simply stood and took a deep breath, taking in the aroma of hot asphalt and burning leaves. He wanted to reach into the nurse's pocket and grab her cigarette and fire it up. But he had quit smoking when he'd quit drinking the hard stuff.

Another woman in scrubs appeared with a stretcher. She rolled it toward his truck, lowered it in one movement, then helped the other woman ease Nellie onto it. Dawn held her sister-in-law's shoulders and still talked soothingly into her ear. Nellie's face was streaked with tears. His eyes held her face because he would not, could not look down at where her knees still seemed to be parted.

One of the nurses pulled a sheet over Nellie's knees and he blew out a sigh of relief.

They rolled past him and Dawn caught his eye. "I'm going with her. Will you stay and bring Jack when he gets here?"

He nodded and, oddly enough, her shoulders sank with what he imagined to be relief. "Let me park the truck and I'll be right in."

He watched for a moment as she followed the stretcher into the E.R. Her silk blouse clung to her back and her once crisp pants held more wrinkles than an old circus elephant. But something about Dawn made him want to take a deep breath, one of those deep cleansing breaths that chased away shadows and cobwebs.

Then again, something about her made him want to sink into her, claim her as his own. A visceral, animalistic reaction—one he'd not had in a while. Her long tan arms and dark tresses were made for wrapping round a man, and her soulful dark eyes hinted at a sensuality he wanted to explore.

Which was a bad idea all around.

He was in Oak Stand to start a new life. After a rotten marriage and a rocky relationship with his daughter, he needed a clean slate. No need to muddy things by lusting after the sexiest thing he'd seen in months. That would be beyond stupid.

Tyson climbed into his old pickup, noting that the Texas dust made his truck's silver paint look dirty gray. A few empty coffee cups from a gas station still sat in the cupholders and he needed to sweep out the gum wrappers that had fallen to the dusty floormats. Thank God, Nellie hadn't had her baby in here.

He parked near a group of medical offices and headed toward the hospital. Just as he crossed the landscaped path two things happened.

First, Dawn emerged from the open E.R., her smile radiant, her eyes dancing. She opened her mouth and yelled, "It's a girl!"

Second, a huge F250 roared into the parking lot with a Longview police cruiser following. Blue lights flashed, tires squealed and a disheveled dark-haired man sprang from the truck and flew toward the E.R.

Jack Darby had finally reached Longview.

In record time, no doubt.

CHAPTER THREE

Dawn watched as Nellie stroked the face of her new-born daughter and remembered the first time she'd held her own son. Only a little fuzzy hair was visible above the tightly bound blanket.

"Can you believe it's a girl?" Nellie said, smiling serenely, not taking her eyes from the bundle in her arms. She softened her voice and murmured to the baby. "And all this time we were calling you a boy. So sorry, sweet girl."

Dawn smiled at her sister-in-law, feeling both incred-ibly happy and exhausted. Amazingly, her headache had disappeared. "I can't believe a lot of things that happened today."

Jack rubbed a hand over his face as he peered at Nellie and the baby. "You think she's going to cause this sort of a ruckus all the time?"

Jack seemed to have permanent shock etched on his face, and she wondered if he might have acquired a few gray hairs over the past hour. It would serve her too-handsome brother right. With Nellie having been so close to her due date, the man should have had his cell phone plastered to his hand. Instead he'd left it in his truck. Luckily, he'd been at a farm just outside Longview when he'd found out Nellie was en route to the hospital.

"No," Dawn said, walking over to the stretcher. She

looked down at the red-faced baby sleeping peacefully after her traumatic entry into the world. "She's going to be the sun rising and setting for you, little brother."

Jack's face emoted into pure love. "For once, I won't argue with you."

Dawn gave her brother a good-natured punch on his arm and looked over to where Tyson stood by the emergency-room curtain. The man didn't look comfortable, but he didn't seem particularly uncomfortable, either. She wondered why she had wanted him to stay. She could have handled everything by herself. But something about Tyson seemed rock-steady and for a few moments, she'd needed his strength.

"Hey, Tyson, let me buy you a cup of coffee." She at least owed him that. The man had gone above and beyond. Besides, the hospital staff was about to move Nellie to a private room and Dawn could really use a break.

Tyson glanced at Nellie. "Sure. I could use a good cup of coffee. Jack?"

But neither Jack nor Nellie paid the least attention to anything other than their baby, lost in the little world they had created.

Dawn's heart pinged.

She glanced back at Tyson and his eyes met hers. He felt the poignancy of the moment, too. She jerked her head toward the exit.

They slipped from the emergency room and headed toward the cafeteria. Her sandals clacked on the polished hospital floor, echoing down the corridor. The sound seemed to heighten the silence between them.

She searched for something to say, but words wouldn't come. The adrenaline that had surged through her body during the past few hours had deserted her, leaving her limbs feeling shaky. She needed to sit down, have something to drink and force her body to relax.

They reached the cafeteria and Tyson frowned at the door.

"What?" Dawn said.

"Closed five minutes ago."

Dawn sighed. "Well, maybe there's a soda machine. I could use a shot of something."

"If I remember correctly, we passed a Starbucks when we got off 259. Let's grab a cup there."

Dawn wavered. She didn't want to leave the hospital. Nellie and Jack might need her help as they got settled in a room. She hadn't been able to complete any paperwork and wasn't sure where she'd put Jack's insurance card.

"Listen, they're not going to even notice you're gone. She's got to be moved to a room, and in my experience that always takes a while. We'll get coffee and pick up a few things for Nellie, like a toothbrush and something to change into." Tyson took her elbow and guided her toward the entrance. Obviously, the man wasn't going to wait for her to argue.

And she had no real reason to fight against his suggestion, so she allowed herself to be pulled toward the double glass doors. His hand on her bare arm felt nice— warm on skin that had grown cold in the hospital's overzealous air-conditioning. But what was even nicer was the thoughtfulness he displayed. Most men wouldn't have bothered to think about Nellie's needs. Still, that didn't mean Tyson was even on her "guy" radar.

He so wasn't.

They stepped into the glow of the evening as an ambulance came screeching around the corner, lights flashing and siren wailing. Tyson stiffened and dropped her arm. His eyes met hers and something dark flashed within.

"You okay?" she asked.

"Yeah, fine," he said, stepping onto the flagstone path leading to the parking lot. "I served a tour in Iraq with the National Guard. The sound of an ambulance always does that to me. Police sirens, too."

"Oh," Dawn said, tracing his footsteps. She didn't know whether his statement invited further questions or not. Many veterans of the wars in Iraq and Afghanistan were tight-lipped about what they experienced in the deserts and mountains overseas. She wasn't sure it was good they didn't talk about their experiences, but she understood not wanting to relive an awful time. It was human nature, plain and simple.

"Not that the sirens sound like the ones I heard. Just reminds me of things I'd rather forget," he said, digging into his pocket for his keys. She watched his broad shoulders ripple with the motion. He was tall, slightly taller than her brother, but his breadth made him seem much larger.

She couldn't stop herself from asking the question. "Were you injured?"

Silence swelled between them before he said, "Only slightly. I took a bit of shrapnel in my shoulder. I was one of the lucky ones."

Which Dawn took to imply that there were others in his unit who were not so fortunate. Damn. This man had been injured in places no one could see. That much was evident to her. She decided not to pursue the conversation any further until they knew each other better. *If* they got to know each other better.

"I'm glad you weren't hurt too badly," she said as

they reached the truck. "Now, which way to Starbucks? I seriously need a shot of espresso."

He unlocked his door and climbed inside, popping the lock on her side of the truck. "Sorry, I should've opened the door for you."

Dawn shrugged. "It's not a date."

"Right," he said, shoving the key into the ignition.

Dawn slid into the sun-warmed interior, aware for the first time how much the cab smelled of him. There were no greasy bags of food on the floor or flyers peppering the dash like in so many guys' trucks. It was virtually clean except for two disposable coffee cups sitting in the cup holders and a few gum wrappers. She inhaled the scent of sandalwood, so manly and so unlike the ocean-breeze scent she had in her own car.

They rode in silence, and seeing the familiar sign, Tyson pulled into a parking spot outside the door. When Dawn entered the café, she felt calm for the first time that day. Something about the familiarity, the jazz flooding the speakers and the half-burned smell of espresso soothed away the anxiety of the past few hours.

She sighed and allowed her shoulders to relax.

"Right choice, I can see," Tyson said in her ear.

She started at his voice so close behind her. His baritone sounded as warm as he seemed. In fact, everything about him radiated warmth. Honey hair, honey smile, honeyed words. For a moment, she longed to lean against him and to feel his solid body against her. She knew how he'd feel—hard and good. She took a teensy step back before she caught herself and moved toward the Order Here sign.

"Absolutely," she murmured, perusing the menu board above the barista who was busy steaming milk. Dawn ordered a café americano with an extra shot and a low-fat blueberry muffin then gestured for Tyson to order. "Go ahead. I'm buying."

He shook his head.

"I insist," she said, before realizing she couldn't pay. She'd left Oak Stand without her purse. "Uh, wait. In all the hubbub, I left my purse." She felt stupid. How could it have slipped her mind she didn't have money? She hated that feeling. Being so out of control. At someone else's mercy.

"Don't worry," he said, sliding a credit card from his wallet and ordering a black coffee. "And don't think I won't take you up on owing me. I'm pretty partial to a good caffeine fix."

Dawn gave him a sheepish smile and found a small table near the window. She sank into the straight-backed chair and sighed. Sitting there felt like heaven. A minute later, Tyson set her drink and muffin in front of her. She took a sip and closed her eyes.

"So that's what it takes to make a woman sigh like that. I've been doing it all wrong," Tyson said, as he sat.

Dawn opened one eye. Was he flirting? He struck her as more the easygoing than flirty type. But every guy had a little flirt in him, though Tyson didn't seem to need it. His smiles were so delectable, they made her toes curl.

Stop, she told herself. "Yep, just give a girl a delicious cup of coffee. Now that you know the secret, you can't tell."

"I feel privileged."

A comfortable silence fell between them. The café wasn't particularly busy at the moment. No doubt business would pick up as couples stopped by for after-movie lattes and teens gathered for legal stimulants. Dawn missed this aspect of city living.

"So about the job, I think it's pretty much yours." In all the chaos, they hadn't had the opportunity to talk about the center. "When Nellie heard you were moving back and starting a contracting business, she'd already signed you up in her head. It's a safe bet she'll hire the dude who rushed her to the hospital and spared her delivering her firstborn on the front steps."

Tyson smiled. "I won't hold you to that."

"But you do want the job?"

He took a swallow of coffee and the muscles in his neck rippled, drawing her attention to the opening of the polo shirt he wore. It was mossy green with a red crawfish on the left breast, and the rich color heightened his amber eyes. "I want the job."

"Good," she said, tearing her eyes from assessing the breadth of his shoulders. "I have a few things I'd like to suggest in remodeling the space."

"Shoot," he said, leaning forward, resting his forearms on the table. At that moment, she didn't think she'd ever seen a man look so intense and yummy at the same time. The attraction hit her like a triple-shot espresso.

She ignored the sudden spike in her internal temperature. "Currently there are five bedrooms and two bathrooms. I think we can make a general gathering place from three of the bedrooms and one of the baths. I only want to take up half of the floor space. I like the idea of other rooms being available for clients who need rest or aren't feeling too well. We don't really have those capabilities on the first floor."

"Well, it's hard for me to judge without looking, but I'll keep your wishes in mind. It's been a while since I've taken on a remodel. I've been designing and building entire subdivisions for the past few years. But, I got my start doing remodeling jobs in college, so it'll come back. Let me look at the space and the blueprints."

She frowned. "I didn't think about blueprints. Nellie would have those. No doubt they're locked in a safe-deposit box at Oak Stand National."

"You want to commit to a time for meeting and reviewing the structure?"

Dawn tried to picture the calendar in her planner, but her brain felt fuzzy. The planner was her secret crutch, a concrete guideline to keep herself straight and from feeling as though she'd fall apart. Without it, she couldn't remember. A bazaar was coming up one Saturday in October, but she couldn't recall which day they'd picked. "I don't have my calendar with me, and I'm sure Nellie will need a little help. But I think it's safe to meet next Saturday afternoon."

"Saturday it is," he said, draining the last of his drink. "I have a few things to finish at Sammy Bennett's place anyway. If you can send the plans to me before then, I'll get something rudimentary drawn up for a starting point."

Dawn nodded and mentally highlighted next Saturday, praying she'd remember it. She popped the last of her blueberry muffin into her mouth, took one more swig of her coffee, then pushed back her chair. "I'd like to pick up a few things for Nellie but I'm afraid I'd need to borrow the money. I'll make sure you get reimbursed."

"No problem," he said, rising and stretching. Again, she watched each movement. Damn. Why did the contractor have to be so hunky? She didn't entirely trust herself to resist this kind of temptation.

"Are you sure?" she stammered, trying to direct her

thoughts to her sister-in-law, who was stranded without even a toothbrush.

"Absolutely," he said, tossing his cup in the trash can beside the door. "I saw a Wal-Mart across the highway. No problem to swing by there."

And Dawn believed him. Tyson seemed the kind who handled everything in an unruffled manner, as though nothing got under his skin. As though he was as steady as the rain starting to fall outside. The man was like jazz, black coffee and faithful dogs. Totally mellow. Likeable. And likely to bring you back for more.

And that was the consolation in the whole attraction thing she had going for him. She didn't like the slow, steady guys, no matter how great they looked in piqué polo shirts. She liked the flashy types, the ones who pressed their advantage, who sent overblown roses and bought her girly drinks designed to make her drop her panties. She liked guys who played it fast and loose. Guys who were totally unreliable at everything except breaking her heart.

Falling for those unreliable ones had been her modus operandi from the moment she first noticed boys.

So she wouldn't have a problem with Tyson. He had *safe and dependable* stamped all over his delicious body. He probably had a first-aid kit in his truck and a condom in his wallet.

No, Tyson Hart wasn't her type at all.

There would be no problem with having him working above her every day, lifting boards with his big, strong arms and taking off his shirt when it got too hot.

She swallowed hard at the thought of Tyson's bared chest.

Stop it, Dawn. Stop picturing the man as a man. He's a contractor. Period.

The contractor in question swung open the door of the coffeehouse and allowed her to pass. She ignored the loose grace of his walk. She ignored the way the truck smelled like him. She ignored the way his arm brushed her shoulder when he threw it over the seat to look behind him as he reversed out of the parking lot.

She sighed in self-congratulation and crossed her legs. Her sandal kicked something underneath the bench seat. She leaned down and saw a first-aid kit lying at her feet.

Bingo.

CHAPTER FOUR

Two things struck Tyson as he walked up the drive toward Tucker House the following Saturday. Elderly people had more energy than he thought. And Dawn Taggart looked extremely hot.

The front lawn was covered with several tables sporting old-fashioned checked tablecloths. He wasn't certain what was going on, but he spotted several plants clustered on tables and assorted blue-haired ladies in aprons scurrying around. Of course, the highlight was the peek of Dawn he'd caught before she disappeared around the corner. Dawn, wearing cutoff jean shorts, a white T-shirt and soap bubbles in her dark hair.

She was barefoot and laughing.

It jolted him unlike any sight in a long time.

"Hey, come on over here and buy some shortbread cookies. I made 'em myself," a frail bird-like woman called to him. Her blue-veined hand beckoned and the smile on her face had him changing directions and veering toward a table showcasing cakes and cookies.

"I ain't seen you around here before," she said, patting her silver bouffant and tossing a look over one shoulder to her friend, who tittered like a wren. Both sets of eyes sparkled beneath the bifocals they wore.

The friend, who wore a striped apron that read "I'm not aging, I'm increasing in value" nodded her head. "I haven't seen you, either."

"Well, now, ladies, I don't mind being the stranger who sweeps into Oak Stand and buys up all these cookies," he said, giving them his best charming grin.

"Why, Grace, he's a sweet-talker, just right for me and you, honey," the silver-headed lady said, setting out several jars of jam.

Grace agreed. "In that case, may I suggest the poppy-seed muffins and the sour cream pound cake? And don't forget Florence Roberts's mayhaw jelly. You just can't buy that off the grocery shelf."

He stuck out his hand. "Sold. And I'm Tyson Hart. My grandfather—"

"Grady Hart's grandson. Well, I'll be darned, Grace. You remember this boy from Sunday school? He's the one who ate the paste and Dr. Grabel had to give him that ipecac."

Grace clapped her hands together. "Of course, Ester. He chased girls all over Oak Stand when he came to town each summer. My granddaughter, Becca, was one of 'em."

Ester peered up at him. "You still a rascal, Tyson?"

He cleared his throat, but was saved from answering by a kid shouting behind him. Which was good because he didn't want to recall a past that involved consuming paste. Or chasing Becca. Obviously, the impression he'd left on the small town hadn't been the one he'd hoped.

"Chasing girls, huh? Wouldn't have pegged you for that type. And paste?" It was Dawn's voice behind him. Damn, he'd hoped she wouldn't hear the ladies' comments. He didn't want her to think he was unreliable or slimy. But why it mattered so much escaped him.

"Never underestimate the power of paste," he said, turning. "It was my secret weapon with the girls. Could hardly peel 'em off me they stuck so hard."

Dawn rolled her eyes then offered her hand. He took it, surprised to find it was wet. She withdrew her hand and wiped it on her shorts. "Sorry. Hunter Todd and I are running a dog wash."

She smiled and something bumped in his chest, not to mention a certain heat built south of the border. Her damp T-shirt clung to her rounded breasts. The shirt was big enough to slide off one shoulder and reveal a lacy bra strap. Her wavy dark hair was in a ponytail, though some tendrils escaped to stick to her cheeks. Her painted pink toes wiggled in the grass. He'd be tempted to say she looked like a teenager, but there was nothing gawky or innocent about Dawn.

She was full-on woman.

He tucked his hand into the front pocket of his jeans, hoping to detract from the stirrings of arousal at her alluring sexuality. Speaking of teenagers. He hadn't felt this way since he'd been one.

Damn. This was supposed to be business.

"Dog washing, huh? Just what kind of operation are y'all running 'round here?" he asked, winking at the two elderly ladies eyeing Dawn and him with more than slight interest.

"We're raising money for some new games. We're short on cash for Wii games, Monopoly and the like. Margo Mott, the assistant director, came up with the idea of a bake sale. And that evolved into a bake sale slash plant sale slash dog wash. Hunter Todd came up with the last one, and since I've been known to kill a perfectly good plant and burn cookies, I got the dog wash."

Hunter Todd raced in between them, dousing them with a squirt bottle. "Gotcha!"

Dawn put two fingers between her lips and whistled.

The boy skidded to a stop. "Cool. How'd you do that?"

"Water stays on the other side of the house. Ester will tan your hide if you get her desserts wet."

Hunter Todd's lower lip poked out.

"But I'll teach you how to whistle like that later," Dawn said, giving him a wink.

"Cool," Hunter Todd said, zipping toward the tub of soapy water he'd left behind.

"Impressive. Will you teach me, too?" Tyson asked.

An emotion he couldn't quite pin down flashed across her eyes before she grinned. "Sure. I'm quite talented with my mouth."

Tyson opened his mouth to deliver a zinger, but Ester beat him to it. "Don't think I'd be giving those kinds of secrets away so easily, my dear."

Tyson couldn't stop the laughter.

Dawn's brown eyes bulged before she choked out her own laughter. "Jeez, the sun is getting to me. Really, I've been around teenage boys long enough to know better."

"Been around teenage boys? Were you a teacher?"

"Heavens, no. I have a nineteen-year-old son."

"You're joking," he said, stunned at her answer. It couldn't be possible. She looked much too young. "But you don't look much beyond…twenty-eight."

His words made her laugh harder and caused a faint blush to color her cheeks. "I wish. Just turned thirty-seven."

The two ladies shifting baked goods around on the table weren't very good at hiding their interest in the conversation. He could have sworn Ester turned up her hearing aid.

"Can you tear yourself away from the pups long

enough to show me the second floor?" he said, stifling the urge to unstick a damp tendril of hair from where it clung to her cheek. His fingers even twitched at the thought of her silky skin beneath them. Silky skin that still looked dewy and fresh. Not like the mother of a nineteen-year-old.

"Pups?" she snorted. "We've only bathed two dogs so far—a Chihuahua and a mutt so I won't be missed. Come on. I'll show you around."

She slid on a pair of flip-flops and called to Hunter Todd that she'd be right back. He frowned but perked up when she gave him a sign and sent him toward the sidewalk to drum up business. Then she led Tyson up the porch steps toward the huge beveled glass door.

Tyson had liked the colossal Victorian the first time he'd seen it. He'd been ten and had been riding by on his bicycle en route to the Dairy Barn for a soft-serve ice cream cone. The house still held the same appeal with its wide porch, white columns and cheerful presence. Nellie's forefathers may have built the huge house to impress, but they didn't neglect its ability to charm with round inset windows, unique arches and a widow's walk.

He followed Dawn inside, where it was clean, bright and engaging. Rocking chairs with cheerful quilted cushions, old-fashioned couches with lacy looking things on the arms and polished oak floors made the house seem like a home rather than a senior adult care center.

Dawn turned toward him before ascending the stairs. She opened her mouth but he beat her to the words.

"I hope I didn't embarrass you out there. I didn't mean to pry."

Her eyes left his face. "You weren't prying and it's no

secret. Andrew's father looked really cute in his board shorts when he showed up at the local pool that summer. Dating a surfer gives a sixteen-year-old, wet-behind-the-ears gal all kinds of perks including a bun in the oven."

Her tone was sharp, and the brown eyes that met his carried a spark of embarrassment. Obviously, she didn't like having to address her past.

"Surfer dude, huh?" he said, trying for lightness. "In Texas?"

She smiled. "Not quite. I'm from California—dairy country. And when that smooth talker came to town, he found a country girl like me easy pickings. Which is why I'm glad I had a son and not a daughter. Girls you got to worry about."

He started to tell her he'd not been granted that luxury. His daughter already wore lipstick and heeled sandals. Thirteen had nearly killed him, and he wasn't looking forward to when she turned fourteen. Laurel's recent leanings were exactly what had led him to Oak Stand and a new life away from the fast-paced city.

But Dawn had started up the stairs, gesturing to the wall on which the grand staircase was fixed. "My first thought was to put in an elevator, but that's expensive. What about one of those chairlifts? Think that would work?"

Tyson nodded, glad she'd shifted the topic. This was a business meeting even if he was totally checking out the sweet curve of her behind as she trotted up the stairs. He also appreciated the fact she'd gotten a little scissor-happy on the shorn-off jeans because they rose a tad too high on the back of her thighs.

He cleared his mind. "I think they've improved those chairlifts quite a bit. But you need to check the disabilities act. You may be required to have an elevator. I included one in the draft."

"Didn't think about that and I should have. See? You're paying off already," she said, stepping into the second-floor hallway before turning around. "I got your estimate. I'm assuming Jack dropped off the original blueprints for the house? I have to check because I'm not sure his brain is functioning. Mae doesn't like to sleep at night."

He looked up at her, silhouetted in the gloom of the hallway. She was just too damn pretty. "Yeah. I got 'em."

She nodded. "Good."

"Is that what they named the baby? Mae? 'Cause it's October."

Dawn's chuckle bounced off the walls. "Not exactly. They had a boy's name ready to go because the ultrasound technician thought it was a boy. Tucker James Darby. Now it's Dorothy Mae Darby. After Nellie's late grandmother."

"I like it. It fits this town."

Dawn snorted. "It should. Nellie's grandmother ran Oak Stand. Her great granddaughter doesn't fall far from the tree. Mae's ruling the roost already."

Dawn began opening the doors on either side of the hallway and calling out the names of each. One was clogged with old books, one a nursery, one obviously Nellie's old bedroom, if the posters of George Strait were any indication.

"So which ones are you thinking about keeping intact?" he called out, stepping inside the last room off the hallway. It was quaintly furnished with a colorful patchwork quilt covering an old-fashioned iron bed. Dawn followed him inside but he didn't realize she was behind him until he turned around and bumped into her.

She stepped back, but he caught her slight intake of breath. His body tightened at the feel of her breasts brushing his arm.

"Sorry," he said, grasping her arms and setting her aright. Her golden skin felt soft under his work-roughened hands. "Didn't realize you were right behind me."

Silence met his apology and the air crackled with tension. They'd both felt the jolt of attraction, but neither would acknowledge it.

"I thought this room and the one next door would work for when our clients need some privacy."

He stepped past her and ducked his head in the adjacent room. "I don't think so. It would be better to use the nursery and this room, since they are closer to the stairs. Let me look around at the structure a bit, and I'll meet you downstairs to show you what I've drawn up."

A furrow creased between her eyebrows. "But that doesn't make sense. These are bedrooms. With beds in them."

Tyson shook his head. "I'll show you what I've drawn up and then we can argue the finer points. Okay?"

She shrugged. "Fine, I'll head downstairs and get that cup of coffee I still owe you."

The blip of sexual tension between them still pulsated in the quietness of the room, but Tyson let her slip out the door without doing anything about it. And his body so wanted him to do something about it. But his mind said no. He had to remind himself yet again why he was in Oak Stand and why acting on such an impulse was not a good idea.

Hell, he hadn't even signed the divorce papers yet.

And that was a good enough reason to ignore the stirrings Dawn caused inside him.

He listened as the slapping of her flip-flops faded away, then he got busy inspecting the soundness of the structure and cementing his ideas for the remodel. He was certain what he'd drawn up would be perfect.

DAWN RINSED AND FILLED the carafe with filtered water. Afternoon coffee was always a good idea even if she didn't need the caffeine. She hadn't been sleeping well, which probably had to do with Andrew's latest attempt to get her and Larry back together.

It all stemmed from an incident several months ago before she'd left Houston. Her ex-husband suffered a burst pipe in the small patio home he leased. Andrew had talked her into letting his father sleep in their extra bedroom. Big mistake. Larry had been on his best behavior, making his famous banana-macadamia waffles and picking up his wet towels. She'd even laughed at his jokes as he flipped the chicken on the grill. But the coziness had given Andrew license to envision his parents together once again.

He'd also complained over the past few months about split holidays and trying to spend time with both of his parents separately. Like every other nineteen-year-old on the planet, he wanted what was easiest for him. Too bad if his convenience didn't work for anyone else. And reconciling with Larry definitely did not work for Dawn. She had to figure out a way to make that point to Andrew wihout alienating him.

So, yeah, she'd take that jolt of caffeine even if it meant tossing and turning all night.

Jolts. There'd been plenty of them going around

upstairs, and she could not, would not, pay attention to them. Look where following her libido had gotten her with the last guy. She'd been instantly attracted to the guy who owned the café across from her design shop in Houston. Murray had been good-looking, suave and totally attentive. He'd also been very married—a little fact he'd failed to mention during their impromptu lunches and romantic weekends. For the first time in a long time, she'd been happy. She'd been in love. And it had been with another woman's husband. The thought still made her want to vomit.

So she wasn't listening to any crazy sexual static. Call her chicken. Or smart. Either way, Tyson Hart would be getting no play.

She glanced at the schedule mounted on the wall. Blue, green, orange and yellow highlighted sections all awaited her perusal. That's how she liked it. No danger. No surprises.

The object of her musings stepped into the kitchen and ran a hand through his hair. The action caused the band on his polo shirt to rise above the sculpted biceps of his arm. The salmon color made his eyes glow. Dawn felt her mouth go dry with desire.

Hell.

"Coffee?" she said, before clearing her throat. She'd sounded like a bullfrog.

"Absolutely," he said, placing a rolled-up paper on the granite countertop. "I ran out to my truck and grabbed the plans I'd worked on. By the way, Hunter Todd had a customer. It looked like a rat, though he assured me it was a dog."

"Herman," Dawn quipped, pulling two mugs from the cabinet. "He's the Chihuahua that belongs to the Sandersons. We've bathed him once already."

She poured him a cup and handed it to him.

"Just the way I like it," he said, before raising it to his lips and taking a sip. "Very good."

"So show me what you've got." She smiled. Another sexually charged statement. Jeez. She was losing it. But Tyson chose to ignore this one, and instead unrolled the plans with the enthusiasm of a boy with his prized collection of baseball cards on display.

"Okay." He set his coffee mug far away from the plans. "Here's the second floor. The rooms aren't labeled but you can see the library, nursery and so on."

She nodded as if she didn't already know what the second floor looked like. As if she'd never walked the halls, slept in Nellie's old room the couple of times she didn't feel like driving out to her brother's ranch.

"These are the plans I've drawn up. First, here are the two rooms you'll keep. We'll divide those into four dormitory-like rooms for resting. Then we'll section off this area and create a bank of bookshelf-style units for storage. We'll install a sink, built-in fridge and a dumbwaiter that will lower to the kitchen on the first floor."

She studied the plans as he ran a finger over the sections, explaining what each would be. Periodically, he would stop to discuss materials or ask for a suggestion. Occasionally, Dawn's interest waned and she watched the enthusiasm he had for the project. Architecture wasn't really her thing, but she could tell he had enjoyed designing the space and that he loved creating something exceptional out of something ordinary.

It was not too different than what she had done in her own redesign shop in Houston. She'd taken old pieces of furniture—things that no one wanted anymore—and created a new piece of furniture. She'd pick up an old chair on the side of the road, repair it, strip it, give it a faux finish and recover it with vintage fabric and, voila, it became a work of art. She liked getting her hands dirty in design work, so she totally understood the pleasure Tyson took in revisioning the space.

"It's fabulous," she said when he'd finished. "I can't believe you can actually do all of that within these four walls."

"Well, part of it is using good design principles. We'll draw the eye upward to give a better sense of space. Using quality materials will offset the lack of square footage. Add some expansive colors, and it will feel airy."

She laughed. "Did you just say *airy?*"

He shrugged. "Okay, so I watch a couple of design shows on HGTV."

Dawn smiled, enjoying his small discomfiture. A picture of him with a notepad balanced on his lap while he took notes from a designer on TV popped into her mind. "I appreciate a man who does his research. So let's talk time frame. When can you start and how long till completion?"

"I can start Monday," he said. "Two months if I can find the right guys to help me. We should be finished before Christmas."

Dawn took a sip from her mug. "Then it's a deal."

"You don't need to talk to Nellie?" he said, reaching for his own mug and taking a long swallow of coffee.

"No, not unless it involves the frequency of nursing or the best diaper-rash creams," she said, rolling her eyes comically.

"Okay, then," he said, putting out his hand. "It's a deal."

Dawn placed her hand in his. It was dry, warm and

enveloped her entire hand. A little frisson of electricity—the kind she was supposed to ignore—shot up her arm. She jerked her eyes to his. He felt it, too.

Then he did something totally unexpected. He pulled her to him. And she went. She could feel the hitch in her breathing, could feel his breath fan her cheek.

She tore her eyes from his and focused on the pulse at the base of his throat. Was it her imagination or was it beating erratically? Her breasts lightly brushed the front of his shirt, prickling immediately at the contact with his body.

She felt his fingers push strands of hair from her forehead. One of his massive arms curled around her, his hand sliding against her back, searing her with the heat of his touch.

She knew he was going to kiss her. She knew it was stupid to let him. Knew it was not what she should want, but she also knew if he didn't press his lips to hers and claim the heat of her mouth, she'd go insane.

She chanced looking up at him.

Her passion was mirrored in his eyes.

He lowered his head and pulled her tighter against him.

She allowed a small sigh to escape her lips. A sigh of acceptance. A sigh of need.

His lips hovered above hers, teasingly.

Then something wet hit her ankles.

Dawn squealed as the wetness wriggled. She stepped back and heard a yelp.

"You stepped on him!" Hunter Todd shouted. "You hurted his paw."

Dawn looked down to see Herman limping around, holding up his front paw. He did indeed look like a drowned rat. And the worried six-year-old didn't look much better. He, too, was dripping on the tiled floor.

Tyson sighed. "Hunter Todd, I think you have about the best timing of any kid I've ever known."

CHAPTER FIVE

DAWN DIPPED HER SPOON into the bowl of Golden Nut Ohs. The planner she'd found under some of Jack's papers sat in front of her, open to the list she'd scribbled in the back. Her secret list that made it into every planner each new year. A list of the things she wanted to undertake by the time she was forty.

Her accomplishments to date were dismal.

She'd never learned sign language. She didn't have two children. She'd never seen the Grand Canyon. Or run a marathon. Or visited the Louvre.

She'd also never had sex on a beach. Why the hell had she put that on there anyway? Gritty sand in hard-to-reach places, sunburn on tender places and seaweed in her hair? Couldn't be good, could it?

Tyson's image popped into her mind. Tyson bare-chested on the beach, sand clinging to his sun-kissed shoulders. Mmm.

How in the name of all that was holy was she going to see that man every day and not get tangled up in him? Even knowing that a man as capable and self-reliant as Tyson could seriously undermine her need to control her life and her sense of responsibility for everyone, didn't stop this wanting. Sorting out where she was going probably wouldn't happen if she got involved with him—she'd be too busy trying to run his life to pay attention to her own.

So okay. She could do it. She could stay away, slide around corners when she saw him coming, and throw up some mental barbed-wire barriers when she absolutely had to talk to him. But something inside, some little know-it-all voice, said it wasn't happening.

She was toast.

"Want some toast?"

"Huh?" Her chin slid from where it rested on her palm. She jerked upright and looked at her brother, who'd obviously used ninja skills and snuck up on her. Stealth dwelt in the arsenal of a younger brother.

"I said—" he yawned "—do you want some toast? I'm making some."

"No. I'm still working on this cereal." She tossed the spoon into the half-eaten mush.

Jack padded around the kitchen in his boxers and snug T-shirt, slamming drawers and banging cabinet doors.

"Are you trying to wake the baby?" Dawn drawled. "'Cause you're doing a good job of trying to wake the dead."

"You're cranky," he said. "Have another cup of coffee."

"I'm not cranky," she groused, knowing she was. She'd been crabby all of yesterday as she'd cleaned out the second-floor rooms at Tucker House. Mostly because she really needed to go over the résumé she'd been prepping to send out to the design firms in Houston. Because that was her future. Oak Stand was temporary. She had to keep one eye on what came next even while she gave this job her all. And that meant today she'd have to help Bubba cart the boxes to the third-story storage. Then she'd have to see the man who'd almost, but not quite, kissed her.

"So what's with you? Is the baby keeping you up? I know our room is downstairs, but the kid has a pair of lungs like her aunt."

She ignored the barb. Her coffee was cold. But she didn't move a muscle to warm it. She ran her finger round and round the rim of the cup. "No, I'm just tired. Got a lot on my mind, I suppose."

"I know things have been tough lately. Hell, there's been so much change in all of our lives that sometimes it's hard to keep up," he said.

Dawned nodded. Two years ago, Jack had been an eligible Las Vegas nightclub owner and she'd been a small-business owner with a teenager in the house. Neither she nor Jack had ever heard of Oak Stand, Texas. And never in a million years had either of them thought Jack would be standing at the kitchen sink, washing bottle nipples, letting his exhausted wife sleep in, or that Dawn would be trying to start her life over again.

"Yeah, it's been…different than what I'd imagined for myself."

Jack pulled out a chair and sat. His blue eyes glanced at her planner then met hers. She saw pity pooling in their depths. She hated pity. He scratched his head, leaving his hair sticking straight up. Dawn might have smiled if she had it in her. "So give yourself some time. You don't have to make any decisions about Houston, or a job or anything else."

"Yeah, I will."

"Heck," he muttered, "I'm so not good with this brother-sister stuff. I don't know what to say. Your life ain't been peachy and mine's about as good as I could ever imagine. How do I make you feel better about Larry and Houston and that married son of a bitch who duped you when I'm so happy?"

She patted his hand. "You don't. You just love me. And I know you do. You're trying your best to take care of me, but I can take care of myself."

She rose and carried her bowl to the farmhouse sink, rinsed it out and loaded it into the dishwasher. Even as she'd said the words, they rang hollow in her ears. Did she believe them? Thus far, very few people would say she'd made good choices. That much was obvious. Every decision she'd ever made seemed wrong. From going all the way with Larry, to trying to start a new business, to accepting the first lunch date with Murray. All a total waste of her time. All wrong.

Except for Andrew.

Her son was the only thing she'd done right. She'd taken that downy-haired baby and raised him into a tall, strong man—well, nearly a man. At nineteen, he was handsome, smart and, outside of trying to arrange dates for her and Larry, had a practical nature. She missed him and wished he'd come to Oak Stand for a visit.

She could feel Jack studying her, so she turned and gave him a brave smile. "I'm off to work. The contractor's coming today to start demoing the space upstairs. And I'm going to look at another rental so I can get out of your hair."

"Do you think we want you out of our hair? Who's going to change all those dirty diapers?"

"Don't worry. You'll get the hang of it. Every daddy does."

Except Larry.

He'd taken one look at Andrew's dirty diaper and vowed he'd never change one.

It was the one promise he'd managed to keep.

"Bubba will be there by nine. He's running out to the

barn to check on Dynamo, but he said it wouldn't take him—how'd he put it?—two shakes of a lamb's tail."

Dawn smiled. Bubbaisms ran rampant on the ranch. The ranch. Jeez. She still couldn't believe her city-slick brother got up every morning, pulled on faded Levi's, and headed out to a barn. The urbane Jack Darby actually loved raising wild broncs for rodeos. When she looked at him now, she saw his life was peachy. The thought lifted her spirits. Gave her hope for herself.

"Okay then," Dawn said, delivering a salute. "Hand me my day planner and I'll be off."

Jack frowned at the planner sitting on the table. "Why don't you use a PDA like everyone else on the planet?"

"Because I like to use a pen and paper. No need to charge a battery."

"Dinosaur."

"Shut up," she said, holding out an expectant hand. "This works just fine. Keeps me straight."

He handed the leather-bound agenda to her with a twinkle in his blue eyes. "It's a crutch. You can't schedule everything in life. Some things won't tolerate being put into a column and highlighted pink."

"Whatever," she said, spinning around and heading out of the kitchen. "I've yet to meet the problem that can't be better handled with proper scheduling. Or at least a list of emergency numbers."

TYSON WATCHED DAWN WALK around the side of Tucker House, digging in her handbag for what he assumed to be the keys. His watch read 7:40 a.m. He'd been here for ten minutes. Dawn was late, but he'd forgive her because she looked too lovely to berate.

She'd braided her hair, though pieces had already

escaped to frame her face. Her light blue shirt was open to a swirly looking yellow-and-blue undershirt. She wore denim trousers that flared just slightly above her trim ankles. He knew they were called crop pants. His ex-wife had worn them. Brown loafers graced her feet. She looked poised and fresh, just right for the first cool October morning, if one could call fifty degrees cool. He knew it would be in the midseventies by lunchtime.

"Sorry I'm late," she called as she mounted the steps, keys in hand. "I'm rarely late, but Jack's damn dog dragged a mutilated, half-rotten squirrel onto the porch and dropped it on my foot."

He raised an eyebrow. "It dropped a dead squirrel on your foot?"

She shivered. "Not just a *dead* squirrel, a *decomposing* squirrel. I have no words for how disgusting it was. I had to shower again."

Tyson dashed away the thought of her standing beneath the showerhead, water sluicing down her delicious body. He shrugged. "No problem. Sorry your morning hasn't been…easy."

Dawn shook her head, an ironic smile curving her bottom lip. "It's par for the course for me, Hart."

Tyson started at the sound of his last name on her lips. Hart? So she was distancing herself. After Saturday afternoon's near lip-lock in the kitchen, he expected as much. But he was surprised at the flicker of disappointment in his gut. He'd wanted her to want him. To want to further their brief encounter.

But at the same time, he knew it was better this way. He needed to focus on his job and on creating a better life for his daughter. He'd agreed to visit Laurel in Dallas last weekend because she absolutely had to see the new Taylor Swift movie, but she'd be in Oak Stand this weekend. He wanted to take her to the Dairy Barn and to the small pond on Gramps's property. Maybe they could crank up the four-wheeler and take a spin. She'd finally see in Oak Stand what he saw—a chance for a new beginning with a very different way of life.

"Well, no one can help when such unforeseeable circumstances occur, like a rotten squirrel on your foot." He chuckled, following her into the dim house.

"Yep. God likes to teach me lessons. 'Cause that totally wasn't scheduled in my planner."

He wasn't sure what she was talking about, but he didn't ask. He'd learned long ago that when a woman was agitated, it was best to let sleeping dogs lie. With or without a dead squirrel.

"So, I'm going to head upstairs and start making some marks on which walls are going to have to go. I hired a couple of local guys to help me, but they won't be here until this afternoon."

She'd already headed toward the rear of the house, but called to him as she ducked into her office. "I'm gonna pop some cinnamon rolls in the oven. We won't have clients until 8:00 a.m. Bubba will be here shortly to move the boxes to the attic. I labeled them clearly with the area in which they should be stored. I'll help when Margo gets here."

He decided to forego the stairs and followed her to the kitchen. "Do you have any ground rules about noise? Because it's going to get noisy at times. Nothing I can do about that."

Dawn smiled. "I'll have them turn their hearing aids down."

He grinned. "Seriously."

She shrugged before pulling open the refrigerator and taking out a tube of ready-to-bake pastries. "I don't foresee a problem. They know there will be ongoing construction for the next few months. We'll just do our best, but I would like to see something in place to prevent dust downstairs. Some of our clients have fragile health and I can't imagine construction dust would be good for them."

"I can handle that," he said. "We'll put plastic at the entrance to the stairs and I'll place a fan in one of the windows to draw some of the dust particles outside."

Dawn pulled out a pan and began unwinding the paper from the cinnamon rolls. Silence fell between them.

"Look, Dawn, about Saturday," he began.

She waved a hand at him, but didn't meet his eyes. "Look, no big deal. It was a weird moment. Let's just pretend it didn't happen."

He wasn't sure they could. He'd learned long ago it was best to not ignore potential problems. Meeting head-on was the only smart solution.

"But it did happen. We can't pretend there isn't something between us," he said, glancing out the window to where leaves floated to the ground on the breeze. Gold, red and orange danced across the yard, scudding against the yellowed grass.

She slid the pan into the oven and stood, straightening her spine like a soldier. Her brown eyes met his. They were guarded. "I can't afford to—" she paused "—dabble with a man. I've made too many mistakes down that road lately. So I want to forget about Saturday. It's easier for me that way."

"Okay," he said, catching a glimpse into her life. His own path had been much the same. Full of wrong turns and rocks in his shoe. "I agree with you. I don't have room to screw up, either. I'll sign divorce papers next month, and I need a fresh start with my daughter."

He saw the questions lurking in the depths of her chocolate eyes. "You have a daughter?"

"Yeah, her name's Laurel. She's nearly fourteen. The divorce has been hard on her. Coming here to Oak Stand, a place where I spent my happiest times, is a new chapter for us. I hope."

"I'm taking a break myself. And I'm looking for a new direction." She caught her bottom lip between her teeth, as though showing her own vulnerability was wrong. He could see the mental shake of her head. "Well, so we agree to ignore any, um, weird feelings? Keep everything business?"

He nodded. "But, let's not call it business. Let's agree to be friendly."

She lifted an eyebrow.

"With no physical contact. Friendship only. I could use another friend in this town. I didn't actually grow up here. Spent mostly summers and an occasional year with my grandfather."

She smiled. "I'm not local, either. And I could use another friend in this town, too. So sounds like we have a deal. But we won't muck it up by shaking on it this time."

Yeah. No touching. And just when his fingers wanted to curl around her upper arms and spin her toward him so they could finish what they'd started two days ago.

But it was over before it began.

"Now we've got that settled, I'll get started." He spun around and nearly bowled over a woman entering the kitchen. She carried several grocery bags and was so small her head would pass under his arm with ease.

"Lordy, where'd you get this hunk, D?" A gold crown

winked at him as she grinned and took him in from the top of his ball cap to the bottom of his work boots.

"I didn't get him. Nellie did."

"Darn, that girl's got good taste," the woman said setting the bags upon the counter and dusting her hands. "I thought she had her hands full with that good-lookin' husband of hers. What's she need another one for? But I'll take this one. He looks a mighty fine specimen of manhood." She cackled and winked at him.

"Hi," he said, "I'm Tyson Hart, the contractor."

She stuck out a weathered hand. "I'm Margo. I help D run this center. And I may look old, but I got a young girl's heart. And her moves, too."

"I don't doubt it," Tyson said, taking the proffered hand and giving it a shake. She looked so regal with her coffee-colored skin and reggae-style braids, he started to bow over her hand. Or lift it to his lips as a courtly gesture.

"Right answer, baby," she said, pulling her hand from his. She started unloading the bags on the counter. She didn't necessarily dismiss him, but she moved on. "D, I've had about all I can stand of that too-big-for-her-britches witch down at the vegetable stand. Her mean ass is running a fruit stand and putting on airs with me. Not to mention her pumpkins are priced too high for anybody to afford this Halloween."

Tyson left Dawn and Margo talking about someone named Ruby Pierson and her overpriced gourds and headed to the second story.

Remodeling a structure the age of Tucker House was daunting, but he felt better knowing he and Dawn had cleared the air about the sexual attraction sitting between them like the proverbial elephant in the room.

They would be friends. Having a female friend would

be a good thing. She could give him advice on what Laurel might want for Christmas. She could tell him whether his new gray sweater matched the pants he'd bought for church on Sunday. She could advise him on what would get chocolate ice cream out of a white T-shirt. Having a female friend would work out fine.

He'd ignore the urge to tuck an errant strand of hair behind her ear. Or to brush against her when she slid past him into a room. He'd stop picturing her naked in the shower. And stop wondering what kind of sweet noises she'd make during sex. He absolutely would not touch her. Her skin was kitten-soft and made him want to stroke her. Make her purr.

Scratch that. He thumped up the stairs. His thoughts were already betraying him.

As he reached the top step, his cell phone rang.

"Hart."

"Where in the jehosephat did you put the remote control? I can't find the damn thing anywhere." The voice was rusty and annoyed.

Tyson sighed. He loved his grandfather, he really did. But the irascible older man was getting harder and harder to keep patience with. Tyson didn't want to admit it, but he suspected the man who'd taken him in when he was ten showed the early stages of Alzheimer's. "I put it on the top of the TV, Gramps. Do you see it?"

"Oh."

"You sure you don't want to come with me to Tucker House while I'm working?"

"Hell, no," his grandfather said, "Do I fart dust? That place is for old folks. I ain't old."

"I didn't say you were, but it might be fun to renew old friendships. Play bridge. Check out the ladies."

Tyson walked through the second floor, picturing the

changes he would make as he talked to his grandfather. He had a lot of work in front of him to get the space ready before Christmas. He knew he could be finished by mid-January at the very latest.

"I don't want no ladies fussin' round me. They'll be bringing me new shirts and casseroles. Trying to knit me booties for winter. Had about all of that I could take with your grandmother."

Tyson smiled. "Yeah, she was a real ballbuster."

"Sweetest thing in Texas is what she was," his grandfather said, emotion heavy in his voice. The man had loved Annie Hart with every fiber of his being and still grew maudlin at the mention of the woman he'd lost twenty-five years ago when Tyson was only a teen.

Their only son, Trent, Tyson's father, had problems almost all his life and as he'd gotten older he'd dabbled in alcohol and drugs. Tyson's mother wasn't much better. Grady and Annie had been the only stable force in Tyson's life. He had bumped back and forth between Oak Stand and towns all over North Carolina as he grew up. At times it had been tough, but he'd survived. His father had passed away five years ago, estranged from his family. His mother lived in Myrtle Beach and rarely called. Grady and Laurel were his family.

"Yeah, Grandma was a gem. Especially to put up with your cranky butt."

Grady grunted.

"So, you got the remote control. Are you good?"

"Course I'm good. I've been takin' care of myself for seventy-six years. Ever since I was twelve years old."

"I know," Tyson said, picking up a long-sleeved white shirt that was hanging on the back of the library door. He knew at once it was Dawn's. She must have left it yesterday when she came to clear out the rooms. Before he could stop himself, he brought the shirt to his nose and inhaled her scent—a clean, flowery smell. Then he snorted. So much for distance. Friends didn't sniff each other's clothing.

"Don't you snort. I had to leave home when I was a wet-behind-the-ears boy to find work. There ain't nothing funny about the Depression and there ain't nothin' funny about going hungry. Somebody had to put food on the table for our family."

Tyson interrupted his grandfather's favorite tirade that would wrap up with a lecture on being a responsible, dependable, teetotaling man. "I wasn't snorting at you. I had some dust in my nose."

"Oh," his grandfather said again.

Tyson told his grandfather goodbye then headed down the stairs. As he stepped onto the landing, he took one more sniff of Dawn's shirt and tried to convince himself it wasn't perverted to stand in an old folk's center and sniff the director's shirt.

Of course, it was perverted. Or weird. Or both.

God, he hoped this friendship thing worked out. But he had his doubts. Dawn had sparked something in him he hadn't felt since before Iraq.

And he knew what it was. It was excitement. Plain and not so simple.

CHAPTER SIX

TWO WEEKS LATER, DAWN carried a pumpkin onto the porch and placed it on one of the pillars flanking the steps of Tucker House. The orange globe grinned with macabre glee—a smile that was Hunter Todd approved. Tyson brought the second one and placed it on the matching pillar. Hunter Todd ran past them and jumped into a pile of leaves Dawn had raked earlier.

"There," he said, "I think those look fine. I wish Laurel was coming for the weekend. We'd show her a true small-town Halloween."

Dawn studied the jack-o'-lanterns, feeling bad for Tyson. Over the past few weeks of "being friends," he'd told her about the pending divorce and the rapidly expanding gulf between him and his only child. He thought moving to Oak Stand would fix everything. That getting back to his roots would give Laurel gravity in her life. Teach her some old-fashioned values. But it didn't seem to be working. Especially since Laurel had contrived reason after reason for not fulfilling the terms of the custody arrangement. Something important always came up—a recital practice, a youth-group function or a bad cold. Tyson said he didn't want to go to court and force his daughter to visit him because he thought the effort would widen the gap between them.

Dawn wanted to tell him his refusal to put his foot

down was the probably the wrong move. But it wasn't her place.

"Yeah, I know. Kids are hard. I can't get Andrew to come for a visit, either. I even dangled caramel apples as bait," Dawn said, wanting to reach out and pluck a pumpkin seed from Tyson's hair, but she refrained from doing so. "Hey, you got a pumpkin seed in your hair."

"Where?" he said, feeling around his hair, missing the thing completely.

"Here. Bend down," Dawn commanded. He tilted toward her and she brushed away the offending seed. She wanted to fan her fingers through his hair, but friends didn't do things like that. Lovers did.

Tyson picked up the seed from where it lay on the walk. "My grandfather roasted some of these for me one Halloween. We stayed up late munching on them and watching old vampire movies."

He sounded so wistful. He missed his child. And he wasn't doing the right thing with her. The situation was only going to get worse. Another good reason Dawn and he were only friends. Tyson had some serious issues that needed his attention, ones Dawn would surely get caught up in.

"It might be cool to do some of those tonight," she said, adjusting the stemmed cap on the jack-o'-lantern. "Did we save the pumpkin guts?"

"Yuck!" Hunter Todd cried, wrinkling his nose as he galloped toward them. "I ain't eating no pumpkin guts."

"They're not real guts, silly. Just the stringy stuff we pulled out. The seeds were in there, remember?" she said.

"Come help me pick them out, Hunter. Then I'll show

you how to roast them," Tyson said, tugging Hunter Todd up the steps.

Dawn pushed her hair out of her face and surveyed the front lawn. She'd have to get those leaves bagged up but not until after the planned festivities. Tonight, Tucker House was holding a special Halloween night out for its patrons. She and Margo had been working all day to set up small stations for the senior adults to operate for the ghosts and princesses who would be showing up when the sun sank into the Texas horizon.

A huge pile of leaves might distract the children while they waited for the ladies who did china painting and ceramics to paint their faces. Ester and Grace were heading up a decorate your own cookie table while some of the men hosted a fish for candy booth and a doughnut dunking booth. Not only would tonight be fun for the senior adults, it would allow busy parents more time for trick-or-treating with their children without having to worry about leaving Grandma or Grandpa home alone.

That was the beauty of Tucker House. Not only did they provide day care for senior adults who could not stay home alone, but they tried to sponsor "Night Out" events that would allow caretakers a chance to go out worry-free. Nellie had been adamant about helping hard-working families with the care of their loved ones. She'd experienced firsthand how caring for her grandmother crimped her own social life. Tucker House even provided sitters for elderly patients who couldn't physically come to Tucker House for the event night.

"Whew! I got the doughnuts from the bakery. Mr. Neely said they were day-old but perfectly good. And the price was right," Margo said, coming out onto the porch wearing a pinafore apron with a ghost on it that Ester had made her.

"Free?" Dawn asked.

Margo's gold crown winked. "Yes, ma'am."

Dawn glanced at Tyson and Hunter Todd hunkered down at the end of the wide porch, picking pumpkin seeds out of the remains of the gourd. She heard a couple of jokes about squishy guts and some high-pitched screams from Hunter Todd. The two heads bobbing together over the task struck a chord of regret in her chest. Regret for Andrew for not having the kind of father who would stoop to such a task, regret she'd not had any more children and regret she'd put the kibosh on exploring something more with the sexy contractor.

It seemed her life would be full of regret.

"Now that's the kind of man you need, D." Margo's words jarred her from her pity party.

"I don't need a man," Dawn said, shifting her gaze from Tyson and Hunter Todd and zeroing in on Margo, who had plopped down beside the jack-o'-lantern.

"We all need a man, baby," Margo said, brushing her bright orange-tipped nails on her apron. "You know, for stuff like fixing a car or killing mice in your house or a roll under them sheets."

"Not me. My track record says differently," Dawn said, climbing the stairs, heading for the front door. She had to check the sugar cookies baking inside.

"So you got a hold of the wrong ones first. Ain't all of 'em good ones, baby. I've had my share of toads before I found my prince. And let me tell you, he ain't a prince every day neither. But I'm glad I got him. Don't close off that door in your life yet, girl."

Dawn stopped and lowered her voice. "I haven't put

any nails in the door. It's still unlocked. It's just not wide open. My life is in shambles right now."

Margo tilted her head. "Why's it in shambles? You got a job. You got a family who loves you. You got a man who's interested."

"We're *friends*." Dawn felt indignant. Why did Margo always have to meddle? She hadn't known the woman but four months, and she was always telling her how to do everything.

"Baby, that don't mean he ain't interested," Margo said with a tinge of smile.

"Margo. Damn it. A friend is all I want." She crossed her arms and glared at the assistant director. How dare the woman remind her of the insane attraction she had for Tyson? They'd been doing great as friends. Just yesterday, they'd sat on the porch, drank lemonade and talked about their favorite TV shows, even quoting some of the one-liners to try to stump each other. They'd laughed so hard, one of the neighbors had peered over a hedge at them. It had been nice. And fun.

Despite that, every second she spent with him made her want him more.

"Well, you tell yourself whatever you need to. But I've been around for the past two weeks, and if I lit a match around you two, we'd all go up in smoke."

Dawn straightened. Margo could feel the sexual tension? Dawn had thought she and Tyson had trampled it down well. Lord knew she'd been trying to play it cool. To stop looking at him so much, to stop thinking about him so much. She thought she had succeeded. Now she knew she hadn't.

"Look. Tyson's a great guy, but you know my past. I can't choose a guy based on mere attraction. Don't you remember what I told you about Murray? It only took one kiss before he had my ankles over my head." Dawn lowered her voice. She didn't want Tyson to hear how easy she'd been. Besides she didn't want him to know how much he occupied her thoughts.

Margo laughed. "I wish I could get my ankles above my head."

"You know what I mean," Dawn sniffed.

"Girl, are you crazy? You didn't know that man was married. You didn't cause that whole scene outside the museum. That was on him. Not you. Why you carrying around that guilt? So you screwed up. We all do that." Margo's dark eyes flickered in the dying sunlight. She looked like an ancient mystic sent to set everyone straight. But Dawn didn't want to hear it.

"I can't help it. I saw his wife's face. Saw their children. I knew exactly what she felt when she saw me standing there holding her husband's hand. I knew because I had felt that way, too, when I found another woman's bra in my own bed. And it wasn't just Murray. Or Larry. I almost went home with some smooth-talking guy I met the night I signed my divorce papers. Seems I can't resist a man who makes me feel pretty, Margo. It's a flaw in my character."

"Uh, uh, uh." Margo shook her head. "You're all mixed up, ain't you? Letting all those old wounds keep you from living. Life is too short, baby. You've got to grab your happiness. But I reckon you ain't ready to reach out yet."

Dawn shook her head. Margo didn't understand how precarious her life felt. She'd had no response to the résumés she'd sent out, and she couldn't depend on her brother forever. She needed a plan. She needed to catch a *break*. Not a man. "I need to check the cookies."

Margo turned her head and looked down the street.

"The sun's startin' to set. All those goblins and witches gonna be out soon."

Dawn didn't answer. She spun toward the door and nearly ran into Tyson.

"Hey," he said, reaching out to steady her, but then stopped and shoved his hands into his back pockets. He was wearing a plaid button-down shirt and well-worn jeans. His eyes in the last glow of the afternoon shone with brighter intensity. "Avery Long invited me over to his place after church to ride on his trails. You wanna come with me?"

"Riding what?" she asked, crossing her arms so she wouldn't brush a string from the pumpkin off his shoulder.

"Four-wheelers, you know, ATVs. I've been itching to take Gramps's Grizzly for a spin. Avery's got several and he told me to bring a friend." His smile reminded her of the caramel apples she'd made for Andrew. She wanted to taste him. "And since we're friends…"

His words threw cold water on the forbidden thoughts involving caramel and his mouth. "Well, yeah, but I don't know anything about four-wheelers…and I'm not sure I want to. What's fun about driving them around?"

He grinned. "Asks the woman who's never ridden one."

Dawn rolled her eyes even though she loved it when he smiled. It made a small dimple appear on his right cheek. "Seriously, what's so hot about driving around on a glorified kiddie toy?"

She'd seen ATVs on trailers, mud-splattered and dusty, and thought the people in the trucks pulling them were idiots. Splashing through ditches and spinning wheelies sounded like something a moron would do.

Or a child. She was a grown woman, not a snot-nosed little kid with Tonka truck fantasies.

"Come with me and find out," he said, the dimple appearing again. She thought about how it would feel to plant her lips right there on that little indention. Just a little angel kiss.

"Anybody got a match?" Margo's voice came from behind them. Dawn didn't miss the amusement within her friend's question.

Tyson peered over her shoulder at Margo. "What do you need a match for?"

"Just making sure we got one. For the jack-o'-lanterns and such."

Dawn turned around and propped her hands on her hips. "We have a lighter inside. And did you hear? Tyson and I are going to ride four-wheelers tomorrow afternoon. You wanna come?" What had she committed herself to? She should never have let Margo's taunts get to her.

Margo blinked. "No, girl, already got my plans set. Me and James goin' down to the lake and do some fishin' after church. You two enjoy the day. My old bones couldn't handle all that jostling around. But I'm glad to see you doing something that ain't on your agenda."

Dawn narrowed her eyes at Margo. "I don't plan everything, Miss Know-It-All. See, I'm being flexible and adventurous."

Margo grinned. "Mmm-hmm. And it just goes to show you're taking my advice and grabbing on to some happiness."

Margo looked way too satisfied, and now, Dawn had roped herself into spending Sunday afternoon with a guy who made her think inappropriate thoughts in the wee hours of the night. "How do you know riding an ATV is grabbing happiness?"

Margo pulled a dead chrysanthemum from the pot sitting at the foot of the steps and shrugged. "I don't, but I'm thinking you better hold on tight, girl."

"Don't worry about her, Margo. I'll make sure she's safe. She'll be back here on Monday morning." Tyson didn't know what Margo meant. But Dawn did.

Margot nodded. "You're the kind to do that. Make sure my Dawn don't get hurt."

Tyson narrowed his eyes. "Okay."

"What time should I meet you at the Longs'?" Dawn resigned herself to going even though it wasn't an ideal date. *Date?* Wait. Not a date. An outing with a friend. She reached out to grab the front door handle, worried about the sugar cookies in the oven turning into brown hockey pucks. Standing looking at Tyson's buttery smile and broad shoulders wasn't a good enough reason to ruin a batch of perfectly good cookies.

He gave her a lopsided grin. Okay, maybe it was.

"I'll swing by and pick you up," he offered.

She pictured Nellie and Jack standing on the porch, waving goodbye as she slipped into Tyson's pickup. She could see the look on Nellie's face. No way. "Don't bother. It's out of your way. I'll meet you there."

Tyson looked as though he might argue, but then shrugged. "Fine. Let's meet for 1:30 p.m."

TYSON STOOD AT THE SIDE of the house, staring at his cell phone. Laurel hadn't called him back. Again. This was turning into a habit. Hell, it had already been a habit for weeks now and wasn't going to get any better if he didn't do something.

He pecked the numbers he knew by heart.

His soon-to-be ex-wife, Karen, answered on the fourth ring.

"We need to talk," he said into the receiver as he toed the fresh lumber he'd hauled in earlier that morning and stacked beneath the window boxes.

"Tyson," she breathed into the phone. "I've been thinking of you. How are things in that cute little town?"

"Fine. But I don't want to talk about me. I want to talk about our daughter."

"Laurel?"

"Do we have another daughter? Yes, of course, Laurel." He had to tamp down the smart-ass tone that crept into his speech every time he talked to the woman who'd cheated on him with his former business partner. It was hard to be nice. "Sorry. Just worried about her."

"Ty, she's fine. Doing better each day. She really wants to come to Oak Stand. But the therapist thinks we need to let her get comfortable with the idea. That's all. I'll bring her soon. I promise."

"I know she's seeing a therapist, but I'm not sure time away from me is better than forcing her to be with me."

"See?" Exasperation crept into Karen's voice. "You use words like *force*. That's part of the problem. We don't need to force her. Let her do things in her own time."

"No. No more. Next week, she comes to Oak Stand. No excuses. I'm putting my foot down. Now let me talk to her, please."

Silence met his demand.

"Karen?"

"What?" Defensiveness crept into her tone. She was hiding something. "Laurel's not here."

He clenched his teeth. "Why not? I thought she had a fever and sore throat."

"Well, she did. Yesterday. She felt much better today so I let her go to Zack Reilly's Halloween party. All the kids were going and she didn't want to be left out."

Now he got the picture. Laurel wasn't sick. She just didn't want to miss the party to spend time with him. And that hurt. What had he done that was so wrong? The divorce was the result of Karen's betrayal. Tyson hadn't thrown his family away. Karen had. So why was he getting the business from his thirteen-year-old daughter?

He tried to shrug off his hurt feelings. "We didn't talk about going to boys' parties. Why did you make this decision on your own?" He couldn't keep the anger from his voice.

"Don't be upset, Ty. The party is well-supervised and I will be picking her up and bringing her home. You know I wouldn't allow her to go to something inappropriate."

This he did know. Karen was overly cautious with Laurel, but that didn't change the fact she hadn't consulted him. And they had agreed to discuss all the big steps in their daughter's life. A party involving boys was one of those.

"Fine. Next time let's talk first, okay? And I do want Laurel in Oak Stand next weekend. It's long overdue."

"We'll talk later this week about the particulars. And, don't forget, she will be spending Thanksgiving with you and Gramps, too." Karen's voice had shifted into sweetness. Placating. Syrupy.

He hated that tone. When they were married, Karen had often used it to butter him up so she'd get her way. In the beginning it had been cute. But her manipulative nature grew old quickly. Now, his first response to her wheedling was anger. But he let it go. No need to pick a fight. His focus was on Laurel. He wrapped up the conversation and ended the call. As exasperating as Karen had been, at least he felt better about his stance on Laurel's visit.

How was he supposed to show Laurel how good life in Oak Stand could be if she wasn't willing to come here? And how could he fix what was wrong between them? His girl had gone from daddy's princess to Tween-zilla. He didn't even recognize her anymore. She rolled her eyes, texted on her phone and insisted on having pedicures. It baffled him that the girl who'd trailed after him even when he mowed the yard had turned into...a real teenager.

Movement through the kitchen window caught his eye. Dawn. Another complication in his life. He knew that his play for friendship wasn't working. He thought about her way too much for her to be only a bud. Her clever jokes and sweet smiles paired with the lushness of her curves had rendered him smitten. He was tired of fighting it. Thus the invitation for tomorrow. He wanted to push her a bit, see if there could be something more than what they'd been pretending for the past few weeks. And nudging her was hard to do with the clients of Tucker House lurking around every corner with bright eyes and hearing aids tuned to the highest setting.

He made his way through the back door to tell Dawn he was leaving. He needed to slip home for a while to check on Gramps...and maybe talk the irascible old man into visiting the center tonight.

The house smelled yummy. Obviously the sugar cookies hadn't burned. He paused inside the mudroom and watched as Dawn pulled the baking sheet from the oven and plopped it onto the burners of the stove. The pan shifted and slid into her wrist.

"Ow!" she yelped.

He started for Dawn, but Margo appeared first.

"You okay?" Margo asked, setting a brown paper bag on the counter, and breaking a piece of aloe from the plant sitting beside the kitchen sink. "Here, put this on it."

"Thanks," Dawn said, taking the plant piece and dabbing it on the welt. She looked at Margo. "This isn't a good idea."

"What? Aloe?"

"You know damn well I'm not talking about aloe. I'm talking about Tyson. I should have said no."

"Why?" Margo said, propping her hands on her hips. "You stupid or something? You ain't screwin' him, girl. You're going to ride a four-wheeler. That won't make your panties hit the dirt."

"Well, my panties aren't going to hit the dirt. Or anywhere else. If I'm going to have a relationship, it's not going to be based on sexual attraction."

"Who said anything about sex?" Tyson said, stepping into the kitchen. He couldn't skulk and listen to the conversation like some Peeping Tom. Though the conversation had been interesting.

Dawn spun around and banged her ankle on a bottom drawer that was sticking out. She yelped then hopped around on her good foot.

"Uh-oh," Margo said, "I'm outta here on this one."

"Coward," Tyson said, stooping down and lifting Dawn's foot into his hands.

Dawn's traitorous friend disappeared swifter than a cat with the family goldfish. Tyson ignored the discomfort of the moment and focused on the reddening mark on Dawn's ankle. He tried to not notice how sweet her ankle was or how he wanted to slide his hand up her smooth calf to sample the curve of her leg.

She tugged her foot from his hands. "It's fine."

He looked up at her and smiled. Her face was red and it had nothing to do with the heat still radiating from the oven. "So what was that all about?"

"Nothing," she said, straightening and testing her weight on her ankle. "It was nothing. Just girl talk."

He rose, all the while trailing his eyes over her from the top of her braided hair to the tips of her tennis shoes. And he lingered on a few spaces in between a bit longer than necessary. "So, did you just say you wanna have sex with me?"

Her eyes widened, and the color on her cheeks deepened.

"Don't answer that. I'm overstepping here. We agreed to be friends. Friends without benefits. Plus, sex on a four-wheeler would be uncomfortable. Though I've never really tried it before," he said.

Dawn closed her mouth. She looked cute, like a confused puppy. "Oh."

"Listen, I'm heading out to the house to check on Gramps. I'll get the strings hung for the doughnut dunk before I go. See you tomorrow at 1:30 p.m. For the, uh, friends thing."

He stepped out into the cool autumn day, feeling much better than he had after getting off the phone with Karen. He had a date with Dawn. Or what had they called it? An outing.

Anticipation built at the thought of having her to himself for the afternoon. It might not result in anything.

But then again...it might give him another horizon to explore in his fresh start.

He whistled all the way to his truck.

CHAPTER SEVEN

THE LONGS' RANCH HOUSE sat on a lovely hill of gold-enrod. Dawn thought the pretty yellow flowers were the only thing that saved the house from being declared condemned.

Shutters tilted drunkenly, the porch sagged and bright plastic toys littered the drive. It could have been a nice house if someone razed it then built another one. But, Dawn ignored the condition of the house because as Texans often said, "They're good people."

Emma Long appeared on the drooping porch and waved, a bright smile affixed to her round face. "Hey, Dawn, don't come too close. Bailey's got the stomach flu and done give it to Avery."

Dawn stepped from her car and shaded her eyes against the sun. "So we aren't going?"

"Heck, no. Well, I ain't, but you and Tyson can still go. Head on around back. He's back there, getting a four-wheeler ready for you." Emma kicked a plastic pail off the porch and picked up a few old newspapers sitting on the steps.

Dawn hesitated.

Because now her outing felt more like a date. Well, maybe not a steakhouse-and-movie date, but close enough to make her wish she'd passed on the four-wheeling thing. But then again, maybe she was being plain silly about the whole thing. She could resist Tyson.

Plus, he'd shown he didn't want to bother with delving into the abnormal attraction they tried to hide from each other.

Okay. No big deal.

So she pulled her sunglasses from her purse, grabbed a piece of gum and locked the doors. Then she headed around the side of the house to look for the object of her somewhat disturbing dreams—dreams that pervaded her thoughts at random moments, dreams she tried to suppress.

She found him bent over a bright red four-wheeler that looked much too big for her to handle.

"Surely, you don't think I can drive that thing?" she said.

Tyson stepped back and critically assessed the machine in front of him. "I think you can handle her."

"You can handle 'er, Dawn. I ain't known you long, gal, but I've seen you in action. Anyone who can get my old man to spit out his chaw before comin' inside Tucker House can handle a little ol' four-wheeler." Avery Long stood on the porch in a T-shirt and jogging pants. He did look a bit green round the gills, but his words were friendly as ever.

"Okay, I trust you, Avery," Dawn called with a friendly wave.

"Y'all have fun," Avery called, before disappearing into the house.

"But you don't trust me?" Tyson asked, wiping his palms on the front of his jeans. Jeans that were a bit too tight on his butt, but Dawn wasn't complaining. Just noticing.

"I won't answer that," she said. The words should have teased, instead they felt potent. Was it him? Or herself she didn't trust?

Probably both.

Tyson's gaze met hers and something passed between them. She'd be crazy to put a definition to exactly what it was, but it made her itchy in her skin. And likely Tyson felt the same.

He turned toward the other four-wheeler, which sat under a Texas sweetgum tree festooned in orange and gold. The green ATV was even bigger than the red one Dawn would be riding. "Let's get going. It'll be dark before we know it."

Dawn eyed the red ATV warily as Tyson set a few items in the storage compartment on his four-wheeler. Then he patted the seat of hers, assisted her onto it and showed her the handbrakes, off/on switch and gave her a rundown about shifting her weight when climbing hills. She dutifully reiterated his instructions before pushing in the brake and thumbing the ignition switch.

The machine roared to life beneath her.

Her heart leaped the first time she hit the gas, but after a minute or so, she discovered driving a four-wheeler was similar to the go-carts she and Andrew raced when he was younger. The scenery rushing past her and Tyson as they steered onto the dirt trails carved into the hilly Texas countryside was much more attractive than the oversize mouse heads she and her son had sped past at the Family Fun Zone.

She redirected her gaze from the view of Tyson's appealing backside, and enjoyed the lacy stalks of wildflowers and the fading green of the expansive stretches of pasture surrounding them. Soon they entered a quiet patch of forest. Branches brushed against her shoulders as the pungent smell of pines, so fresh and primeval, invaded her nose. Light fell through the trees in soft patterns and the lush green was interrupted only occasionally by the surprise of autumn color.

Peace settled inside her as her body melted into the drone of the machine. Perhaps all those silly folks who splashed through Texas on loud four-wheelers knew something she did not.

They rode for thirty minutes before Tyson slowed and pointed toward a path that broke off from the one they were on. It disappeared around a curve as if swallowed by hungry trees. She nodded and followed him as he charged into the unknown.

A few minutes and a couple of near decapitations later, they emerged into a clearing bordering a pond. The still beauty of the sparkling water made her catch her breath.

Tyson rolled to a halt and killed his ATV. She did the same.

For a moment, neither spoke. They simply took in the awesome beauty before them.

"A hidden pond," Dawn breathed, aware of the freshness of the air she took in.

"Not so hidden. I think I fished here as a boy. We're on the Pattersons' property."

Dawn slid from the seat. Her legs felt a bit shaky as she stepped onto the dying grass. "So we're trespassing?"

Tyson swung off his seat and strolled toward the water's edge. "No. Avery said several of the property owners carved these paths out so they could do exactly what we're doing. We're good."

Dawn joined him at the edge of the pond. Small minnows darted into the murky depths as she stepped beside him. Birds cawed overhead as squirrels scampered in the heavy brush skirting the water. Again, peace nestled within her.

"I brought some iced tea. Want one?"

Dawn shook her head. "I'm trying to break my afternoon caffeine habit. Not sleeping too good lately."

"Jeez, that's what an old person would say," he said with a smirk.

She propped her hands on her hips. "You calling me old, mister?"

"Well, if the shoe fits and all that," he said, digging around inside the compartment under the four-wheeler seat. He pulled two bottled iced teas from the depths, along with a couple of red apples. "This one's decaffeinated."

She took the bottle and waved off the apple. Her hands felt dusty, and left small streaks of muddy water against the chilled glass. It was hard not to request a wet wipe.

Tyson popped the lid on his drink and held it aloft. "To our friendship and a fine autumn day."

She clinked her bottle against his, suddenly wishing the tea were a glass of wine, that this was a real date and they were toasting each other in a nonfriendship way.

Damn.

She couldn't help herself. What the hell was wrong with her? Couldn't she forget about wanting to run her hands up Tyson's naked chest? Or tracing his earlobe with her tongue. She was seriously whacked. That was all.

Her eyes slid to Tyson as he gulped the tea. Heck, even his throat moving as he swallowed turned her on.

She lifted her own bottle and took a sip. It was good tea. It didn't help quench her true thirst at all though.

"Look," Tyson said, breaking the silence. He pointed toward scrubby brush a few feet away. A small brown hare sat perfectly still before twitching an ear in their direction. At her slight intake of breath, it hopped into the tangled brush.

"I love rabbits," Dawn said, her eyes searching the woods for another trace of the hare. "I used to have little decorative rabbits all over my kitchen."

He narrowed his eyes. "Why do women do that?"

"Do what?"

"Decorate with stuff like bunny statues. That's weird." He drained the last of his tea.

She snorted. "And men aren't weird? You spend all Sunday monitoring your fantasy football teams, key word being *fantasy*. And don't make me bring out the fact men sit on a toilet for, like, hours."

"To get away from women," he said.

"Well, don't get a woman if you don't want to deal with her. You could save your kitchen from being attacked by bunnies and never worry about putting the toilet seat down." Dawn grumbled, digging the toe of her sneaker in the scattered pine needles. She silently drew her initial in the sandy soil.

"I can think of better things to do with a woman other than get away from her." His words were sensual, implying fulfillment of her naughty dreams.

It was a temptation she couldn't resist.

"Oh?" she said. "What kind of things would you do to a woman?"

Her eyes finally met his. The golden depths betrayed the desire within. She played with fire, but like a pyromaniac she couldn't stop. She kept lighting matches. And she knew why. She wanted him too much to stop.

"I'd start with her earlobe. I've always like a woman's ear. So delicate." His gaze followed her hand as she tucked a strand of hair behind her ear. He took her half-filled bottle from her and set it beside his empty one.

Dawn could feel her breath speed up.

"I like to trace the outside with my tongue. Just the barest of touches, like a butterfly's wings. Soft. Then I like to suck the earlobe right into my mouth before kissing my way down to that pulse beating in her neck."

Dawn swallowed as his gaze dipped to that very spot which had quickened in tune with her breathing.

His eyes returned to hers. They had darkened and she wanted to step closer and look deeper into the whiskey depths, to find the true man beneath the outer toughness.

But she didn't have to because he stepped toward her. She held as still as the rabbit who'd leaped into the woods. But she was aware. Oh, so aware.

His hand touched her cheek, the barest of caresses, before cupping her chin and tilting her head back.

"Then I focus on the mouth. I do love a mouth like yours, Dawn. Sweet and ripe like cherries. Corny, I know. But true. It makes me want to taste. To immerse myself."

She forgot how to breathe as his lips brushed against hers. Again, it was soft like a wisp of gossamer. He did it once. Twice.

She didn't allow a third time, for she lifted on both toes and pressed her mouth to his, fully and not so gently.

Tyson didn't seem to mind. He took her lead and curled his large hand beneath her head, angling her head so he might sample her lips fully.

And it was good. He tasted like warmth, crackling fire and butterscotch schnapps. She couldn't stop tasting him. Her hands slid to his shoulders and threaded through his hair, bringing his mouth down harder.

He hauled her closer so her breasts pressed against him. Her stomach nestled against his hips and she felt his hardness. A dam broke inside her and need came gushing out, flooding her body. The woods faded around them. All that existed was this man, this incredible man who did incredible things with his mouth.

He cupped her face and drank of her, and she'd never felt anything like it. Ever. She wanted to crawl inside him. Have him crawl inside her. Or thrust inside her. Take her to dizzying heights. New peaks.

One of his hands snaked down her back and cupped her bottom, bringing her against his erection, rocking her against him. A frenzy built as she absorbed herself in Tyson.

She was so sucked into the world they'd created nothing penetrated until Dawn heard the most shocking word she'd ever hear when being held by a man.

"Mom?"

She ripped her mouth from Tyson's. "Andrew?"

She dropped onto her heels and looked at her son standing in the clearing. Her brain felt foggy and it took a moment for the sight to penetrate her senses.

Andrew was here.

How?

She blinked. She felt as though she'd been tossed into a movie. It was too coincidental to be real.

"What the hell are you doing here?" her son said, anger flooding his face.

Dawn dropped her arms from Tyson's shoulders and took a shaky step backward. She couldn't seem to form words. She couldn't understand how he had appeared out of the blue, like some spy, a seriously pissed-off spy.

The answer to that question stepped beside Dawn's son.

Marcie Patterson. Her son's latest flirtation was whip-thin with high breasts snug in a top that left little to the imagination. A blond-streaked ponytail brushed her shoulders. It didn't escape her that Andrew had likely been looking to do much the same thing she and Tyson had been doing. Creating opportunity with a girl who was more than willing.

Dawn found her voice. "For one thing, I live here. And don't you use that language with me. I brought you up better."

Andrew took his ball cap off then put it on again. He turned on Tyson. She could see ire crackle in Andrew's eyes before he shifted them back to her.

"Seriously?" her son said. "You're, like, getting on me for my language, and I just found you doing some dude in the woods?"

"We were only kissing, and what I do with a man is none of your business, young man."

She could feel Tyson stiffen beside her. This wasn't his fight, but she appreciated the supportive hand he placed on the small of her back.

She stepped forward, feeling irritation flood her body. How dare Andrew show up on her moment? How dare he act so rudely? Make her feel small when she'd sacrificed her whole life for him. He didn't have the right.

Besides, her son hadn't even bothered to let her know he was in Oak Stand.

"Hi, Ms. Taggart," Marcie chirped, slipping her arm through Andrew's. He shook it away, refusing to be soothed by the girl.

Dawn didn't really care for Marcie, but she gave a small smile to the girl. "Hello, Marcie."

"So are y'all, like, riding four-wheelers or something?" the girl asked, pretending they had met up at Wal-Mart. As though coming upon her boyfriend's mother making out with a total stranger was an everyday occurrence.

Again, she tried out a smile. "Yeah, it's a nice day for taking a ride. This is my friend, Tyson Hart."

Dawn gestured to Tyson. He nodded at the girl.

"Oh, hi," she said, flashing him a practiced smile, the one she used on every male she encountered. The girl was a man-eater in training. "Those your four-wheelers?"

He nodded. "Well, one of them. I've been teaching Dawn to ride."

Andrew's mouth turned down. "Yeah, I see that. I thought you were going to Houston this weekend, Mom. To see Dad."

"No, you were mistaken," Dawn said, folding her arms across her chest. "I thought you were in Houston."

Andrew's eyes flashed with something. Guilt? Anger? "Guess neither of us did what we said we'd do, huh?"

She ignored his sarcasm. "Tyson, this is my son, Andrew. I wasn't expecting him this weekend," she said, allowing the anger to creep back in her tone. She'd been asking her son for weeks to come for a visit. He'd claimed fall baseball practice and difficult classes had him too tied up. Obviously, the ropes had loosened. Or maybe Marcie had more power than a pathetic mother with no future and no real home.

Andrew didn't extend a hand toward Tyson. Rather, he crossed his arms and dismissed him. "I came for Carter Harp's Halloween party."

"Really? So where'd you stay?" Dawn asked, crossing her own arms. Marcie shifted in her trendy running shoes and looked away. The girl knew when battle lines had been drawn. Tyson remained silent, but he rubbed small circles on her back.

"I slept over at Marcie's house. With Marcie," her son said, his lips twisting into a smirk. Dawn felt it. Felt what he tried to do—punish her. Flaunt his inappropriate behavior in front of her while looking down his nose at her—the double standards game.

"Oh, really?" she said. "Well, I hope you were responsible. I don't need Nick Patterson standing on Jack's doorstep with a shotgun. Nor am I ready to be a grandmother."

Marcie turned the color of the sweetgum leaves on the tree behind her. Andrew didn't look embarrassed in the least. "We're good. It's a lesson Dad beat into me, if you remember."

She didn't say anything. Her heart hurt too much. She'd missed her good-natured child over the past few months. Why was he so angry? Because she'd kissed another man? Because she hadn't fallen for his prearranged weekend with Larry the Snake? Because she wasn't bending over backward to please him?

Tyson patted her back one last time before dropping his hand. "Well, we'll be on our way now we know you two are being conscientious sex partners. Come on, Dawn." He held out his hand. She looked at it for a moment before taking it.

They walked to the four-wheelers parked just off the trail. Dawn climb on hers while Tyson tossed the bottles into the storage compartment and climbed on.

Andrew stood like a statue, his face fixed in belligerence. Poor Marcie searched the bushes for escape. She looked like the brown hare except much more desperate. The whole situation couldn't have been more uncomfortable.

Just before she hit the button to bring the engine to life, Andrew stepped forward with his hand up. "Hey, Tyson, I appreciate your acknowledging my sexual responsibility, man. I'd appreciate it if you do the same. She's my mom, and someone's got to look out for her."

Andrew tossed her a meaningful look and strolled toward the pond.

Smart-ass.

Tyson turned and looked at her. She couldn't stop the tears from springing to her eyes. This whole outing had been a colossal mistake. She now reaped the benefit of her impulsiveness. Of her stupid desires. This was a reminder. She needed to stay focused on her future. On figuring out where she would be this time next year. She had to stick to the plan. And Tyson Hart had never been part of any plan.

As she cranked the four-wheeler, she cranked up her resolve to stay the path.

No more straying. She'd sacrifice the hidden ponds and sweet kisses for an actual destination.

CHAPTER EIGHT

JACK BALANCED HIS DAUGHTER in his lap and frowned at Dawn. "He's nineteen, for Christ's sake. What did you expect?"

"I know Andrew's age and I'm not so stupid I don't realize he's sleeping with Marcie, but he didn't even call to say he was in town. And even worse, he's trying to set me up with Larry. I don't get it. Ever since that weekend Larry stayed in our guest room, he's been shoving us together. Time to get over the ol' parents' divorce, don't you think? But I'm more angry he didn't come by the ranch."

Jack cradled the baby so he could take a big bite from a caramel apple sitting on the table beside him. "He was looking for his treats elsewhere."

Dawn wanted to throw something at her brother. She didn't even want to entertain the idea. The whole situation made her sad. And angry. When had things fallen apart between her and her son?

"Well, I don't want to talk about it," she said, kicking off her running shoes. She'd just gotten in from a run around the ranch and decided she needed trail shoes. The rocky Texas ground had caused splinters of pain to shoot through her knees. The run hadn't cleared her mind anyhow. Only cluttered it more.

"Don't want to talk about what?" Nellie said, slipping

into the den and whisking her daughter away from her husband.

"Hey, give her back," Jack said. "We're making faces at each other."

"Honey, that's her poopy face. Unless you'd rather change the diaper?" Nellie said, picking up the toile diaper bag at his feet.

"Nope. Wouldn't want to stop you from practicing your craft. You get the diaper perfect. I'm just in your shadow." Jack hit the lever on the recliner and launched himself back.

"You need more practice," Nellie said, sticking out her tongue while still managing to look about as content as a woman could—a beautiful newborn baby in one hand, a husband at arm's reach and a future that looked as secure as Fort Knox.

Future? Dawn didn't want to go there. Hers was like a rickety bridge spanning a gorge. The one from all the movies—old, fraying, missing planks. Skeletons scattered below. Precarious. Very precarious. Which was a bad thing for a gal who liked to plan out which panties she'd wear for the week.

Little Mae mewled like a kitten as her mother set her on the striped couch and kissed her baby feet before tugging up the pink gown covered in yellow duckies. "So what are we not talking about?"

"The fact Andrew came to town and didn't tell Dawn. And the fact he's pissed off because she was with another man," Jack said, tugging a dog-eared copy of *Sports Illustrated* from beneath a pile of *Child* magazines.

"He's dating the Patterson girl, isn't he?" Nellie said, making kissing faces at Mae. Dawn wanted to tell her the baby couldn't even see her mother at that distance, but didn't. Nellie likely wouldn't stop anyway.

"Yeah, he's been seeing her off and on again for a while. I don't expect it to go anywhere. She's a small-town girl who fascinates him," Dawn said, sinking into a chair beside the stacked stone fireplace.

Nellie called the den Jack's man cave, but Dawn liked the room better than any other. It reminded her of her father's office when she was a girl. The walls were painted adobe and the room boasted comfy overstuffed furniture and rustic Texas decor. The wood floor beneath Dawn's bare feet shone lustrously in the warm lamplight. A Navajo patterned rug centered the room underneath an antler chandelier.

"Nothing wrong with a small-town girl," Nellie said, focusing on her sister-in-law.

Dawn had foot-in-mouth syndrome. She figuratively removed her socked foot from her mouth. "Sorry."

"No offense taken. We country gals roll with the punches. But why does it bother you that he's seeing Marcie?"

Andrew seeing Marcie wasn't what was bothering her. It was Andrew seeing her and Tyson in the woods preparing to rip each other's clothes off. But she didn't want that kernel of information out there. In any form. She still had issues with what they had done. Guilt and want balled up into a massive knot of confusion in her brain.

"No. I shouldn't be one of those moms who thinks her baby is too good for a girl. I'm just bothered that he and I are on two different wavelengths. I feel like I'm not even a part of his life anymore. We always had an honest relationship. Well, as honest as a boy can be with his mother."

"Exactly," Jack said, not looking up from the magazine. "Mothers never know their children as well as they think they do. You don't want to know the stuff I hid from our mother."

"But I do," Nellie said. Her eyes sparkled in the dim room.

Jack eyed her. "Trust me. You don't. It's killing me to know I have to raise a daughter. I know too much about horny boys."

Nellie laughed. Dawn didn't. Her son was obviously one of those boys. Maybe all boys from thirteen to ninety were like that. Maybe that's all Tyson wanted, too. She didn't know his heart nor his intent for her.

This thought stilled her. Another good reason to redraw the line of friendship and not cross it.

"I guess it hurts to know Drew didn't want to see me. I haven't seen him since the beginning of September. And even then, he spent much of his time with Marcie while I washed his socks. You'd think he'd want to at least come by and say hello." She probably sounded whiny, but she missed Andrew desperately. Didn't he get that? He was her baby. Always would be.

"Nope," Jack said, making her want to slap him. "It's the natural progression of things. In fact, maybe his trying to hook you up with the Lar Man is his way of protecting you from being lonely. Maybe he's worried about you after the year you went through. Maybe he feels bad he's not around anymore."

Dawn tilted her head. "Huh?"

"Like if you're not alone, he doesn't feel guilty."

"Then why would it have to be Larry? Why would he be mad I was with another guy?"

"'Cause Larry's his father. That makes it easier. There is no unknown."

Dawn frowned. That twist had never crossed her mind. "You're not really helping."

"So what about Tyson? Did you have fun riding on the four-wheelers?" Nellie was good at changing the subject. It was as though she could smell an argument coming on.

Tyson.

The taste of his mouth had popped into Dawn's thoughts more than she cared to admit as she'd pounded the trail stretching across the ranch. She kept reliving their kiss in her mind. How good he'd felt pressed against her. How he'd tasted like sweet tea and temptation. And how wrong it had all been.

The trip to the Longs' house had been awkward. Her emotions had been swirling like a Texas-size dust storm. When they'd finally rolled into the yard and killed the engines, she couldn't force any cheerfulness. They'd said the minimum, called out "thanks" to Avery, who'd come out to wave goodbye, then Dawn had driven away.

"Dawn?"

Her head snapped up as Nellie called her name. "Yes?"

"The four-wheelers?"

"Oh. We had a nice time. Avery and his brood have the stomach flu, so it was just Tyson and me. I actually enjoyed the ride. Go figure."

Nellie cast a worried look at the baby. "You didn't get around the Longs', did you?"

Dawn smiled. "No, Avery popped his head out the back door and said hello. No contact."

Her sister-in-law released her breath. "Well, I'm glad you liked the ride. Although, I thought it was an odd activity for a date."

"It wasn't a date. Just an outing."

Jack snorted. "Right."

Before Dawn could make a sarcastic comeback, the

phone rang. Jack scooped up the cordless handset from the table beside him and answered while Dawn gave her sister-in-law an exasperated face. Nellie grinned and patted Mae's back. "It's probably Lila. She's been calling every day to check on Mae."

"Mom can't wait to get her hands on that grandbaby. I can't believe she took that trip with Dad. She hated Wyoming last time. He told her they'd be back in time for the birth. Guess a freak blizzard and an impatient baby shut that down."

"She may never forgive me or Wyoming," Nellie said, kissing the baby's head.

"Or Dad," Dawn said. Her mother still hadn't gotten over the fact her father had cashed in on the promise she made him so long ago—the dream of his own horse ranch. Of course, Tom Darby built her an exact replica of the California farmhouse in which she'd been raised in order to entice her south. Having a new grandbaby had sweetened the deal.

Jack placed the phone on the table. "That was Tyson. He won't be in tomorrow. His grandfather had a heart attack and he's at the hospital in Longview with him."

Dawn's own heart dropped to her stomach. "Oh, no. That's horrible."

Nellie murmured much the same. "Terrible. Mr. Hart's about all he's got family-wise. Well, except for his daughter."

"I better head over to the hospital."

"Dawn, it's nearly eight o'clock and Longview's so far away. Just call him," Nellie said, nuzzling the baby's downy head as she began to fret. Mae bobbed her head against her mother's shoulder in that frantic rooting motion all newborns performed when it was time for dinner.

"He doesn't have anybody else, Nell. I'm his friend and that's what friends do. Did he say how bad it was?"

Jack shook his head. "They just got to the hospital. He said he thought Grady was stable, but Tyson is stuck in the ICU waiting room while the doctors work on Grady."

Dawn picked up the socks and shoes she'd abandoned next to the chair. "I'd better go, but first I'm grabbing a shower. I can't offer a sweaty shoulder."

She almost missed the look Nellie shot Jack.

"Maybe I should drive you," Jack said, lowering the footrest on his recliner.

Dawn shook her head. "I know the way. Stay with Nell and the baby."

Jack shrugged his shoulders at Nellie and disappeared behind his magazine. His wife cleared her throat. He ignored her.

"Nellie, I'll be fine. I've got my cell. I'll call you when I get there and let you know how Grady is."

She could tell Nellie didn't like the thought of her going alone, but her sister-in-law nodded and went back to fussing with the baby.

Sometimes having a family was a pain in the ass. She often wished she could rent a boat, drive them all out into the middle of the ocean and shove them off into watery depths. No more meddling, drama or guilt-trips. Other times, family made her feel gooey like a chocolate-chip cookie fresh from the oven.

This was a chocolate-chip moment.

THE SOUND OF HER SNEAKERS squeaking on the polished hospital floor brought back a sense of déjà vu.

Had it only been three weeks ago she'd met Tyson and her newest niece?

Seemed impossible. She felt as if she'd known Tyson much longer than a mere three weeks. More like a lifetime.

The hospital was virtually empty except for the shadow of a passing nurse or orderly. The smell of disinfectant and despair lurked around each corner, and the elevator smelled like feet. After a wrong turn and a stop to the visitor restroom, she finally made it to the ICU waiting room.

Tyson was the only person in the room. He sat, head propped in his hands. She couldn't tell whether he was asleep, praying or lost in thought. But he looked pretty damn lonely. She was glad she'd come.

"Hey," she called softly from the doorway.

His head snapped up and for a moment she saw fear in his eyes.

"Oh, good," he said, before standing. She could see the relief radiating off him. "It's you."

She gave a little shrug. "Thought you might need a friend."

He sank onto the faux-leather chair. "Thanks."

He didn't say anything else, but his shoulders relaxed a bit, as if having someone else there had lessened his burden.

She slid into one of the bright orange cushioned chairs and patted his arm. "Know anything yet?"

"Not really. I guess they're still running tests. I don't know." He rubbed one hand over his face and sighed. "These damned places take so long to do anything."

She rubbed his arm. "When did it happen?"

His hand covered hers and he squeezed. He shifted their joined hands to his thigh. Hers fit nicely in his.

She liked the way his calloused fingers stroked the skin between her thumb and fingers, the way his large hand contrasted against her smaller one.

"We were watching the Saints game. I'd fixed some cheese sticks—his favorite—and the second quarter had just started. He told me Drew Brees threw off his back foot on the last play then he stopped talking, gasped and went still. I couldn't get out of the chair fast enough."

"Oh, Tyson, that's so scary."

"Yeah, but he seemed okay. He started complaining about how the marinara sauce must have given him horrible indigestion. But I didn't think so. I had this gut feeling like something was wrong. So I carted his stubborn ass to the truck. He fought me the whole way. But when we were outside Longview, he started sweating profusely then passed out."

She squeezed his hand.

"Scared the sh—mess out of me. I got here and they said it was probably a heart attack." He swiped his arm over his forehead and leaned back, but he didn't let go of her hand. "Hell."

Dawn knew she couldn't make his obvious distress disappear. She really didn't know what to do other than sit there with him. So she did.

For twenty minutes they waited, neither one making any sort of conversation. She stared at a Western landscape hanging crookedly on the utilitarian wall and the scuffs on the tiled floor caused by the chairs being moved around. Finally a plump nurse in green scrubs whose name tag read Delilah Newhouse, RN, popped her head into the room. Tyson's grip on her hand tightened.

"Mr. Hart?"

"Yes," he said, his voice calm though Dawn felt a tremble in his hand.

"Your grandfather's stable. Dr. Quimby wants to talk with you."

Tyson closed his eyes for a moment before opening them again. "Good. Thank you."

"You can come back and see him now."

Tyson stood, but didn't drop Dawn's hand.

The nurse gave him a quick smile. "Your wife can come, too."

Dawn opened her mouth to say she wasn't his wife, then realized it didn't really matter. What did Delilah care?

As she rose, Tyson's cell phone went off. He pulled it from his pocket with an apologetic look at the nurse. "It's my daughter."

"You'll probably need to call her back. Dr. Quimby gets off in ten minutes and you need to speak with him." Delilah didn't give him a chance to answer. She merely held the door so he could pass.

The phone kept repeating a most annoying ringtone. Tyson looked at it then looked at Dawn. "Will you talk to Laurel and tell her about Gramps?"

"Me?" Dawn said. "Laurel doesn't know me."

He shoved the phone at her. "Doesn't matter. Talk to her then meet me in ICU."

He disappeared through the door, leaving her with the possibility of offending a thirteen-year-old who was likely afraid for her great-grandfather.

Dawn flipped open the phone. "Tyson Hart's phone."

Jeez. She sounded stupid. Why didn't she just say hello?

"Um, who's this?" a breathy voice asked.

"Hi. Laurel?"

"No, this is Karen Hart, Laurel's mother. Who is this?"

Oh, crap. The almost ex-wife.

"Oh, hi. Um…my name is Dawn Taggart. I'm the director of the adult care center Tyson's renovating," Dawn said, wanting to slap herself for sounding so silly. What did that matter? She was acting like some crazy teenager who wanted to justify being with Tyson during an emergency.

"Okay," Karen said. "And you're answering Tyson's phone because…?"

Dislike bristled inside Dawn. "Because he's with the doctor now."

"Oh," the voice said. "Well, Laurel's been worried about Gramps. I have, too, of course. How is he?"

"I don't know. Tyson said the doctor thought he had a heart attack, but the nurse—"

"Never mind. Have Tyson call us when he is through talking to the doctor."

"Certainly," Dawn said.

Karen didn't bother to say goodbye. Tyson's ex didn't sound like a pleasant person. Didn't sound like she was worthy of a guy like Tyson. Of course, Dawn's dislike for the woman could be a result of the jolt of jealousy that ripped through her. He had loved Karen, made a baby with her, shared his dreams with her. And that made Karen so not her friend.

Dawn shook her stirrings of jealousy away. She had no claim whatsoever on Tyson. They were friends. But as a friend, she was free to dislike Tyson's former wife.

She pocketed Tyson's phone and headed toward the ICU unit. Delilah waved her into one of the small rooms surrounding the nurse's bay where Tyson stood alone, looking at his grandfather. Grady had tubes, drips and blipping monitors attached, yet he slept peacefully.

"Hey," she whispered, hesitating outside the room door.

Tyson let out a deep breath and motioned for her to come closer. "They've given him a sedative."

"What did the doctor say?"

Tyson rubbed a weary hand over his face. "Definitely a heart attack, but they think he's out of the woods. They're going to keep him here tonight and do some tests tomorrow so they can tell how much damage was done to his ticker."

She touched his shoulder. "That's good. Your wife wants you to call her."

"Who?" he asked. "Oh, you mean Karen. Funny, I don't think of her as my wife. Haven't for a long time."

Something warm flooded Dawn's body at those words. She'd never liked that she lusted after someone who was still technically married, even if it was in name only and would be undone in a matter of days.

Tyson smiled at her. Then like in the waiting room, his hand covered hers. But this time he wasn't content to merely hold her hand. He pulled her into a hug. "Thank you for coming."

Dawn curled her arms around him and rested her cheek against his chest. His worn T-shirt was soft against her face and he smelled like warm male with the faint scent of fried cheese. He turned his head and rested it against hers.

They stood that way for a few minutes—Tyson pressed to her, seeming to draw comfort in her presence.

And it felt right. For once, she felt no guilt for being in his arms.

A monitor bleeped and he drew back as a nurse hurried in and pressed a few buttons. She smiled reassuringly. "Don't worry. He's stable. These machines go off all night."

Tyson tried to look convinced, but failed.

The nurse patted him. "Go home. If there's any change, we'll call you. Nothing you can do now but get some rest."

She bustled out, not waiting for a response.

"Man, the nurses are bossy around here," Tyson said, shoving his hands into his pockets.

"They have to be to put up with patients. People in pain are not the easiest to deal with," she said, missing the comfort of his arms about her. Of course, she didn't need comfort, but it had felt good.

"I guess. You think I should leave him?" Tyson asked, walking her toward the swinging doors that would take them back to the ICU waiting room.

"That's your call. The waiting room doesn't look comfy, and they have given him a sedative."

Tyson pressed his lips together. He looked determined. "I've slept in worse. I'll stay. I wouldn't sleep at home anyway."

Dawn nodded. She could admire his selflessness, something she'd rarely seen in the men in her life. Tyson was different. Deep down she knew that, and it scared her. Because he stirred hope deep inside her. Hope that her attraction to him would result in something good this time. Hope that she could find something like what Jack and Nellie had, something to build on, to nurture, to grow.

And hope felt awfully dangerous. Because it made her believe in falling in love.

Love had never been her friend.

CHAPTER NINE

NEARLY THREE WEEKS LATER, Tyson opened the truck door and glared at his grandfather. "Come on, move your butt. I've got a job to do, Gramps."

Grady didn't budge from the passenger seat. "I didn't agree to this. This place is for old folks and I ain't one of 'em."

"It's either this or the home health nurse around the clock. And, I swear, I'll find the biggest, ugliest one they have," Tyson said, aggravated enough to bend the door frame with his grip. He'd had about enough of Grady's antics. Over the past two weeks, he had to check the old man's mouth every night to make sure he didn't tongue his medications. And he didn't want to think about the whole diet change deal. He'd learned to duck fairly quickly when he delivered whole-wheat pasta or an egg-white omelet. Grady seemed to think his heart attack was "just a little episode" and didn't merit any change in his sedate lifestyle. He regressed into a toddler. Laurel was never as difficult.

So he'd done the only thing he could do. Once his grandfather had been cleared to venture out, Tyson had enrolled him in Tucker House's program.

"I don't give a damn! I ain't going to Tucker House!"

Except Grady didn't yell "Tucker House." He used the naughty word that rhymed with Tucker.

"Grady Hart, watch your mouth. Don't make me bring out the spoon and vinegar on the first day," said a voice obviously trying to choke down laughter. Luckily, Dawn had a sense of humor.

Tyson spun to find her and Elvera Griffin coming down the drive. Dawn wore a dark blue sweater that wrapped around her lush breasts in a way that made Tyson's mouth water. A skirt the color of wet concrete swished around black heeled boots. For a moment an image of Dawn in a black lace bra, garters and those heeled boots flashed in his mind.

Sweet mother of all that was wicked. She'd look spectacular.

"Don't tempt her, Grady. She can be meaner than a snake." Elvera gave Dawn a little wink. At least, Tyson thought it was a wink. Could have been the glare on Elvera's overly large, hot pink glasses.

Grady still hadn't moved from the truck. He stared at Elvera who wore a pair of overalls with bright green flowers all over them. "You that gal I took to Fred Jones's barn dance back in '46? Vera Trisk from Iron Bridge?"

Elvera put a withered hand over a mouth painted to match her glasses and giggled. "Why, Grady Hart, you know it is. You're supposed to say I haven't changed a bit."

Grady's blue eyes lowered a bit. Mostly in the general vicinity of Elvera's generous chest. "Well, you ain't changed where it matters."

Dawn's mouth dropped open, Tyson snorted and Elvera giggled before moving toward Grady. She extended one hand and grasped his grandfather's sleeve. "You old scoundrel, come on and let me show you what

I'm doing in the garden out back. I might need your opinion on where to place the bird feeders."

Grady hefted himself from the truck with a grunt. With a slight swagger, he took Elvera's arm and led her up the drive.

"Well, I'll be," Tyson said, grinning at Dawn. "I guess all it took was a pair of green eyes batting in his direction."

"Not sure it was the pair of eyes, though." Dawn laughed, taking a bag from him. The sound was plain musical and did funny things to his heart. Along with a region much lower than the one that thumped against his ribs.

They walked up the drive, silent in the beauty of a spectacular autumn morning. The sun peeked from behind clouds illuminating the first truly crisp morning they'd had thus far. It made a man feel as though he could do anything and Tyson embraced the thought that all things were possible.

Dawn shifted the bag from one hand to the other, causing a piece of dark hair to escape from her hair clip. He wanted to touch her, so he reached out and pushed the errant tress behind her ear.

She stopped.

He took two more steps and turned back toward her, smiling because he felt like it. A beautiful morning, a beautiful woman and a day not having to convince his grandfather he'd have to start riding the exercise bike.

"What are we doing?" she asked, setting the bag at her feet and crossing her arms. A tiny furrow gathered between her pretty brown eyes. She frowned way too much for his taste.

He knew what she was asking, but didn't really want

to go there this morning. "We're going inside so I can catch up on my work."

She shook her head and the piece of hair dislodged again from behind her ear. He sighed, put down his sander and carpenter's box, and shoved both hands in his pockets.

"You mean, between us."

She nodded, her eyes meeting his. For a moment, he looked at her, at this woman who'd made him feel for the first time in a long time. But she looked so serious and slightly grumpy that he couldn't remember why she made him feel like whistling show tunes. She just did.

She unfolded her arms, turning her palms upward. "We agreed to be friends, but this doesn't feel like friendship. I guess I'm being honest because I don't know where to go. How to handle you touching me like that."

"Does it bother you? My touching you?"

She bit her lip. "No, and that's the problem. I like it and I want you to touch me…and kiss me…and…" Her sigh ended the thought.

She looked pained. And that seemed so wrong. She acted as though where they were heading was a bad place. "So what's wrong with feeling that way? I like you. You like me. At least, I think you do."

A sudden wind swept through the oak trees, throwing dappled sunlight across Dawn's face. Her skirt flapped against her boots. She reminded him of Mother Earth, of all things feminine and mysterious. A goddess among her elements.

"You are still married," she said.

"But if Gramps hadn't gotten sick, I wouldn't be." Tyson had been scheduled in with his lawyer to finalize the divorce the week Gramps had had his heart attack.

Admittedly formalizing the end of the marriage—a marriage that had been over for a good while—had taken a backseat for Tyson while he focused on his grandfather. "I'm signing the papers in five days. I'll be free. So that's not a reason to put on the brakes."

"You don't get it, Tyson," she said, straightening her shoulders. "I promised myself I wouldn't get tangled in a relationship. The last one I had was…disastrous. People got hurt. It was bad. So I can't risk that same result right now. Living in Oak Stand is temporary. Fleeting. I can't—no, I *won't*—base a relationship on my wanting to strip you naked and mount you."

He couldn't stop the grin. Or the rush of desire that flooded him. But he knew this conversation was important. He pressed his mouth into a grim line. "So what you're saying is you're unwilling to take a chance."

Her eyes widened. "No, that's not what I'm saying. I just mean the timing is off for this. And in fairness to everyone outside of you and me, I can't get involved with you until that changes."

He did smile at that. "So you think you can schedule love or attraction or whatever this is? Put it in that little planner you're always toting around?"

"Love?" Her voice rose three octaves. She glanced at the wide porch surrounding Tucker House. Tyson followed her gaze to see Margo disappear with the swish of her broom skirt. Nosy woman.

"I didn't mean love as in what's going on between us, so simmer down. I'm talking about opportunity for growth. You're refusing to give what we have between us a chance because it's not convenient for you."

Dawn took a deep breath. It made her chest rise, pulling his attention to her generous curves. Yet again. Hell. He couldn't seem to help himself from wanting to unwrap her from that flapping skirt like she was a present meant for him alone. He wanted her the way he'd never wanted a woman. Or at least one he could remember.

"Stop looking at me like that," she said, rolling her eyes and jerking a thumb toward the house. "Don't think they can't see the way we look at each other."

"I can't help it," he said, shrugging. If she thought he'd stop looking at her, she was crazy. She was a feast for the eyes. Hell, even the old men couldn't seem to stop checking out her butt every time she trotted past the table where they played dominoes.

Her shoulders slumped. "I'm too old for this."

"First of all, you aren't old. You're beautiful. And let's not spend so much time putting up guidelines for our relationship. This is how I see it. You are an attractive, single woman. I am, well, a single guy."

"You know you're attractive," she said, a slight smile finally appearing on her face.

"Whatever. We are two people with no commitments, embarking on a friendship that may lead to something more. Right?" He needed her to agree with him. Especially if he wanted to kiss her again. Which he did.

"I guess."

"Stop being afraid. Surviving Iraq and this divorce have taught me life is too short to spend it cowering in the shadows. Everyone's afraid of getting hurt. That's human, but you can't quit living just because you brush shoulders with heartache," he said, reaching out and cupping her face. "Take a chance. And stop guarding your heart."

"Any other don'ts?" she muttered, leaning into his hand.

"No, but I got a whole list of do's." He chucked her

on the chin. "We won't cover all of them right away. We'll start with numbers one and two tonight."

"Tonight?" Her brown eyes narrowed.

"I'm making my famous Burning Hart chili, sans the fat and cholesterol. The Cowboys are on *Monday Night Football*. Care to join us?" He hadn't planned on making that meal, but he could wing it. Pick up some ground turkey from the grocery store and whip up a mean low-fat version of his tailgate chili.

"Well, okay. How's that meet the requirement for number one?" She tilted her head, a spark of humor returning to her warm eyes.

"Number one is learn how to relax. Although, I'm not sure football is relaxing. Last time, the quarterback's bad throw gave my grandfather a heart attack. We'll just go with the flow." He picked up his sander and carpentry box and started toward the house. He wanted to stay and flirt with Dawn, but they both had work to do.

He hurried up the back stairs, tossing a nod toward his grandfather and Elvera, who were wandering around the backyard staring assessingly at each tree. Leaves crackled underfoot and through the screened back door he could smell something fragrant cooking. Again, possibility welled within him.

He felt Dawn behind him, knew she was struggling with the bag she'd taken from him. He reached back and scooped it from her grasp.

"And don't forget number two."

"What's number two?" She held the squeaky door open wide so he could squeeze through.

"I guess you'll find out."

DAWN GROWLED AT HERSELF in the mirror. Her stupid hair wouldn't curl properly on one side and the golden sand eye shadow made her brown eyes look squinty. But her lips looked good. She'd raided Nellie's supply of designer makeup and found iced mocha latte lip gloss. The neutral color made her mouth look kissable.

Which was a good thing.

Because she planned on using those puppies tonight. As the hot water had sluiced over her body in the shower, she'd decided kissing would be okay. Tyson had been right. She'd been guarding the door to her heart a little too closely. A few dates here and there wouldn't hurt. They weren't falling in love, merely exploring the boundaries of a relationship.

She relifted her breasts in the red lace push-up bra before slipping into the wool dress. It covered everything appropriately, but would allow a peek of red lace if she shifted just right. Some small part of her liked the thought of driving Tyson crazy.

And that surprised her.

Because she'd never been the teasing sort. But something about Tyson made her feel flirty and naughty. Maybe it was the way he looked at her as though he wanted to undress her. Or the way he found excuses to brush against her throughout the day. She blew out a breath as Nellie entered the room.

"You look awesome. What's with all the sighing?" Nellie asked, placing a stack of folded laundry on the bed.

"Oh, nothing. My hair is flat on one side. Wow, you folded my laundry?" Dawn pointed at the stack Nellie had set down before turning toward the mirror and threading a silver and turquoise dangle earring into her ear. Then she tugged her bodice down and pulled on the knee-high black boots she'd worn earlier that day. They totally made the dress.

"Yeah, Jack mixed some of your T-shirts in with mine. He can't tell the difference." Nellie plopped onto the bed. Her sweatshirt carried spit-up stains and she'd pulled on a pair of maternity shorts. She looked tired—kinda like every new mother on the face of the planet. "Hey, you forgot to put on your other earring."

"Thanks." Dawn threaded the other earring in her ear and gathered her hair up so she could put it in a ponytail.

"No, leave it down. Guys love to run their hands through long hair," Nellie said, stifling a yawn with her hand. She flopped back onto Dawn's bed and stretched.

"I'm not planning on his hands in my hair. I'm just going over for supper. And a football game." Dawn released her hair and tossed down the holder. Maybe Nellie was right.

"I saw your bra strap. Red lace? Yeah, right," Nellie said, picking at the eyelet trim on the pillow sham.

"You know, you're starting to sound like my brother."

Nellie laughed. "That's what they say happens to married couples. That and no more hot sex."

Dawn spun around. "Well, you just had a baby. You can't exactly do the deed yet."

Nellie pushed herself up on one elbow. "But Jack's acting all weird and stuff. You know, about me and my body. I tried to initiate a little hanky-panky last night, and he kissed me on the forehead like I was his elderly aunt. You'd think he'd be all over a little fun. He was before Mae arrived."

Dawn waved her hands. "Stop. Don't need to hear this."

Nellie shifted until she sat cross-legged. "You think it's my boobs? All the, you know, leaking and stuff?"

Dawn shook her head. "Nah, he sees you differently now. You know, as the mother of his child."

"But I don't want to be only the mother of his child. I want him to lick whipped cream off my stomach like he used to."

She laughed. "Again. TMI. And things will get back to normal. Give him a couple more weeks. But I would make one recommendation."

Nellie stood and tugged her sweatshirt past her still shrinking midsection. "What's that?"

Dawn picked up her purse and headed for the door, unable to resist throwing a saucy grin at her sister-in-law. "Get yourself a red lace bra, sister."

The last thing she heard as she glided down the hallway was Nellie calling, "They don't make nursing bras in red lace, smart-ass."

Dawn couldn't stop smiling. For the first time in a long time, she felt the stirrings of happiness. Sure, Andrew was ticked at her while still suggesting she call his dad. And Larry kept calling and hinting around about a big deal she might want to get in on…along with dinner, of course. And Margo kept complaining about horny old men who touched her butt. And, still, there was the whole no job, no ideas for her future thing. But, tonight those things didn't matter. She felt giddy like a girl with her first crush. She had a bloom in her cheeks and a bounce in her step.

So maybe not thinking was the best alternative. Even if the thought of not planning her days made her a little nauseous, that habit hadn't gotten her very far. There were so many parts of her life that weren't how she wanted them, despite all her strategizing. So for the moment, she was going to be a fly by the seat of her pants kind of gal.

The kind of gal who wore a red lace bra and planned for a night of flirting…and maybe something more.

"Big date?" Jack's voice emerged from the den.

"Not really a date," she said, flipping her hair over her shoulder and walking toward him. She leaned down and kissed the soft hair atop the infant sleeping on his chest. Jack's Lab woofed from the pillow beside the hearth. "I'm not kissing you, Dutch. Forget about it."

Jack laughed softly. "Yeah, buddy. Those lips look primed for someone with two legs."

Dawn tapped her brother on the head.

"Ow," he whispered. "You're gonna wake her up."

"Not my problem. Auntie Dawn is heading out the door."

"You're seriously wicked, woman," Jack said, dropping his own featherlight kiss atop his daughter's head. He looked up at Dawn, his expression shifting from tenderness to seriousness. "You sure about tangling with Tyson? You said that you weren't going to mess around with any guys until—"

"I'm not *tangling*. We're hanging out. I'm trying not to schedule stuff. Your advice. Remember?" Dawn's stomach fluttered a bit at that thought.

"Since when have you ever listened to me?"

"I don't listen to you. I listen to me. And I'm an adult and so is Tyson. I don't have any ties and his divorce will be final in a matter of days."

"Divorce?" Jack's words were louder than intended. The baby stirred and he patted her back. His blue eyes met Dawn's, meaning clear. Jack may be her baby brother, but he was a man. A man who clearly felt protective of all the women under his roof.

"Leave her alone, Jack," Nellie said, entering the den, wearing a clean and noticeably tighter T-shirt. Jack's gaze zoomed right in on his wife's abundant breasts. "Tyson's a free man. He and his wife have been separated for two years. His wife already moved in with the guy she cheated on him with. Why shouldn't he?"

"Cheated on him?" Dawn said, dumbfounded at her sister-in-law's offhand words.

"You didn't know? She cheated on him with his business partner while he was in Iraq."

Dawn blinked. Karen cheated on Tyson? It was the first time she'd heard the reason for their breakup. She'd assumed they'd split because of his absence in Iraq. The thought Tyson had come home to heartbreak made her ache for him. Made her blood heat with anger at Karen. And made her stomach sink. Tyson was on the rebound. Everyone knew not to date someone on the rebound. Well, at least not someone who'd been so utterly devastated in a relationship.

"It's nothing to worry about," Nellie continued, smiling at her husband with a little sparkle in her emerald eyes. "Go get lucky tonight."

Jack frowned.

Dawn shook her head and shouldered her purse. No way was she getting lucky tonight. The last bit of information Nellie imparted had her rethinking the wisdom of going with the flow. The wisdom in not not thinking. "I'm not worried about getting lucky."

It really was a shame, though. And such a waste of a great bra.

CHAPTER TEN

"THAT SONOFABITCH needs to block for him. How in the hell is he supposed to fight off defenders and get to the goal line without any help?" Grady yelled at the TV.

As if hearing the elderly man, the announcer concluded much the same.

"Exactly," Grady said, yanking up the footrest of his faded leather recliner with satisfaction.

Tyson grinned at Dawn and shook his head. He pointed to the kitchen and jerked his head. She wasn't sure she wanted to be alone with him. She wasn't sure of anything anymore. Not after what Nellie had revealed about his wife and her affair. Dawn couldn't even be sure Tyson was over his ex-wife and ready to embark on another relationship.

But she pushed herself from the seventies-style olive tweed couch and followed Tyson to the kitchen. If Grady noticed they'd slipped away, he didn't acknowledge it. He yelled at Jeremy Whitten, who Dawn had learned was a tight end and usually a good blocker.

As she entered the kitchen, Tyson spun her into his arms and kissed her.

And, damn, it felt good.

He tasted so delicious, like yeasty beer, salty pretzels and all things manly and warm. She couldn't stop herself from leaning into him, from wanting him.

Heat flooded her body and swept her away.

And even though she knew it was a bad idea, she didn't stop him when he deepened the kiss.

After a moment, he drew back. "I've been waiting to do that all night. I'm so turned on I could supply the electric company for the month."

Dawn licked her lips and tried to focus on the coffee machine flashing the time over his shoulder. Reality-check time.

She leaped as his fingers traced the top of her dress. "And don't think I haven't seen what you're hiding underneath this prim little dress. It's driving me crazy."

Mission accomplished. Couldn't say she hadn't done what she'd set out to do. But his fingers against her heated skin dashed all thoughts from her head. The man's hands were magic. Her body begged him to dip his hand inside her dress and find her breast, cup it, caress her, take her over the edge. Yet the small sliver of sanity that remained urged her to run out the back door. To move before it was too late.

But she forgot all about escape when Tyson lowered his head to her neck and dropped little kisses along her collarbone.

It felt beyond good. She couldn't stop herself from clasping his head to her chest and reveling in the sweet desire unfurling deep in her body. Her traitorous knee even slid up the side of his thigh, bringing him closer to the heart of her.

One of his hands cupped the back of her knee, helping to guide her leg and curl it around his thigh. He maneuvered her against the kitchen counter, bringing his body hard against hers. She could feel his erection straining his jeans and she wanted nothing more than to unbutton his fly and feel him fill her hand. Then feel him sliding inside her. It had to be the only way to extinguish the fire raging out of control.

Tyson lifted his head and took possession of her lips once again, ruthlessly plundering her mouth. She moaned and met him stroke for stroke, growing nearly frenzied with passion.

It had never felt this way, as though she must have this man or die trying.

So caught up in the moment, she was barely cognizant of someone calling Tyson's name.

He lifted his mouth from hers as he cocked his head. His whiskey-colored eyes were glazed, the pupils dilated. Ragged breath aside, Tyson almost sounded normal when he called, "What?"

Tyson obviously didn't care his grandfather was in the next room. His hand left the back of her knee and glided up her thigh, stopping at the barrier of her matching red panties.

"Bring me another beer when you come back," Grady hollered, over the referee's whistle sounding in the background.

His finger had just slipped beneath the lace edge of her panties when she dropped her leg to the floor. It was one of the hardest things she'd ever done. She wanted to see what he would do. *Really* wanted to. But she had let this get out of hand. "Stop."

His teeth nipped her ear. "I don't want to stop."

She pushed at his chest. "Stop."

He stepped back, his arms falling to his sides. "Why?"

She rubbed her lips together and refocused on the blinking numbers of the coffee machine. She needed to pull herself together. To use her mind and forget about how turned on she was.

"We're in your grandfather's kitchen," she said, refusing to meet his eyes. She didn't want to look at him yet. He was too damn appealing. And appealing, turned-on men were her weakness. Obviously.

He caught her about her waist and pressed a kiss against the side of her neck. "So?" he whispered.

Dawn literally had to grit her teeth before stepping away. "We can't do this in the kitchen. We probably shouldn't do this at all."

Tyson pulled back, his eyes mirroring confusion though he gave her a silly grin.

Her heart plinked.

"Well, I gotta agree with you, darlin'. We don't have a good track record with getting it on in kitchens. Last time we ended up with a soaked Chihuahua and a five-year-old holding a squirt gun. But what's with the not doing this at all? I thought we'd agreed to let things run their course?"

Dawn sighed and scooted even farther away from him. Distance had to be good. "But not this fast. We haven't known each other long enough—"

"I've seen you nearly every day for more than a month. This is what? Our third date?" He crossed his arms and looked much like a father giving a lecture to a wayward schoolgirl.

"My coming to the hospital was not a date, Tyson," she said, finally meeting his eyes. She couldn't quite read his expression. She didn't know whether he was amused or aggravated. Or both.

"That night you came to the hospital I felt more alone than I ever had. Even when I was in Iraq. We connected on a level I knew existed but had never reached. You're special, and I know we have the potential to build something good together."

She closed her eyes, and damned if her heart didn't contract in her chest. But he was moving too fast. No one felt that way that fast. He had to be still reeling from Karen's betrayal. He was looking for something that wasn't there. Not yet.

"Look, I don't know where we're headed, but I think it's worth making the journey. Even if I have to convince you to put on your hiking shoes, lady."

Dawn opened her mouth to speak, but he cut her off. "Plus, I know you, Dawn Taggart. I know you push your hair back from your face when you're nervous. You have two sweeteners in your coffee. You cheat at UNO. You slip Margo extra money for her son who's in college. Your favorite color is blue. You like to put hot sauce on your eggs. You—"

"But I don't know you, Tyson." Dawn crossed her arms over her chest. "I didn't even know the details of your whole divorce with Karen. About her cheating on you."

His eyes narrowed a bit as he stared at her. A full minute passed before he spoke. "Why is that important?"

"Why is that important?" Her voice rose. She paused, took a cleansing breath and counted to five. "It's important because I'm not risking my heart on some rebound relationship. It's a fact—women don't get a future with a guy who's been dumped a few months before. He isn't ready. And I don't want to waste time on something that's going to have me crying into my cereal bowl next month."

Tyson shoved his hands in his pockets and shook his head. "First of all, it has been over two years since I've been with Karen. Technically, it's been three. You really are a piece of work. You think you can control everything? You can't. You can't control your heart. Or your son. Or whether you'll get another job next month. There is no formula for life, Dawn. You have to creep around like the rest of us, finding comfort where you can, savoring the feeling that makes you feel like moving forward."

"Is that what I am to you? Comfort?" That bothered her. She didn't want to be used. She'd already felt that way too often in her life. And rebounds were about comfort. Hot sex. No strings. No ties.

Tyson sighed and gave her a small smile. "Yeah, you are, but not in the way you think."

An irritated voice came from the other room. "What in the tarnation does a guy have to do to get a beer around here?"

Tyson shook his head and called, "You've already had your limit, Gramps."

Grady muttered a word that should have made Dawn blush. But she was the mother of a nineteen-year-old boy. Very little made her blush anymore.

"I should go," she muttered. She wanted to get away from Tyson. Away from his words. Away from the damage of his life. Of her life.

"Yeah," Tyson said, surprising her with his easy acceptance. After his minilecture, she thought he would want her to stay. So he could hammer his point home and make her feel even more emotionally immature.

"I'll say good-night to your grandfather and then slip out," she said. She resisted tucking her hair behind her ear. For the first time, she felt awkward around Tyson. Just moments ago she had wanted to wrap her legs around him. Now she wanted to slink out like a thief with the family silver.

"I spent a lot of time in Iraq studying tactical

strategies," he said, grabbing an O'Doul's and popping the top. Her eyes followed his hands as he poured the nonalcoholic beer into a Texas Rangers mug.

The foam reached the top of the mug and he looked at her. But he didn't say anything. Just studied her as she picked at a sliver of skin next to her thumbnail.

She stared back.

"I wouldn't call this a retreat, but I know when I need to halt, reassess the situation and gather my ammunition," he finally said.

"You think this is some kind of battle for my emotions?" Dawn couldn't stop feeling annoyed. The man seemed positively cavalier. Way too lighthearted for a guy who'd been turned down. Well, sort of turned down.

"No. I refuse to surrender to your fears. You're grasping at straws, looking for anything to prevent you from taking a risk with your heart."

"I am not," she said, gritting her teeth, knowing he was correct in his assessment and not liking it one bit. He'd figured her out a little too easily. So, she was scared? She had reason.

He arched an eyebrow. "Let's see. First it was things are too unstable, then it was I can't build a relationship on sexual attraction, now it's the rebound thing. What are you going to drag out next to keep me at arm's length?"

"I don't need a reason."

"Yes, you do. Because I'm not giving up. I think what we have between us is worth pulling on my camouflage and polishing my gun."

"I'll let that innuendo slide."

His bark of laughter must have reached Grady, who

called out, "Stop all that lollygagging and get in here. Dallas is on the four-yard line."

"Coming," Tyson hollered as he picked up the beer. He slid past Dawn and dropped a gentle kiss atop her head. "If you want to go ahead and wave your flag, it's all good. Otherwise, I'll see you tomorrow."

"What's with men and war analogies anyway?"

He turned and smiled. "You know we can't resist invading hostile territory, especially when it's as good as yours."

She planted her hands on her hips. "I'm not hostile. And just so you know, I don't cheat at UNO."

His laughter was the last thing she heard as she picked up her purse and left.

She couldn't help thinking she was a coward. And that she'd been rude in not telling Grady good-night. And she'd never found out Tyson's number two rule.

She thought about his kiss. About his hands stroking her body.

Well, maybe she had.

CHAPTER ELEVEN

"NOW PICK UP THE RAFFIA and tie it in a loose bow around the stalk. Like this," Dawn said, demonstrating the technique on her bundle of wheat shafts. Then she watched as eight pairs of blue-veined, care-worn hands mimicked her actions. Tuesday was craft day at Tucker House.

"I told Essie that I'd be bringing the centerpiece and not the fruit salad this year. And do you know what she said?" Ida Franz asked.

The group of elderly ladies all replied with a chorus of "What?"

"She said we don't need no centerpiece. The men were gonna eat Thanksgiving dinner in front of the TV anyhow."

"Shameful," one of the ladies tsked as she pulled out her lopsided bow and retied the raffia.

Ida shrugged. "Well, that's what Earl gets for marrying a woman from Shelbyville. No culture whatsoever."

Linda Taylor piped up. "My grandson's girlfriend is from over by Shelbyville. He said her momma gave him lemonade in a jelly jar."

"They do no such thing," Elsie Greer piped up. "I've known plenty people from Shelbyville. It's a nice town."

Most of the women nodded. Dawn tried not to laugh, but couldn't help herself. She loved when she was able to hold a craft class. The conversations that went on kept her tickled for the rest of the week.

Holding such classes and events was important to Dawn. It kept Tucker House feeling more like a community center than an adult day care where clients were sent out to molder under the eye of an indifferent nurse. The ladies and gentlemen who came to Tucker House still had much to give, so she and Nellie had worked up a schedule that kept them plugged into their community.

While the ladies worked on Thanksgiving Day centerpieces, the owner of Carter's Auto Service Center was holding a discussion on winterizing automobiles for the gentlemen on the back screened-in porch. Dawn wasn't quite sure it was the best of topics being half of the men no longer were allowed to drive and East Texas wasn't exactly blizzard central, but it didn't seem to matter. As she'd passed through the kitchen earlier, she'd heard a vehement debate on the merits of using a certain type of air filter.

As she finished wiring the bright oversize sunflowers into the display, Margo appeared at the door. "D, you've got a call."

"Bring me the phone. I've still got to attach the acorns we painted."

Margo shook her head and mouthed "Larry the Snake."

Dawn sighed and pushed herself from the table with a promise to return to show the ladies how to secure the acorns to the project.

She took the phone from Margo and stepped out to the porch. The cool November wind caused the windchimes to clang together, but otherwise, all was quiet outside. "Good morning, Larry. What can I do for you?"

"Hey, darlin'. How's my favorite girl?" Larry's voice was as smooth as ice on a hockey rink.

Dawn rolled her eyes. "Fine, but busy."

"Glad to hear it, baby," he continued, obviously not taking the hint she didn't have time to waste. Of course, he did everything on his own schedule. Whatever Larry wanted regardless of cost to anyone else. Being married to him for fourteen years had been like raising another kid.

"I don't have time to chat, Larry. I'm in the middle of something."

He sighed, a heavy put-upon sound, before muttering, "Well, then I guess I'd better get to the point, sugar pants."

"Larry," she warned. She'd talked to him once before about using pet names. The man never listened.

"Fine. I wanted to check on your plans for Thanksgiving next week. I'm not going to L.A., so I thought I'd spend a few days in Oak Knoll with you and Drew. Drew said you'd love to have me."

Dawn closed her eyes and gritted her teeth. The idea of Larry at the dinner table regaling everyone with dazzling stock-market deals and dropping the names of movie stars he'd played golf with made her stomach lurch. She wouldn't be able to choke down any of Nellie's famous chicken and dressing. "The name of the town is Oak Stand, and I'm not sure that's a good idea. We're eating with Nellie and Jack. I don't feel comfortable inviting you without asking them."

"Hell, doll, ask them. I miss hanging with my boy Jack anyway," Larry said.

I bet, Dawn thought. Larry always had a get-rich-quick scheme in the works. And he always needed capital. Jack was the favored target.

"Look, Andrew will be in Houston for part of the week. He's doing strength and conditioning for baseball. You can see him there and not worry about coming here," Dawn said as Tyson emerged from the rear of the house, carrying a stack of lumber. An old plaid shirt stretched across his broad shoulders and tight worn Levi's molded to his thighs. He looked as delicious as apple pie with a side of vanilla ice cream. How did the man do it?

"Dawn?" Larry's voice prodded her from her mini-daydream about the man she had sworn last night she'd stay away from. The same vow she'd made almost four times before. Of course, she wasn't very good at listening to herself. At least not where Tyson was concerned.

"Hmm?" she murmured, still checking out Tyson as he winked at her. He disappeared around the side of the house, giving her a nice view of how well his jeans fit his backside.

"I asked if you'd just check with Jack. I don't want to spend the day by myself," he said. Guilt picked at her conscience. She thought about Andrew and his almost incessant desire to be near his father. She could feel herself wavering.

"Larry, it won't work. Talk to Andrew and find a different solution. I'm sorry." She couldn't tolerate Larry hanging around. He treated her like a personal assistant. *Dawn, do you know how to get this stain out of cashmere? Take a look at my bank statement and see where I made the error. Would you mind paying for dinner? I'll get it next go around.* Yep, the last thing she needed was Larry and his load of hot air.

"Fine. Whatever," he groused.

Tyson appeared again, pulling his work gloves off

and doffing his work-stained ball cap. He was heading her way.

"I wanted to talk to you about Andrew's tuition, but I can't now. I've gotta go," she said into the phone, pressing the end button before Larry could say anything more.

"Hey," Tyson said, balancing his work boot on one of the steps.

"Hey," she said, tugging down her cranberry-colored sweater and refusing to push her hair behind her ear.

"I'm glad you came to supper last night," he said, his gaze warmed her as he swept her from head to toe.

"Really?" she said, wetting her lips. He made her so warm she wanted to thank the breeze for cooling her cheeks.

"Yeah, really." Posed the way he was proved how great he looked in his work clothes.

"It gave me a lot to think about," she said, scuffing the tip of her boot around the freshly painted porch planks.

"Good." She thought he would say more, but he didn't.

"I'm not a coward. I simply don't want to complicate my life."

He lifted an eyebrow. "Who does?"

"So maybe I'm willing to take a chance," she said. Which was absolutely not what she meant to say. In fact, it was the opposite. So why had those words come out of her mouth? Had Larry driven her to it?

But she knew Larry wasn't the cause of her impulsiveness. For some reason she trusted Tyson.

So she'd waved the white flag. Obviously, Tyson had no problem with the easy surrender. His sensual lips curved into a smile. He looked confident, as though whatever battle plans he'd drawn up after his retreat last night were already effective. Maybe his plan of attack involved those jeans he wore. They were good ammunition for a thirtysomething gal who hadn't had sex in a while.

"Great. I had some thoughts for this weekend. I wanted to spend time with you before Laurel gets here on Sunday. She's definitely coming for Thanksgiving."

"I'm glad to hear she's making it."

He nodded. "Finally. She ran out of excuses, and I ran out of patience. So, are you up for a little trip?"

"Trip?" she echoed as visions of tangled hotel sheets cropped up in her mind. How would Tyson look wrapped in those sheets, all sleepy-eyed and scruffy from an exhausting night of passion?

"Nothing big. Maybe a couple days in Jefferson. I need to look for a few things and there are lots of antiques shops. You game?"

Jefferson, Texas, was a historic little town known for cozy bed-and-breakfasts and an abundance of antiques shops. She'd been dying to visit ever since she'd moved to Oak Stand. Antiquing had once been part of her livelihood and she missed poking through dusty stores. Plus she'd heard the cornbread sandwiches at one of the little cafés were to die for. And she'd love to visit the bookstore that was also a hair salon. But a weekend jaunt with Tyson would be…scary? Moving faster and faster in the direction of serious relationship? Still, all she could do was nod. "Sure. I've been wanting to check out Jefferson. I hear it's nice."

"Good. Oh, and Nellie called and invited me, Gramps and Laurel to Thanksgiving dinner next week."

Dawn gave an inward sigh of relief, happy that she'd stood her ground with Larry. The thought of Larry and

Tyson sitting next to one another over turkey and cranberry sauce nearly gave her hives.

"Good." She swallowed. Hard. "That's great. I'll get to meet Laurel. And Nellie is a terrific cook."

He grinned. "I know. She liked to cook even as a kid. She always snuck into the kitchen at camp and whipped up brownies. The cooks loved her at Pine Forest. I can only imagine what she'll do to a Thanksgiving feast." Dawn had almost forgotten he had met Nellie at summer camp. They'd formed a bond over Nellie's inability to pass her archery skill test.

"Well, I guess I'll see you around. Got to get back to Centerpieces 101."

Two steps later, his lips were on hers. Hard, possessive, Tyson left no doubt that their weekend trip wasn't just an outing. It was a real date.

"Later," he said, disappearing around the side of the house again, whistling a James Taylor song.

"Mm…hmm. Just what I thought," Margo's voice came from behind her.

Dawn whirled around and handed the phone to her assistant. "Shut up, Margo."

Margo's bark of laughter followed her into the house, but Dawn didn't have time to worry about what her friend thought. In the course of ten minutes, she'd totally done an about-face. No longer was she putting the brakes on her relationship with Tyson. Instead she was lumping coal on the fires of a train speeding out of control. She could only hope the tracks didn't fall out from under her.

WHEN DAWN CLIMBED INTO Tyson's truck on Friday afternoon, her first words were about Andrew.

"My son has lost his marbles," she said, handing him

her overnight bag and settling her purse at her feet. "He told me I am acting like a teenager."

Tyson didn't want to talk about anything to do with belligerent kids, or grandfathers who refused to eat right or ex-spouses who wouldn't behave. He wanted to escape reality if only for two days. But he shrugged and went with the conversation. "That's a good thing, isn't it?"

She smiled. "Depends. My irresponsible teen years led to an unplanned pregnancy."

"I think you've learned that lesson. So why is he so opposed to you doing something for yourself?" Tyson pulled away from the curb and headed in the direction of Jefferson.

"He's spoiled and wants me to do what I've always done. Cater to him."

"Can't say I've had much experience with mothers. My own bounced back and forth between a psycho June Cleaver and a hanger-swinging Joan Crawford. I was never her first priority."

Dawn made a face. "Rather the opposite for Andrew. He's got a bug up his ass, that's for sure. But he's a big boy and has to learn that I'm a big girl and can take care of myself."

It was the last she said on the subject of Andrew, but he knew her son's displeasure bothered her. The rest of the drive was slightly tense and uncomfortably polite.

A quintessential small town, Jefferson was as busy as a one-legged man in a butt-kicking contest when they reached it. All Friday afternoons in fall were traffic-filled—had something to do with high school football games. Pity the people—like them—looking for a place to park.

Tyson drove down the street in front of the Jefferson Historical Museum several times before finally spying a sports car pulling out of a tight spot in front of an old general store. He might make the truck fit.

"There's a place over there." Dawn pointed toward a much larger spot in a lot off the Excelsior Hotel a street over.

"That'll work," he said, putting his foot to the pedal and careening across oncoming traffic. He had one shot to take the parking spot.

Dawn yelped and grabbed the handle above the door.

They slid into the space just as a convertible full of young girls pulled into the lot, music blaring, totally off-kilter with the whole stepping back in time thing Jefferson had going on.

"Whew," he said. "Thought we'd never find a place."

The woman next to him smiled, seemingly much more light-hearted now they'd reached their destination.

"Here, let me take your bag," Tyson said, opening her door and extending his hand.

"I've got it. It's really light. I figured I wouldn't need too much." The brightness of the afternoon sun couldn't hide the red that stained her cheeks. "I didn't mean it that way. It's a short trip."

Disappointment lodged in his gut. He'd booked two rooms, but hoped there would be need for only one. Still, he didn't want to push her too hard. A weekend away didn't necessarily mean a marathon between the sheets.

But a man could hope.

Pulling her to him and draping his arm around her shoulders, he started for the hotel sitting prominently on the brick-paved street. The white building laced with black ironwork didn't look as grand as its name. Rather, it looked homey.

They entered the lobby and were immediately sucked back into the mid-1800s. Old-fashioned wallpaper, deep red drapes and an antique walnut desk met them. A display of the house's history sat to the left for further exploration as was a glimpse of a parlor dressed in blue and gold.

Tyson headed toward the man at the check-in desk.

"I have a reservation for Tyson Hart. The Grant Room and the Lady Bird Johnson room, I believe."

The man welcomed them to Excelsior House Hotel then typed into the computer. "Okay, that's the historic Grant Room with two double beds and the Lady Bird Johnson room with a king." He looked at them. "You sure you want both rooms? For only the two of you?"

Tyson nodded just as Dawn said, "I'll pay for mine."

If they weren't going to have sex, it *had* to be separate rooms. No way he could stay in the same room with her and not press her to take their relationship to the next level. He wanted her too much, wanted to get lost in her until the first fingers of her namesake crept over the windowsill. But only when she was ready.

"Well, I had a cancellation for the Jay Gould room. It has lovely antique walnut furniture imported from Russia plus a nice claw-foot tub. Good for a long soak after a day of walking around Jefferson or—" he eyed them "—whatever else might exhaust you." A devilish smile curled in his goatee.

Dawn gave a nervous laugh. "That sounds nice, but I think we better keep the ones we booked."

The clerk nodded and tapped away at his computer. Dawn still refused to meet Tyson's eyes and he wondered what she was thinking. Was she already regretting her decision to take this trip with him?

The clerk handed him their individual key cards. "I went ahead and gave you the Jay Gould, Mr. Hart. It has a king-size bed you might find more comfortable. Enjoy your stay."

"Thank you," he said, stepping from the desk and regarding a small table of brochures. He picked out a few showcasing local restaurants and turned to Dawn. "What would you like to do first? Eat?"

Dawn fiddled with the strap on her bag. "Whatever you want. I didn't even bring my planner."

He feigned clasping his heart and staggering backward, drawing a laugh from her.

"Well, let's drop off our bags then we can decide."

The bloodred carpet lined the stairs and led to a corridor lined with several doors. It didn't take him long to find his room, insert the key into the lock and swing the door open.

Dawn passed him as he stepped inside the spacious room. He stuck his head out as she disappeared inside the room not far from his.

"Hey," he called.

She peeked back out at him. "Yeah."

"Ten minutes good?"

She nodded. "I'll be ready."

CHAPTER TWELVE

DAWN STARED AT THE lovely room before her. Warm as its namesake, it displayed Southern charm and graciousness.

But she didn't want to be there.

She wanted to be in the Jay Gould room testing out that king-size bed. So what was holding her back?

Andrew's adultlike lecture? The fact Tyson wasn't legally free? Her own past mistakes with the wrong guy?

Maybe it was all of them.

She caught her reflection in the mirror. *Chicken*.

Before she could think much more about all the reasons why she shouldn't, she scooped up her overnight bag and backed out of the room.

Ten long strides later, she knocked at Tyson's door.

Tyson swung the door open, while flicking the light off. "Hey, that didn't take—"

Her mouth covered his, cutting him off. She twined her arms around his shoulders and pressed herself to him. The man wasn't stupid. He wrapped his arms around her, deepening the kiss, and pulled her into the room.

The door clicked shut.

Dawn broke the kiss, pulling back. The room was dark and she couldn't read his expression. "Let's try out that king-size bed."

She felt his body's response. His arms tightened, his breath quickened. He bent his head to hers.

"Are you certain?" he whispered against her lips.

Dawn knew there wasn't much that *was* certain in her life. She didn't know where she'd live next year, what job she'd be doing or if taking the next step with Tyson was a good idea. All she knew was she was tired of thinking, planning and reasoning her way through life.

And she knew she was certain about one thing: she wanted Tyson.

Her answer was to press her lips to his, more firmly than before. Her hands wound around his neck, fingering the hair that brushed his collar. He needed a haircut, but she wouldn't complain. She was totally digging the rough-around-the-edges, bad-boy vibe he was putting out. She was also digging the way the man kissed.

One of his hands slid beneath her ponytail and cupped the nape of her neck, maneuvering her head into the right position for deepening the kiss. His tongue traced the edge of her lower lip before plunging into her mouth. No, this man didn't dally when it came to kissing. The man was eating her up.

Amen.

Desire surged through her veins, cavorting through her body, causing her softest parts to throb with need. Oh, my, it felt good. So, so very good.

She felt a tug at the base of her neck and her hair slipped from its clip and tumbled down her back. Tyson's response was to bury both hands in the mass of waves, pulling her even harder against his body. His mouth still wreaked havoc on hers, causing a groan to escape her lips.

She surprised herself with how fast she'd revved up. Well, it *had* been a while.

Tyson leaned back to smile at her. She stared, trying to control her breathing, trying to settle her riotous pulse into some pattern of normality. "I want to take your clothes off with my teeth, but only if you want this. No tears or angry words hurled my way after we do this. No regrets, okay?"

She opened her mouth, but he silenced it with his finger. "Once we go there—" he jerked his thumb toward the four-poster bed sitting prominently in the center of the room "—we aren't going back."

"Who said I want to?" she said, taking his finger from her lips and pressing his hand to her chest. "We've been dancing round this since we met. So, are you going to stand here and talk me out of this or are you going to get busy with those teeth?"

A predatory grin flashed across his face before he muttered in her ear, "You asked for this."

Dawn would have squealed had she been the type, but all she could do was laugh as he tossed her over one shoulder and strode to the bed.

"Animal," she declared as she landed on the over-stuffed mattress. She hadn't landed gracefully, either. Kinda all sprawled out and awkward.

"You have no idea." He tugged his shirt over his head, dropping it on the floor. She could see his teeth flash in the afternoon light sneaking past the ornate drapes. It made her all shivery inside.

She pulled the clip hanging drunkenly from one of her tresses and tossed it toward the bedside table. It missed the mark and clattered to the floor. Then she slid her leather moccasins from her feet allowing them to fall with a thump. She glanced at Tyson as she pulled the socks from her feet, as well. He was working on his belt. The man didn't play around when it came to getting busy. The observation had her body thrumming like a car engine.

She reached for the bottom of her sweater as he dropped his jeans. He was magnificent. Hefting lumber and jackhammering concrete all day had left him heavily muscled in all the right places. His broad chest was sprinkled with golden hair. He wore plaid boxer shorts that strained with his arousal. His thighs and calves were just as muscled. She wished he would turn around so she could check out his backside. Nothing better than the back of a naked man whose physique looked like Tyson's.

Her hands forgot she was supposed to be undressing. She just drank him in.

"Hey, leave that to me," he said, climbing onto the bed, hovering above her on hands and knees. She dropped back, allowing her head to fall onto a needle-point pillow. Her hair fanned around her and though she was almost fully dressed, she could feel the heat from his body.

"What?" She breathed in his smell, remembering the day she'd first met him. She'd been struck first by his warmth. And that's what she recalled as she lay beneath him. He smelled like autumn, as though she could burrow inside him and absorb his strength.

"I want to take off your clothes," he said, bending his head and placing tiny kisses upon the pulse fluttering so wildly in her neck. His hot breath fanned her throat and for a moment, she felt like a wild creature beneath the paw of the hungry lion. She was helpless.

And that loss of control excited her.

His hand slid across her stomach, searing her through

the merino sweater. His fingers slipped beneath, skimming her bare flesh. She sucked in her breath. Then released it slowly. He caught it with his mouth.

Tyson allowed his mouth to slip from hers to nibble her lower lip. She tasted so good, like honey and wildflowers, like something so fresh and new. He had no time for poetics. Earthly pursuits awaited them.

He allowed his hand to tease her stomach, enjoying the way her flesh retracted at his touch. He tugged her sweater upward, allowing his hand to glide over the bared skin beneath her breast. Just the slightest of touches, brushing the underwire of her bra. Then he hooked one finger beneath the silken barrier and allowed her breast to pop free. With the weight of her breast in one hand, he could tease no more.

He slipped his other hand beneath her, pulling her to him, fitting her body against his. He was hard, pulsing for her softness. He wanted to go slowly and savor making love to Dawn. But, now, he wasn't sure it was an option. It had been a long time since he'd indulged in such hedonistic pleasures of a woman's body.

He gathered her to him, sliding his hand onto her bottom, tugging her against his arousal. She hooked her leg over his hip, pulling him even closer, rubbing herself against him, causing him to groan.

She pushed his hand from where it lingered on her breast and tugged off her sweater. His hands found the button to her jeans and he had them halfway down her thighs by the time she'd divested herself of her bra. She kicked the denim from her legs and lay before him clad in the tiniest of bikini panties, edged in lace and tied on either side with satin ribbons.

His very own present.

And with that thought, he knew he must relish in the unwrapping of the gift.

So first, he made love to her body with his eyes. He took in her beauty. From her deep brown eyes dilated with desire, to her luscious mouth, silken shoulders, heavy breasts, firm stomach, flared hips and finally lean legs. All for him.

He nuzzled her neck. "You are perfection."

She snorted.

His lips found her earlobe. "But you are. Let me convince you."

His hand traveled across from shoulder blade to shoulder blade. "Here you are delicate. Very feminine. So smooth and soft."

Her eyes found his and she watched his face as his hand moved on her body.

He slid his hand to her breasts. They were large and still very firm, topped with two dusky nipples, like cherries atop a delicious bowl of cream. "But here, here you are exquisite."

One finger flicked her nipple, eliciting a sigh from her.

He moved quickly, closing his mouth around the pebbled peak. Dawn moaned and lurched upward, clasping his head to her, urging him to continue. He loved her responsiveness. And though he thought it impossible, he felt himself grow even harder at her sweet little moans.

He lifted his head. "But your stomach, it's the sweetest gateway I've seen yet." His hand glided across her quivering stomach. Her gently rounded belly felt so soft. He drew circles around her navel, enjoying the way her muscles trembled.

"Stop," she protested with a giggle. He glanced at

her face, meeting her eyes. Damn, but he was having a fine time.

He ripped his eyes from hers and looked at her decadent panties. "What's this? A gift?"

He fingered the two bows anchoring either side of her hips. "I hate to skip right over those two fine legs you have and those delicious feet, but I could never resist such a nicely packaged present."

He shot her a look he hoped conveyed his wicked intent. "It would be rude for me to ignore such a gift. Right?"

She nodded.

"Well, then, shall I open it?" He slid one finger across the top of the panties. "Or should I just take a peek?"

He lifted the edge and leaned close to her stomach. He allowed his breath to fan her belly, allowed his cheek to glance her flesh. She responded by groaning and lifting her hips from the bed.

"Tyson," she begged, twisting her hips.

"Yes?" he asked, allowing his lips to kiss a path across the skin above the lace band. He could feel her heat, could feel her slipping beyond control. It made him heady with power.

"Please, take them off," she said, her own hands slipping down to help him out.

"No, no. This is my present, angel," he said, stilling her hands and placing them at her sides.

He delivered a wink. Then he used his teeth to untie one little satin bow. "That wasn't too hard," he breathed against her flesh. "Now for the other one."

He did the same to the other bow, allowing the ties to fall onto the coverlet of the bed. Slowly he nipped the satin with his teeth and pulled the panties away from her body. He released them from his mouth.

"I can't believe you actually used your teeth," she said, propping herself upon both elbows. Her breath had grown even more labored and there was a spark of admiration in her eyes.

"I'm a man of many talents," he said, allowing his hand to brush against the heart of her, feathering through the neat line of dark hair outlining the very part he'd dreamed about. "And I'm really liking my present, angel."

Suddenly her hands were on his chest, pushing him back. He fell onto the bed and Dawn rose above him.

"Enough," she panted, tugging down his boxers so he sprang free. Her hand sought him, and at her touch, he nearly launched off the bed. Her hand was a silken vise, incapacitating him. Her other hand divested him of his undershorts, tossing them somewhere onto the darkness of the oaken floor.

"No more Miss Nice Guy," Dawn said, releasing him and straddling his hips. He could feel how wet she was. How hot. How sexy. He was on fire.

"Condom?" she whispered into his ear. He wanted to answer, but he'd forgotten how to talk with a goddess astride him. He reached up and cupped the breasts swaying before him.

Finally, he managed to murmur, "Side pocket of my overnight."

She launched herself from him and padded naked across the floor. He watched her in the dim light, loving the way she moved, the curve of her hip, the sweet view presented as she bent and rummaged through his bag.

She pulled out a string of condoms from the pocket. "Think this will be enough?"

She laughed, the musical sound fell upon him and something like sheer joy gathered deep inside him.

She scurried to him, climbing upon the bed as graceful as a lioness. She seemed to be playing with him. The roles had been reversed. He didn't mind. His huntress ripped a package free from the row with her teeth and straddled him again.

The sight of her creamy thighs on either side of him made his mouth go dry. She smiled at him and ripped open the condom, again, with her teeth. "I know. Don't tell my dentist I'm using my teeth to open these things. And I won't tell anybody what you used your teeth for."

Tyson laughed and took the condom from her, jammed it on his length and pulled her down for a kiss. "I won't tell if you don't."

She laughed against his lips before lifting herself and sliding onto him.

If anyone had asked him at that moment to describe how good she felt sheathed round him, it would have come out as gobbledygook. There were no words.

It must have been the same for Dawn.

She released an "mmm" before starting to move. He held her smooth hips and let her have her wicked way with him. She was mesmerizing. So wild and lovely with her hair streaming down her back, eyes closed and utter concentration on her face. Her mouth fell open and she licked her lips as her hands lifted to pull her hair up. It made her breasts rise like two tempting orbs.

"This is good," she said, not bothering to open her eyes. Her rhythm increased and he lifted his hips to meet her stroke for stroke before sliding his hands up to cup her breasts. He pulled her down and filled his mouth with her succulent flesh.

Her hands framed his face and her ebony hair fell

round them, cloaking them with the smell of green-apple shampoo.

He rolled her over and increased his pace. She wrapped her legs tight around him, giving him deeper access.

He could feel his release building in his lower belly, tightening his balls.

"I can't last much longer," he whispered in her ear, as he slid his hands down to grasp her bottom and lift her. The words had no more escaped his lips than he felt her tighten around him and the first tremors hit her body.

Her head arched on the bed and a groan ripped from her throat. He covered her open mouth with his and joined her in that most majestic place as wave after wave of pleasure rolled over him.

Finally, he lay still, cradled in her arms, only the harsh sound of their breathing filling the room. Tyson rolled off her, flinging one arm out on the bed and leaving his other beneath Dawn. A canopy stretched above them, a reminder they lay in a bed carved many years before, in a room designed to remind them of the past.

"Oh, my," Dawn said to no one in particular. And for a moment, her words took him back to the time when paddleboats sailed the lake a mile or two away from the hotel. This woman could have easily been the mistress of his cotton plantation and he her master. Or more likely, Dawn would have been some luscious senorita sent to tempt him with her kohl-rimmed eyes and a low-bodice gown.

A horn sounded on the street below him, totally ruining his crazy daydream of post–Civil War trysts. Orgasms did that for him. Every time after he came, he turned into some daisy-chain weaving little girl bent on fantasy.

Of course, the reality was that he was lying on a fancy bed, utterly exhausted by the best sex he'd had since Clinton was president, still wearing a spent condom. "I hope we're not sharing a bathroom with any of the other guests."

Dawn gave a sleepy laugh. "He said a private bath with a claw-foot tub, remember?"

"I was too busy thinking about how I was going to lure you into this bed to listen much to what he had to say," he responded, sitting up. "Be right back."

He found the bathroom easily enough and made short work of cleaning up.

When he returned, Dawn was sound asleep, sprawled out naked and looking as delectable as a Southern Maid doughnut. Desire stirred within him though he couldn't fathom burning the coverlet up for a second go around. Yet. Instead, he pulled the covers back and ever so gently eased Dawn beneath them. She snuggled right up to him and within seconds he joined her in the soundest slumber he'd had in a while.

CHAPTER THIRTEEN

"YOU GONNA EAT THAT? I'm starving," Tyson said eyeing the decadent orange-blossom muffin sitting on the side of her plate.

She lifted a fork. "Touch it and you'll be missing a finger."

He grinned. "God, I love it when you talk tough."

She swirled her fork at him. "So I recall."

Silverware clattered in the breakfast room surrounding the wrought iron table at which they sat. Their table perched just inside the courtyard of the hotel where doors opened to the crisp morning breeze. The scenery out the doors was picturesque—herbs overflowed iron planters, a ginger cat curled up on an ancient brick paver and Texas sunshine fell onto the purple pansies and golden chrysanthemums frolicking around the enormous stone fountain. It felt as if the world celebrated the lovemaking they'd shared throughout the night.

"Sorry we didn't make the dinner reservation," she said, pushing a bit of egg around the toile-patterned plate. When they'd woken from their nap, dinner was long past so they'd settled for an appetizer at a nearby grill before hurrying back to their room to pursue other pleasures.

He dashed away the hair hanging in his eyes, and said, "Are you kidding? I'd rather have what I had than a steak."

Pleasure filled her. "Are you comparing me to beef?"

"Well, you do have pretty brown eyes. You know, like a cow." As soon as the words left his mouth, he must have realized what he said. "Wait, what I meant is you have eyes with those thick lashes. And cows, well, they actually have pretty eyes. And—" He snapped his mouth shut.

She arched one eyebrow, a little trick she'd taught herself after watching all those glamour-pusses in the old black-and-white movies on AMC. Then she totally ruined it by smiling.

He shrugged. "Sometimes I'm not so good with the compliments."

"So I see."

A few minutes passed in companionable silence. Dawn took time to notice the little things about the man who'd taken her to dance among the stars quite a few times over the course of the night. He drank his coffee with one sweetener, and he liked lots of pepper on his eggs. He passed over the strawberry jam for apple jelly and didn't eat the fat on the bacon. He also didn't look at anyone else in the room but her. It was a nice change and showed the man Tyson truly was.

And he *was* different from every other man she'd known—something she'd known from the moment she met him. So, if he was different, the relationship could also be different than any she'd ever had. Perhaps, the old wives' tale was correct. The third time was the charm.

But still, she felt cautious. As though maybe the reason she felt so happy, so absolutely free to pursue possibilities with Tyson was because she wasn't in her reality. Instead she was fifty miles away from her temporary home, enjoying orange-blossom muffins and tea in a century-old hotel on a weekend adventure with a man who'd moments before treated her to a naughty bubble bath in a claw-foot tub. This was nothing like reality.

Maybe she was being way too pragmatic. She didn't want this to be only a fling, but she wasn't sure if she was ready to tumble into love. For the time being, she'd stop overthinking. Stop expecting the worst. It wasn't as if Tyson's wife was going to show up with two kids in tow and catch them necking in front of the Houston Museum of Natural History.

No, Tyson's soon-to-be ex-wife would stay in Dallas. But his thirteen-year-old daughter would be here on Sunday.

Now that was a romantic fantasy killer.

"What are you thinking about?" Tyson asked, polishing off the last of his coffee.

"Your wife," she said, taking a sip of her spiced breakfast tea.

Tyson looked as though he might choke on the last of his omelet. "Please. Let's not think about my ex-wife."

"Almost ex-wife. And we haven't talked about the elephant in the room. About her cheating on you."

He set his fork on his empty plate. "There's not much to say. It's history. I haven't been with Karen in years. She left me for my business partner. Remember?" He seemed so matter of fact. Something like that would crush most people. Something like that had crushed her.

"How come it doesn't bother you?" she asked, looking around to make sure there weren't any nosy folks catching juicy tidbits. No one seemed to pay attention to them.

"It bothered me. Still does. I came home from some godforsaken country to find my wife and daughter so different I barely knew them. And then my partner Corbin acted strangely. I knew something was up. When I found out, it hurt. In fact, it hurt pretty badly. But what good is it to carry pain around and wear it for the world to see? I can't change what happened. I can only move forward." By the way he'd said it, she could tell he didn't want to talk about the past anymore.

Maybe he was right. Maybe that's what she'd been doing. Carrying around the pain of her mistakes. Perhaps her baggage blocked the view into her future. She'd have to think more about that idea.

But not today. Today was not about the reality of life. No broken dreams, battered pride or leaky faucets. Today was about sunshine, antiquing and stealing kisses.

"Okay, I get it," she said, tossing her napkin beside her nearly empty plate. "Let's not talk about things like cheating spouses or Mr. Thompson's gout or how many times Mae wakes me up during the night. No unpaid bills, diet shakes or ungrateful kids."

Tyson laughed. "Mr. Thompson's got gout?"

"Stuff it," Dawn said, scooting her chair back from the table. "I'm ready to shop and shop some more."

"Spoken like a true woman," he said, trying to dredge up a frown. But he couldn't. His topaz eyes shimmered with something similar to what welled inside her.

She was pretty certain that something was joy.

"You sure you want to come with me? I mean, I could go antiquing by myself," she said, picking up her purse. She'd been putting aside some cash to buy Christmas presents. Surely, today would be the perfect day to get some of those on her list checked off.

"Are you kidding? I live for exquisitely crafted wood. No better place to find it than in antiques shops. Plus, I'm still sleeping in my old bed from junior high. Slats fall out underneath if I sit down too hard. I'd love to find an old rice sleigh or bed."

Dawn dug inside her purse for her Costa Del Mar sunglasses then popped them on. She also pulled out a pamphlet. "I've got a brochure right here with a map of the stores. Some have only knickknacks, but others have serious furniture."

"Lead on," Tyson said, waving to the front-desk lady and grabbing Dawn's hand.

She wondered if a glow of happiness surrounded her. Because it sure felt that way. For the first time in the longest time, she felt taken care of. She felt bubbly and silly and fun. She felt like there was something more than merely existing.

"HERE, HOLD THIS. I'm going to win you that pink elephant," Tyson said, handing her his half-eaten candy apple. Dawn grabbed the apple and immediately took a bite. The crackling of the sugar coating along with the crisp flavor of Granny Smith apple filled her mouth. Yum. She'd forgotten how good one of these could be.

She watched as Tyson approached the carnival booth and dug money out of his pocket. Men. They loved to throw balls at anything.

All around her people swirled, laughing and fussing, holding hands and high-fiving, and chasing kids and kissing them. She and Tyson had happened upon a Thanksgiving carnival hosted by an Episcopal church, and Tyson had insisted they make a donation, aka, eat funnel cakes, buy raffle tickets for a handmade quilt and play silly games. They'd already won a goldfish throwing Ping-Pong balls. They'd named the fish Homer and given him to a kid who'd been in near tears because he couldn't win one. His mother hadn't looked too pleased, but the boy had grinned from ear to ear. He'd reminded her of Andrew at that age.

"Here you go. One pink elephant," Tyson said shoving the fluffy stuffed animal her way and taking his caramel apple. "Hey, you ate some of my apple."

"Not all of it," Dawn said, looking down at her new acquisition. "So you won it, huh?"

"Sure," he said, devouring the other half of the apple in three bites. "I thought you were watching. I was trying to impress you with my arm speed."

"Oh, you impress me all right. I haven't had this much fun in…well, I'm not sure I've ever really had a true date to compare it to."

Tyson pulled her to him as they walked over to a display of yarn-crafted tissue holders. "Never had a date? You're kidding."

"Well, my parents refused to let me date until I was sixteen, which proved wise since I was a late bloomer. I even wore reading glasses. I wasn't exactly a nerd, just a non-entity. Boys ignored me."

"Can't imagine that," Tyson said as he picked up a fluorescent yellow-and-green tissue box. "What's this for?"

Dawn laughed. "Tissues."

A girl of about thirteen blinked at them through the same sort of glasses Dawn had worn at that age. "That's only five dollars."

Tyson smiled at her. "Did you make these?"

Her eyes shifted away. She was a shy one. "Yes, sir, my grams and me made them."

"Well, I'll take it," Tyson said, digging more money out of his wallet. "You did a nice job."

The girl took the money and placed the tissue box in a plastic grocery bag. Tyson took it and winked at her. Dawn swore the girl puffed her chest out a bit as they walked away. That was her Tyson—saving the female race one prepubescent heart at a time. Hell, who was she kidding? He was saving her very adult heart, patching it up and filling it again.

"What are you going to do with that?" Dawn asked.

"Christmas present," he said, eyeing a booth advertising apple cake and pumpkin bread. "You were telling me why you didn't date."

"Oh, yeah, I lost the baby fat, tried out for cheerleader and got a perm. It did wonders for my social life. Not to mention, my pops finally let me go out with my friends. So I went to the movies, drank wine coolers and basically tried to be as cool as a chick could be in a California dairy town."

They stopped so he could buy a few loaves of bread before continuing toward the carnival rides set up in the park across from the church.

"I remember the night I first saw Larry. I didn't know it at the time, but he'd been sent to stay with his aunt because he'd been getting in trouble in L.A.—skipping school to surf and smoke pot. He was all Malibu sunshine and swagger. And, ol' Larry knew how to cull the weakest from the pack. I was ripe for the picking. We didn't really have a date. He just got me in the backseat of his aunt's Crown Victoria and next thing I knew my panties were on the floorboard."

Tyson studied her.

"Yeah, I know," she said, "I was young and stupid. Larry didn't have to do much sweet-talking.

"I wasn't looking at you because of that. Because, lady, you didn't give it up easy to me."

Dawn laughed. "I've been burned twice. It kinda makes a girl more careful with charming, good-looking guys."

He tugged her toward the Ferris wheel and waggled his eyebrows. "Why thank you, my dear."

"So, next thing I know, Larry's moved on to Marla Baker and I'm suddenly very queasy. Long story short. My dad raised hell, Larry conceded and I pulled on my Sunday best. We came to Texas to live with my aunt and uncle. Larry went to work in my uncle's vacuum cleaner repair shop, and I changed dirty diapers and got my GED."

He pressed his lips together and stared down at her. "Tough to do when you're still a kid yourself."

She nodded. "Yeah, but what doesn't kill us, huh?"

"Still."

"So no time for dates, although that didn't stop Larry from having a few."

Tyson didn't say anything, but she thought she felt his outrage. Something in the way his jaw tightened. "I held that marriage together for almost fourteen years. Mostly for Andrew's sake. I felt he deserved to have a whole family. And also because I got used to what I had. Just existing."

"Why did you end the marriage?"

"I found Larry's girl of the week's bra in our bed. He'd never brought one home before. I decided I didn't want Andrew having that kind of father in the house after all. Plus, I was finally pissed. Wanted to kill Larry. I'd rather have Andrew have one parent who could actually take care of him. Maybe mold some values in him, help him grow into a good man."

Tyson nodded. "Couldn't do that from jail, could you?"

Dawn laughed. She rarely talked about her past, mostly because it dredged up too much shame, but, so far, Tyson wasn't heading for the hills. Yet. "No, I couldn't. Plus, leaving Larry was a long time coming."

They found themselves in a long line. "Wait here, I'll get some tickets."

Dawn really didn't want to ride the Ferris wheel, but Tyson looked like a kid at the opportunity. The ride whirred above her, a dizzying blur of motion. After a minute or so, the ride stopped, stranding a cluster of teenagers on top who took great delight in throwing popcorn down on kids waiting in line.

"Got 'em," Tyson said, slipping in line behind her and curving his arm around her waist, pulling her to him. He kissed the shell of her ear. "I love the Ferris wheel. Makes me feel like I'm a kid again."

"I can tell," she said.

They stood, content to brush against one another as they waited their turn. Finally, the operator opened a swinging car and motioned for them to climb inside. After making sure the bar clicked in place, she settled against Tyson's arm where it stretched across the back of the seat.

A moment later they were climbing into the Texas sky. The car came to rest at the very top.

"Wow." He pointed out the sun sinking into the horizon. Lofty pines looked like grass beneath their feet. "This thing really gets up here, doesn't it?"

Dawn gripped his hand.

"Not good with heights?" he said, pulling her closer

to his side. He felt so warm and solid. So Tyson-like. She relaxed.

"I haven't ridden one of these in a long time. I'd for-gotten the cars swing. My stomach feels funny." She clutched his hand tightly and stared at the golden orb creating art in the darkening sky. Orange and pink rib-bons curled into the azure canvas.

"Wait, you said two good-looking guys charmed you. The second didn't take you on dates, either?"

She stiffened against him and remained silent. It was bad enough she had failed where Larry was concerned. Her marriage was destined to fail. Larry wasn't cut out to love anyone but himself. But talking about Murray was harder. He was a mistake that haunted her.

"Look, I'm sorry. We're not supposed to drag out the dirty laundry. We said this weekend wasn't about leaky plumbing or dirty socks." Tyson sighed and pointed to the cakewalk being played out beneath them. "Let's do that next."

"I've never really talked about my failures before." She hesitated a moment. "But, it feels good to do it. With you."

"That's what all the women say," he quipped with a mischievous grin.

She rolled her eyes. "Oh, please. Walked right into that one."

His response was to pull her into a kiss. A slow, sweet kiss. A dating kiss.

She pulled away and studied him in the fading light. He smiled at her. "I'm glad you feel comfortable enough."

"Okay. So the next guy came along about a year ago. I still had my business open. Again, a failure. But anyway, I had a shop, and across the street was this great little

Italian bistro. The guy was very similar to Larry. Handsome, charming and made me feel like a new penny. I didn't know he was married."

She stopped and took a deep breath. "I know what you're thinking... I should have known. But funny thing was I didn't get it. We met for lunch, flirted, things progressed. I even thought about how wonderful it was he settled for seeing me during the day. My nights were filled with taking Andrew to practice and business classes at the local community college. Stupid, huh?"

Tyson squeezed her against him. "Not stupid. Sometimes we don't want to look too hard because we're afraid of what we might find."

His words seemed to be pointed at himself, as well as her.

"True, but I should have guessed. We were out for lunch one day when we walked right into his wife and their two kids. I was kissing him when I heard her voice. I'll never forget the way she sounded. At that moment, even before I turned around, I knew. I'd heard the same sound in my own voice when I asked Larry why he'd been out, why he smelled like perfume."

She closed her eyes against the memory of the suburban blonde and her tragic green eyes. Devastation. Anger. Pain. Dawn hadn't known what to do. Murray had launched into some contrived story. She'd slipped into the restaurant they'd exited and been sick in the bathroom. The betrayal had been that visceral.

"Damaged," he murmured, as they swung almost a hundred feet up.

"What?"

"Both of us. We're a bit damaged."

"I guess you could say that," she said. Worded that way, she wasn't so sure they should be meeting up like two ships passing in the night. Two dinged-up ships. Those kind of ships went down to watery graves.

He looked at her, meeting her eyes. "I guess not too many people get to be our age without having a few dents. Lots of people have it worse."

"Are you calling me old?" Dawn said, allowing a smile to hover around her lips. Hell, she was damaged. So the hell what? Did that mean she wasn't worthy? That she and Tyson couldn't carve out some sort of relationship from the ashes of their ruined romances?

"Never," he swore, as the ride started up, dropping them with a sudden plunge.

She shrieked as they swooped past the operator grinning at them with a jack-o'-lantern smile. Then she laughed.

And she couldn't seem to stop. Tyson joined her, wrapping his arm around her and tucking the pink elephant in between them.

Dawn was tired of the past. Finally, she wanted to look to her future.

CHAPTER FOURTEEN

WANTING TO LOOK TOWARD her future had made sense
in Jefferson. After hot sex, mondo Christmas shopping
and lots of laughter, she'd vowed to claim a better life
for herself. To believe in dreams again. However, being
back in reality, otherwise known as Oak Stand, was
another matter.

"Mom, I'm home!" Andrew's voice barreled into
the kitchen, where she stood washing baby bottles for
Nellie.

Her son appeared in the doorway, reminding her of
when he was a toddler. Hurricane Andrew. He wasn't
much different, other than being nineteen years old.
And towering over his mother.

"Hey, honey," Dawn said, popping him with a towel.
"I wasn't expecting you till later. Thought you had
practice."

Andrew opened the refrigerator and perused the con-
tents. "Coach let us go early. Hey, what's this?"

Her son held up a bottle filled with what looked to
be watered-down milk. He swirled the liquid around,
his brown eyes studying the bottle with scientific un-
certainty. She noticed he'd gotten a haircut recently and
the barber had nicked his hairline over his ear.

"That's expressed milk," she said, stacking the baby
bottle in the dish drainer.

"What kind of milk is that?" he said, screwing up his face as he started to unscrew the lid.

"Breast milk," she said, turning off the faucet.

"Nasty," Andrew said, quickly shoving the container back into the fridge. "Aunt Nellie needs to mark that sh—stuff."

"It's not nasty. It's a perfectly natural part of being a mother. I nursed you."

Andrew clomped to the pantry and rustled around inside. His voice came from the depths. "Don't remind me of stuff like that, Mom. It's sick."

Dawn laughed. She was so glad to see him. She'd missed him something terrible when he'd left for school. They'd always had a good relationship, then suddenly the house in Houston had been so empty. And if her house seemed empty, her heart had dust bunnies. Being in Oak Stand had softened the empty-nest ache. Over the past few months, her big city heart had remembered the barefoot girl she'd been back in California. Sure small-town people were nosy, but they cared. Her mind flashed to Emma Long and her pear preserves, Ms. Ester who'd given her a funny T-shirt that said It's not PMS, it's you, and Bubba, who weeded the flowerbeds of Tucker House because she'd once mentioned the need. All things she'd never had in Houston.

So she'd been thinking a lot lately about staying here. It wasn't far from Andrew's campus. He could visit whenever. With Marcie Patterson in the picture, he'd be making the trip anyway. She could sell the house in Houston and get one in town. The possibility of continuing to run Tucker House crept into her mind along with the idea of something more permanent with Tyson. But it was too soon to think in that direction. She wiped the thoughts away as she wiped down the sink.

"Did you talk to your father?" she asked, tossing the towel onto the gleaming granite countertop.

Her son emerged from the pantry with a bag of animal crackers. "Yeah, he was bummed. I wanted to spend the holiday with both of you. Maybe he can come up later."

Dawn's heart sank. She wanted to spend time with Tyson and his daughter. Get Andrew onto better footing with Tyson. She and Tyson had agreed a casual hangout vibe would be good for both their kids, maybe have some apple cider and shortbread cookies and hang out on the ranch's enormous back porch. But if Larry came to town, things would be too weird.

"We'll see," she said, using her standard mom-ism. Andrew always said that *we'll see* meant *no*.

Her son grunted.

"Honey, I wanted to talk to you about something. About that afternoon by the pond."

Andrew tossed a cookie in his mouth and stared at her.

"The guy I was with, well, his name is Tyson Hart."

"I remember," he said, grabbing a soda from the fridge and popping the top.

"We've been seeing each other and I really like him. I'd like for you to give him a chance." Her words sounded rushed. As if she was nervous. Which was silly. Andrew was her son, and he was a good boy—a good boy who'd always wanted the best for her.

"You think you should be dating? I mean, Dad might come up here to see you and all," he said, shoving another cookie in his mouth.

"Drew, your father and I have been divorced for almost five years. We're friends." Which was a total lie. She would never consider Larry the Snake a friend. He was a sperm donor. Okay, more than that, but not a friend. Friends practiced give and take in a relationship. All Larry knew was take. But Andrew didn't get that. She had never let him know what a waste of skin his father was.

"Why?" Andrew asked. He set his soda can on the counter and crossed his arms. He looked so much like a man, even though his brown eyes mirrored little-boy pain. "Why'd you make him leave to begin with? Things were fine. I never got it."

How had a conversation about her dating turned into this? Why did her son still harbor hope for reconciliation?

"Honey, this is probably not the best time to talk about what happened between your dad and me. I care about him because he's your father, but our marriage wasn't working. We weren't in love anymore." Or ever.

Larry was what he was—a man who would never grow up. Andrew never saw Larry's flaws. He thought his good time Charlie father was the bomb. That the greasy little worm was cool, pimp, all that and a bag of chips.

Of course, what child wouldn't? She'd done the laundry, met with the principal, driven a wheezing Andrew to the hospital, punished the child when he'd lied about stealing a chocolate bar. She'd been the caretaker, disciplinarian and errand runner. She'd made the sacrifices to raise a child. Larry had been the opposite. He showed up late to games with new baseball gloves. He came to the hospital with video games. He allowed Andrew to go to the Astros game even when he was supposedly grounded. He called the principal a loser and degraded the man for picking on his son. Larry was the hero, while she was the enforcer.

Andrew's inflated opinion of his father was her fault. She'd made excuses for too long.

"He still loves you. He told me so," Andrew said, shoving his hands in his pockets. "I don't know why you want to see this Tyson guy. We're still a family. You said we'd always be a family no matter what, but obviously that isn't true. I have to spend all my holidays split between the two of you."

Dawn rubbed a hand over her face. "I'm sorry. But do you expect me to make something out of nothing just so it's easier for you? That's not fair to me. And you're too old for this."

He shrugged. "Whatever."

"You're an adult now, right?"

He nodded, even though she wasn't certain she could call her baby an adult. His body looked every inch a man, but his psyche was still building Lego creations. She knew. She'd been a mother at seventeen still looking through magazines for prom dresses she would never wear.

"Then you know relationships between men and women are complicated. Your dad and I both love you. We just don't love each other in the way it takes for us to get back together."

"But Dad said—"

"What your dad says and does are two different things, Andrew. They always have been. He cares about me in the same way I care about him. As friends. That's all."

At that, her son closed his mouth. He didn't say anything further, just glared at her.

"Let's try to keep an open mind and work on having

a nice Thanksgiving," she said, patting her son on the back. She stood on her tiptoes to kiss his scruffy jaw. "I love you, Drew, and I'm glad you're here."

"Whatever." Andrew headed for the back door. She could see Jack sitting on the porch, balancing Mae on his knee.

Pain punched her in the chest as sudden tears sprang to her eyes. Fighting for her and Tyson's relationship wasn't going to be easy. Andrew stubbornly clung to some crazy belief his parents would somehow reconcile. To make life easier for him.

Yeah, sure. She'd get right on that.

All she could hope was Tyson was having an easier time of it with his daughter. Thirteen-year-olds could be more than difficult to deal with, and when they were thirteen-year-old girls, well, that could be like dancing with the devil's wife—dangerous and uncomfortably hot.

TYSON PULLED AT HIS collar as he stared at his soon-to-be ex-wife. "I still can't believe you're here."

Karen turned eyes the color of an Alaskan lake on him. "What's not to get? I promised Laurel I would come and stay. After all, we're signing the papers and that's been difficult on her. She's having problems in school. She's really vulnerable right now."

"But it's my time with her," he mumbled, propping his arms on the tailgate. "I haven't seen her in over a month."

Karen flipped her auburn hair over one shoulder and leveled him with a killer smile. "Tyson, honey, she's our daughter. I don't like carving this up into 'my' time or 'your' time. It's crass."

Tyson snorted. "Crass?"

"Don't go there. We're past the accusations and playing the blame game, Ty."

Tyson shrugged. Karen might be past it, but he would always nurse a small kernel of betrayal. There would always be conflict between them because of the very nature of their breakup. Karen had chosen the path they were on. "I still think this is pretty shitty of you. But if you're staying in Oak Stand, you're getting a hotel room. There's a little bed-and-breakfast in town and a small motel."

Karen smiled. "Already taken care of. I'll be staying at the Tulip Hill Bed and Breakfast. Laurel will stay here with you and Gramps, of course."

"But I can stay with you, too, right, Mom? You know, like, if I want to," Laurel said.

Tyson turned to find his daughter right behind them. He thought she'd stayed inside the house with Gramps.

"Pumpkin, if you need to go stay with your mother, you can. I hope you don't want to, though. I've missed my girl." Tyson took Laurel in. He hadn't seen her since she got her braces. They made her look so much more like a teenager. Laurel was slim and athletic. Her long brown hair hung past her shoulders and her wide blue eyes were startling against her tanned skin. She would be a heartbreaker. Hell, she already was.

"Thanks, Dad," she said, pulling a pink phone from her pocket and flipping the screen on it. She didn't say anything else, just started tapping into the phone, shoulders slumping, eyes glazed.

"Is this what she does all the time?" he asked Karen as she lifted a Louis Vuitton bag from the depths of his toolbox. He watched as Karen checked the bag over, likely for scratches.

"Well, sure. She's a kid, you know. They all do that. Facebooking and Twittering and texting," she said as she handed Laurel's bag to him. "I'm sorry I couldn't bring my car. I had no idea it would take so long to repair. You won't mind giving me a ride into town, will you? Or do I need—wait, do they even have cabs here?"

Tyson should have taken Karen to the B and B first, but he'd agreed to let her say hello to his grandfather. Besides he still reeled with shock at finding her packed and ready at the end of the drive right beside his daughter. He couldn't believe she'd connived her way into his holiday. But Karen had cornered him, whispering about how uncomfortable Laurel felt with the custody arrangements and how perhaps they should talk to the lawyer again.

Laurel not comfortable with him?

He was her damn father. Why wouldn't she feel comfortable with him? He'd only been in Oak Stand for three months. Before that, he and Laurel had spent almost every weekend in a cramped apartment in Las Colinas going shopping, watching movies and scarfing down pizza while Karen played with his ex-business partner. What had changed? Surely, Gramps's house was better than an apartment that smelled like mildew and smoke.

Perhaps he should have stayed in Dallas. Maybe tearing Laurel from her world had been too much.

But he was certain he'd done the right thing returning to East Texas. He needed to put the brakes on Laurel. She looked and acted like a spoiled heiress. All she needed to complete her look was Herman the Chihuahua in a bag under her arm. She was too good of a girl to fall prey to the things of the world so easily. Oak Stand was a road bump for his daughter. She'd have to slow down here.

If he had to fight for that right, he'd do it. He had to get things straight for her.

He sighed and looked at Karen.

"Sure, I'll take you into town. Let me tell Gramps." Tyson headed toward the ranch house he now called home. Laurel was sitting on the porch in one of the rockers, absorbed by her phone. She didn't even acknowledge him as he passed by. "Laurel, wanna go with me to take your mom into town? You can see the house I'm working on."

His daughter didn't look up. "Nah, I'll just hang here."

Disappointment lodged in his chest. He hadn't seen her in over a month and he'd missed her the way a prisoner misses open spaces. When he'd gotten back from Iraq nearly two years ago, there'd been no more kisses on her forehead, no silly jokes, no triple-fudge ice cream cones. The pigtailed little girl he'd left behind years ago would have jumped at any chance to ride beside him in the truck. This new creature, not so much.

What had happened to her?

But he knew. Laurel was another casualty of a father gone to war, of divorce and of being a teenager in today's world.

He swallowed the hurt of her indifference. "Okay, then. Be back in a bit."

Tyson set Laurel's bag inside the foyer, yelled to his grandfather to keep an eye on his great-granddaughter, then went to the truck. He watched Karen open the passenger door and dust the seat with her hand before stepping daintily into the truck. She'd spent the past two hours in the same spot, so it was a diva move. He rolled his eyes before putting the truck in Drive.

He didn't talk to Karen. He was afraid of what he might say to her now that they were alone.

"I get you're probably mad, Ty, but I really had Laurel's best interests in mind. Truly."

He didn't respond. Just turned to look at the woman who sat with her legs crossed and her hands folded elegantly in her lap. She looked incongruous in his old pickup.

She met his eyes with not the least bit of apprehension in the blue depths. She looked good. She'd lost some weight and wore her designer jeans and blouse like a Plano blue-blooded heiress. She had manicured fingernails and ruby-red lips. Her perfume wafted across the cab, tickling his nose, reminding him of how she'd always dabbed the expensive French scent between her breasts before she came to bed. She was lovely. Always had been. Beautiful smile, beautiful body and lots of maintenance.

He was glad to be rid of her.

"I don't really want to talk about it, Karen. I'm too pissed."

She patted his arm. "Don't be mad, Ty. We'll spend Thanksgiving together. We're still a family, you know."

Her words sounded like a purr. What the hell?

"You will always be the mother of my child, but we are not a family any longer. And you are not spending Thanksgiving dinner with us. Hope the bed-and-breakfast has something planned."

"Come on, Ty. Don't be like that. You know we will always have something." Karen rubbed his arm then patted his thigh. The move surprised him. His former wife had not shown any affection toward him since before he left for Iraq. He wondered if she and Corbin were on the outs.

He picked up her hand and put it back in her lap. "Yes, we will have something—Laurel. But that's it. You made that choice."

Karen folded her arms. "I don't know why you have to be so nasty. We went through counseling so we could accept the good and bad in each other. Don't you want this to work?"

Tyson waved at Marvin Settler as the mailman passed in his ancient Cadillac. "Define *this*."

"Our relationship."

He snorted.

"You are the father of my child. We'll always have that between us." Karen studied her hands. She no longer wore a wedding band on her left hand, but she wore a large ruby ring on her right. "I've missed you, Tyson."

Tyson was tempted to slam on his brakes, toss her onto the side of the road and haul ass back to his grandfather's. The nerve of the woman. To show up on his time, intrude on his holiday then say things about missing him and still being in a relationship. But he didn't toss her out. He kept driving.

"Haven't you missed me a little?" Karen asked. He could feel her eyes on him. Eyes he'd once loved and looked into as he kissed her. But he didn't love her anymore.

"Karen, I don't know what you're doing, but I need you to stop."

"What?" she said, pretending to look out the window at the small clapboard houses on the fringe of town. Sweetgum and pecan trees dazzled orange and gold against the darkening sky. Most of the houses had neatly trimmed yards and planters of festive mums. Dogs barked, children biked and neighbors called out to each other as they arrived home from work. More and more, Oak Stand burrowed into his heart. He knew he'd be happy making his permanent home here. Dawn flashed into his mind. Dawn sitting on a porch swing, barefoot and scrumptious, at the end of the work day.

"You're playing games with me," he said, turning onto the street beside the square. Tucker House was to the left and Margo sat on the porch with Mr. Levitt and Clara Jennings. He tooted his horn.

"Who's that?" Karen asked, ducking her head to get a glimpse.

"That's the house I'm working on. It's an adult day care center," he said, hooking a turn down Beech Street heading toward the B and B.

"Oh," she said, dismissing the topic. "Come on, Ty. I'm not playing games. I've been doing some thinking is all. I've been wondering if I made a bad decision not staying with you. I saw you pull up to our house last month and all those feelings came flooding back. And you looked so good. So tan and in shape and I—"

"Karen, it's too late for that." He stopped the truck in front of the gingerbread house. "We're past that now."

"We still haven't signed the papers. We could try again."

He couldn't stop the curse word that slipped from his lips.

"You don't have to be crass," Karen said, narrowing her eyes. "Are you seeing somebody else?"

He remained silent.

She bit her lip before pouting. "You're not, are you? Seeing someone?"

"Karen…" he started.

"But we're not even divorced yet," she said, placing her hand on his shoulder.

"For Christ's sake, woman, you slept with my best friend while I was in Iraq writing you love letters. You've got to be shitting me you're upset because I've moved on. Two signatures will do away with those vows we took. So hand me the papers you brought from the attorney before you climb out."

Anger welled within him. And perhaps a smidgeon of guilt. Here was Karen, smack-dab in the middle of Oak Stand, dredging up bad memories and playing head games with him. Dragging Dawn into his mess felt selfish when he still had to deal with the instability of his former life. But with Dawn he couldn't help himself. He knew she was his future. But his past had just opened up a big ol' can of crazy on him.

Karen remained silent. Tears glittered on her mascara-laden lashes and her ruby-red lips trembled slightly. "I said I was sorry about Corbin. I missed you and he was there, you know?"

"No, I don't know. But, I've forgiven you both and it's time we all move on. With no regrets." Tyson didn't wait for her to respond. He opened the truck door and slid out into the twilight settling around the small town. He didn't bother opening Karen's truck door. He just pulled her three bags from the depths behind the seat and set them on the curb.

She appeared at his elbow.

"I'm sorry, Tyson. For everything. But I can't stop my heart from feeling the way it does about you. No matter what, I always come back to you. I always have." Her auburn hair brushed his shoulder as she rose on her toes and kissed his cheek. "Thanks for the ride."

Tyson muttered, "You're welcome," then watched the

woman he'd once loved struggle with her bags as she walked the cobbled path to the Tulip Hill's door. She disappeared within the soft glow of the parlor.

He shouldn't have let her come with Laurel. He should have put his foot down.

Hell.

He started up the walk after her. He'd take her back to Dallas. But then he thought about his daughter. The words Karen had whispered about Laurel crying herself to sleep at night, about her grades slipping, her refusal to take piano anymore.

And he stopped.

If he and Dawn had a shot, they'd have to deal with everything life threw at them. That included crazy ex-wives and drama-queen daughters.

Go with the flow.

Easier said than done.

CHAPTER FIFTEEN

DAWN LOOKED AROUND AT the ladies gathered at the craft table. Several chattered as they secured the glazed squash and baby pumpkins to their arrangement. A few ladies bit their lips in concentration as their arthritic hands wielded the hot glue guns. Mary St. John stared at her arrangement in disgust.

"Problems, Mary?" Dawn asked, collecting stray pieces of raffia and torn leaves.

"This whole thing looks like a hat my aunt Millicent wore once," Mary said, pointing to the clump of leaves, sunflowers and wired raffia. Dawn had to admit it was a bit of a mess.

"Well, surely, it's not that bad," Dawn said, standing behind her and trying to find a good side to the arrangement.

"My aunt Millicent was blind and insisted on making her own bonnets. Trust me, it's bad."

Dawn laughed as Tyson appeared in the doorway. Her heart leaped and she gave him a smile that also encompassed the long-legged girl standing beside him. Laurel had straight brown hair and eyes so blue Dawn could see the color from across the room. "Hey, look. Help has arrived."

Mary focused her trifocals on the doorway. "Surely, you don't think a man could help with this. That one's not even gay."

How well Dawn knew. Nothing feminine about her Tyson. Odd, how easy it was for her to claim him as her own. Yet they'd made no promises to one another. But Tyson acted as if they were heading toward some sort of permanent status. Or maybe she just nurtured that hope in her still vulnerable heart.

"Morning, Tyson," Dawn called. "Have you brought us some help?"

"Morning, Dawn. Ladies," Tyson said stepping into the room. He wasn't wearing work clothes today. Instead he wore a pair of khaki trousers and a burnt-orange rugby-style shirt.

Dawn moved across the room and extended her hand to the girl. "Hi, Laurel. I'm Dawn. It's good to meet you."

Laurel snapped her phone shut, tucking it into her back pocket, then looked at Dawn's hand. Reluctantly, she offered her own, giving Dawn's a brief tug. "Hey."

Tyson smiled at his daughter. "I told Dawn all about you and told her maybe you'd help with the craft project this morning. You've always loved crafts."

"I've never loved crafts, Dad."

"Sure you have. Remember all those bracelets you made that summer?"

Laurel rolled her eyes. "Yeah, when I was, like, nine."

Dawn shot Tyson a questioning look. It was obvious Laurel didn't want to be here. "Well, you don't have to help. If you like games, some of the gentlemen in the parlor are having a boxing contest on the Wii."

Laurel blinked. "Seriously? They're playing Wii?"

"Yeah," Dawn said, as she pulled a bag of glue sticks from a drawer. "They're like kids your age. Obsessed with video games."

"They're morons," Ester said.

At this Laurel laughed.

Ester winked at the girl, her glasses flashing beneath the chandelier. "Boys don't change much, honey. If they can find some asinine thing to occupy their time, they'll do it."

"Ester, I'm standing right here," Tyson said.

"Well, I can see you, honey. My eyes work, but I'm too old to temper my words. Just go ahead and be offended," the silver-haired woman said with a grin, wrapping another piece of raffia around the hurricane vase in the middle of her centerpiece. She turned to Grace and asked for a few acorns.

Dawn pulled a face, trying not to laugh. Tyson shook his head, a bemused smile on his face.

He patted Laurel on the back. "I'm going upstairs to meet with the inspector. It won't take long. Hang down here for a bit and then we'll head to the Dairy Barn for lunch. And don't let Ester eat you for lunch. Old hags like to devour young girls."

Ester's only response was an appropriate cackle.

Dawn couldn't hold back the laugh this time. Tyson winked at her and slipped out the door.

Laurel said nothing. She plopped into a chair by the door and pulled out her cell phone and started texting.

So much for getting to know her. Dawn had wanted to form some sort of tentative relationship with Tyson's daughter, but it felt so damned awkward. The girl didn't want to be here, maybe felt some sort of vibe existing between Dawn and her father, and probably thought old people were lame.

Dawn looked at Laurel, whose shining hair fell around her face, hiding her from the rest of the world. "If you decide you want to make a centerpiece, I can give you the materials. Or if you want to help poor Mrs. St. John out, you could do that, too."

"Mary is hopeless," Ester said. "I'll get down there and see if I can help her salvage that monstrosity she's put together."

Dawn started to admonish Ester, but Mary beat her to it.

"Oh, shut up, you old windbag," Mary said, tossing an acorn Ester's way.

Ester laughed and scooted her chair back. Being that they were former sister-in-laws, Dawn snapped her mouth shut and let them at each other. It seemed to amuse everyone else at the table.

"Hey, Mom."

Dawn spun around to find Andrew filling up the doorway.

All the ladies around the table called out hellos. They loved when Andrew came to the center. He'd only been by once or twice, but he flirted with them and took time to notice them. She loved when he showed how kind he was.

"Hey, honey, what are you doing up and about this early?" Andrew usually slept till at least noon on vacation days. She looked at her watch. It was only 10:30 a.m.

"Uncle Jack wanted to meet the inspector and see the contractor's progress. I told Jack I'd ride in with him. We're going to head to the Dairy Barn for lunch."

"We're going there for lunch, too." Laurel had lowered her phone to her lap. Her eyes were on Andrew.

Her son leaned inside the door to find the voice. "Hey, when did y'all start taking in girls?"

"Who says we ain't girls?" Grace tittered.

Andrew blinked. "You know what I mean, Ms. Grace. I mean, like—"

"Hotties?" Ester piped up from the end of the table where she stood mashing Mary's centerpiece with both hands. "'Cause I'm a hottie."

Andrew laughed, his rich baritone filling the room and making the ladies giggle. Dawn looked at her son dressed in a fitted Hollister T-shirt and worn jeans. His hair looked windblown and he'd forgotten to shave. Objectively she could say he was all-American-boy beautiful.

"Yeah, the center for hotties," he snorted.

Dawn swore Laurel's mouth opened wider at Andrew's teasing of the older ladies. She snapped it shut and gave him a shy smile. Then she ducked her head, focusing on the cell phone in her hand.

"Drew, this is Tyson's daughter, Laurel. She's spending Thanksgiving break with her father. Laurel, this is my son, Andrew." Dawn motioned toward the girl who looked as if she were pretending to study her phone's little flip screen, but was really darting glances at her son.

"Hey," Andrew said, clasping either side of the doorjamb and leaning into the room. "You'll like Charlie Mac's onion rings. They rock."

Laurel flipped her hair over her shoulder. "I don't eat fried stuff. It's bad for you."

Andrew looked stunned. "Sucks for you. You're missing out. I'll let you try one of mine, if you want."

"Really?" Laurel asked, rising from the chair. "Maybe just one then."

"Okay, cool," he said. "I'm heading to the kitchen. I smell Margo's blueberry biscuits."

Dawn nodded. "Sure, but come back before you leave for the Barn. I may want a club salad."

Laurel hovered by her chair. "I think I'll go see what my dad's doing."

The two kids disappeared, leaving Dawn shaking her head. See what her dad was doing? Yeah, right. More like trail behind Andrew toward the kitchen. Well, at least Laurel expressed some interest in something. Too bad it was misplaced. Dawn had a feeling Laurel was growing up way too fast. She wore too much makeup, clothes that were too tight and seemed to pay attention only to her cell phone and boys. Well, maybe that's how all thirteen-year-olds were nowadays.

Still, it worried Dawn.

If she and Tyson stayed together, rambling into some sort of future together, it would be difficult. They each had a child. A child who didn't want change. They each had an ex. Hers seemed to think she was his unpaid assistant. She had no clue what to expect of Karen, who obviously had decided to stay in Oak Stand no matter she wasn't invited. Dawn didn't even know if, in light of Karen's unexpected appearance, she and Tyson could share Thanksgiving dinner together.

Difficult was not even the word.

Her world felt a lot like Mary St. John's centerpiece looked: a jumbled mess.

"I can't redeem this thing," Ester declared, tossing down a bunch of artificial sunflowers. "Stick a pot of mums on the table or something 'cause this isn't going to work."

"I guess it really is a mess," Mary said, looking at the ruined decoration.

Dawn wasn't sure she could use the centerpiece as

a prophecy, but something told her she'd be sticking a pot of mums on her own table.

Whatever the hell that meant.

"So what did you think about Dawn? She's nice, isn't she?" Tyson asked Laurel as he set the tray on the table. Around them the Dairy Barn hummed as usual. The place had been running for years. He'd had his first milkshake sitting at a table over by the door when he'd been seven years old. Charlie Mac, the owner, still made a hell of a milkshake. His hot, crispy French fries weren't bad, either.

"She's okay, I guess," Laurel mumbled, shoving a forkful of lettuce into her mouth. It seemed his daughter no longer ate cheeseburgers. Her new lunch of choice was a grilled-chicken salad. "Her son is totally hot, though."

Totally hot? Was this coming out of the mouth of his thirteen-year-old daughter? Wasn't she too young to notice boys? "What?"

"Her son, Andrew. He's way hot. How old is he? Do you know?" Laurel darted another glance at the glass front door of the eatery. She'd been steadily watching it since they'd sat.

"He's too old for you, like, against-the-law old," Tyson said, swiping a fry in the glob of ketchup and tossing it into his mouth. "When did you trade Build-a-Bear for boys?"

Laurel giggled. "I still like my Build-a-Bear stuff. I just like boys, too. Especially Andrew."

"He's in college. Don't even think about it."

At that moment, the door to the burger joint swung open and Jack and Andrew stepped in. Okay, it all made sense now. Laurel had been waiting for the boy wonder to show. Jack caught Tyson's eye and nodded. Andrew caught his eye and glared. Great.

"Oooh, there he is. He said I could have one of his onion rings." Laurel slid out of the booth before Tyson finished chewing his bite of burger. He couldn't protest without choking.

His daughter made a beeline for Andrew and Jack.

"Great, just great," he muttered to no one in particular. He watched Laurel extend her hand to Jack before flipping her hair over her shoulder and hitting the glowering boy with a smile Tyson had never seen her use before. Holy crap. She was flirting.

He wadded up his napkin and threw it on the table. With a terse "Be right back," to the busboy, he strode over to Jack and Andrew. Laurel stood beside Andrew, chattering about how good the salad was and how cool the retro diner was.

"Jack," he said. "Long time, no see."

Jack smiled. "Yeah, it's been a long time. If I'd known y'all were headed here, I'd have given you a ride."

"That would've been awesome," Laurel said, "I mean, we walked. You can maybe give us a ride back?" Laurel smiled again, her baby blues zeroing in on Andrew.

Dawn's son shifted uneasily, obviously uncomfortable with the younger girl's testing of her feminine wiles.

"Sure, we could probably give y'all a lift. Might be a tight fit." Andrew looked to Jack for confirmation.

Jack didn't reply, but a smile hovered on the man's lips. Tyson knew exactly what the man was thinking.

"That's okay," Laurel said, wetting her lips with a flick of her tongue. She flipped her hair over her shoulder again and tucked her hands into her back pocket. The move was made to entice, causing her small breasts to thrust forward.

Tyson stared at his daughter as if she'd sprouted a tail and horns. Maybe she had. He'd heard raising a teenage girl was rough. He wondered if he needed to fit her with a chastity belt. And throw the key in a river.

"No need. We'll be walking back. Gotta walk off this cheeseburger," he said, rubbing his stomach. He tugged on Laurel's arm. "Come on, honey. Let's finish our lunch and allow them to order."

His daughter shrugged out of his grasp. "Okay. But, hey, don't forget you promised me one of your onion rings, Andrew."

Laurel whirled and sashayed back toward their booth. Tyson shrugged. "Sorry about that. She's a bit, uh, headstrong."

Jack laughed and Andrew dismissed Tyson, not giving him a chance to greet him, instead turning toward the order board. Andrew would be a tough nut to crack. Tyson had a feeling neither Andrew nor Laurel would accept his and Dawn's relationship easily. It already felt like a whole lotta uphill hiking with boulders in his backpack.

Before heading back to the booth, he took a moment to clap Jack on the back. "Don't laugh, big boy. You've got one of those to raise yourself."

At that Jack fell silent. Then he frowned. "Hell."

When Tyson reached the booth, a sulking daughter met him. She'd shoved her half-eaten salad aside. "Why'd you tell them we couldn't ride with them? I don't want to walk back to that lame place."

Tyson leveled her with a look. "Okay, missy, enough with the diva routine. First of all, you're acting like a spoiled brat. And, second, you can lay off Andrew. He's too old for you—"

"I'll be fourteen next month," Laurel said with a roll of her eyes.

"I don't care if you were sixteen. You aren't dating a college guy who's that much older than you. He could get arrested. Forget about it."

"Mom would let me—"

"No, she wouldn't and don't pretend she would. And even if you are living several hours' away from me, you won't be dating until you are at least fifteen. And there will be guidelines. And you will respect them or I will come to Dallas and horsewhip you."

"Daddy!" Laurel protested. "You wouldn't."

"I'll do whatever I have to do to protect you. Even if it's from yourself. I love you."

"But you've never whipped me," Laurel said, her blue eyes now the size of the platters hanging on the wall behind Charlie Mac's gnarled figure.

He knew he'd never raise a hand to Laurel. It wasn't in him to strike the child, though his own father had walloped him good upon occasion. No, there were other ways to make her understand what he expected of her.

"You're going to make the right decisions—" he let his words sink in before continuing "—or your mother and I will make them for you. Got it?"

Laurel ducked her head and pouted. "Fine."

"What was that?" he asked, crossing his arms and hitting her with another deadly Dad stare.

"Yes, sir," she muttered, shoulders sinking.

"Good." Tyson picked up his cheeseburger, which had grown cold during his parental tirade. Laurel propped her chin on her hand and pretended as though he wasn't in the universe.

Well, wasn't Thanksgiving turning out ducky?

Laurel showed up looking like a miniature Britney

Spears and gave him lip. Karen wanted to reconcile or something he didn't want to think about delving into. And Andrew wanted to gut him and fry his innards. Not to mention, he'd forgotten to get the divorce papers his lawyer had sent via Karen.

Sitting 'round the table together ought to be a gas.

Bring on the flippin' turkey.

CHAPTER SIXTEEN

"SOMEONE HAND ME A POT HOLDER, please?" Nellie said, balancing a huge pan of corn-bread dressing in one hand.

Jack handed her a cross-stitched oven mitt and cleared a spot on the granite counter.

"I'm finished chopping the pecans. Want me to mix up the topping for the sweet potatoes?" Dawn asked, dumping the last of the nuts into a mixing bowl.

"Go ahead," Nellie said, sliding the pan of dressing onto the counter and wiping her brow with the back of her frilly apron. "Whew, I haven't cooked for this many people since the Ladies Auxiliary tea almost a year ago. I've gotten out of practice."

Jack spun his wife into a kiss, silencing her quite handily. Dawn laughed. "No time for sucking face, Jack. You've got to get the turkey off the smoker."

Jack broke off the embrace with Nellie and saluted his sister. "Aye, aye, Captain."

"I love when he follows orders," Dawn said, dumping brown sugar and flour on top of the pecans. A smack followed by a stinging on her backside had her jumping then spinning around. Jack stood behind her, grinning like a fool and dangling a damp hand towel.

"You'll pay for that," Dawn said with the certainty of an older sister who knew how to put a younger brother in his place.

"What's with you Darbys and your towel snapping? Just plum immature," Nellie said, though she smiled, happy as a clam. Nellie had once told Dawn that she loved her kitchen full of family, mischief and decadent foods. It was something she'd missed out on as a child.

A tapping at the window over the sink drew their attention. Tyson's face appeared. He beckoned Dawn with a finger.

"Go ahead. I'll finish up the topping. We're on the downhill anyway," Nellie said, shoving her husband toward the doorway. "Check the turkey then go make sure our little pumpkin's sleeping."

Tyson made a face at Dawn and suddenly all of her worries about the complexity of the day slid away. She lifted the apron over her head and tossed it on the table.

She grabbed a sweater from the hook in the mudroom and slipped out the door to embrace the kiss of the November wind. The day had dawned overcast and belligerent—just right for Thanksgiving Day.

Tyson stood in the middle of the screened porch balancing an enormous pot of chrysanthemums. They were bright yellow and happy against the gray palette of the day. And they made her laugh.

"What?" Tyson said, sheepish smile in place. "You don't like this kind of flower?"

Dawn kissed him on the cheek and took the pot from him. "No, I love them. It's a bit of a joke between me and the gals at the center."

Tyson grabbed hold of her and kissed her. His lips were cold and tasted like peppermint. He pulled back. "Now, that's a proper greeting. Wanna take a walk before everybody gets here?"

Dawn opened the door and set the flowers in the mudroom. She would put them by the hearth in the den later. They'd look festive next to the crackling fire they'd enjoy after the game of flag football. Jack rustled everyone up for an impromptu game every year. After they watched the first half of the Dallas Cowboys, of course.

"Where is everyone else? Laurel's not with you?"

He took her hand and tugged her outside. The brown leaves crunched beneath their feet as they headed toward the small stand of woods directly behind the ranch house. It was the only bit of lushness in the endless sea of rolling pastureland.

"She was still getting ready. Who knew it took so much time to get ready to eat turkey? Gramps is waiting on his sour cream pound cake to finish baking. I didn't know it, but my grandfather considers himself a master baker. Karen said she'd drive them over. She came by to wish Laurel a happy holiday."

"Oh," Dawn said, matching her stride to his.

Tyson stopped and pulled her behind a large sycamore tree. His cold hands sank into her loose hair before he tilted her head so her eyes met his. The emotions swirling in the whiskey depths made her heart squeeze and a familiar warmth pool in her pelvis. "I had to get away and see you. I've missed you. Seeing you, but not touching you, not kissing you, not hearing you make those little moans in the back of your throat…"

His voice grew harsh as he studied her lips. She licked them in invitation.

He accepted, placing his mouth over hers, teasing her with his tongue, stamping her as his. He hauled her against him and Dawn fell into that place where nothing else existed but Tyson. She curled her arms round his neck, twining her fingers in his recently cut hair, and kissed him back with all the longing she'd felt over the past few days.

It had been agony.

She'd gone crazy thinking about him. Wondering if he'd changed his mind about her. About their possible future.

"Tyson," she murmured against his lips before inserting a little distance between them. "We've got to figure this out soon. I want what we had in Jefferson. I can't stop thinking about being with you."

"Me, too," he said, grasping her hips and pulling her against his hardness. "Lady, I wish you were wearing a skirt because I do believe we'd have that thing round your waist by now."

"Incredibly short-sighted of me." She nipped his bottom lip and he groaned. His hand moved up her rib cage toward her breast. She wanted him to fill his hand with her flesh, but they needed to stop before she stripped down naked in her brother's backyard and cavorted like an oversexed wood nymph.

"Wait," she breathed against the citrusy smell of his neck. "We'll have company soon and we've already had one bad experience the last time we kissed in the woods. We don't need anyone else to happen upon us making out like teenagers."

Tyson released her and stepped away. "You're right. We've got to handle this the right way. I already have Andrew wanting to string me up by my toenails for kissing his dear momma. If he knew what I did to you in that hotel room, the buzzards would be picking at me."

Dawn shrugged. "I don't think he'd resort to murder."

Tyson snorted. "You don't know men very well then, do you?"

At his words, she stiffened. Her past mistakes had proven that much true. She *didn't* know men very well. Her heart had suffered for it. And how did she know Tyson wouldn't break her heart the way the others had? She didn't. It was a sobering thought, cooling her ardor. She shivered against the gust of wind that shot through the grove.

"This isn't going to be easy," she said, pulling her sweater tighter against her. "You sure you want to do this?"

Tyson shook his head. "Don't get cold feet on me just because we're going to have to face-off against our kids. You're worth it, babe. I'm worth it, I promise."

He tugged one of the hands she'd tucked beneath her breasts loose and embraced her. He tilted her chin up so she stared into his eyes. "Listen, we agreed we had a right to be happy. Others have taken it from us, but this time we stand firm. We've got something worth fighting for and no one, not even our children, is going to keep us from carving out a piece of happiness for ourselves."

Dawn closed her eyes and sent up a little prayer he was right. That they were doing the right thing. And that no one would get hurt.

She opened them and nodded. "Right."

"Good," Tyson said, dropping a tender kiss on her forehead. "Because you make me happy. And every day I feel like I'm falling more and more—"

"Daddy?" The word split the air like a stray bullet.

What had Tyson been about to say? Was he falling in love with her? Or had he meant to say something else? Her emotions whirled like a cyclone, but outwardly she remained still as well water. Maybe she was jumping to conclusions. Nothing about her and Tyson was set in stone. Nothing.

But she didn't have time to ask. His daughter crunched closer and closer to them.

"Daddy! Where are you?" Laurel's voice carried on the wind.

"Shit." Tyson stepped away and shoved his hands into the navy blue hoodie he wore.

Dawn hurriedly picked up a few pinecones scattered at their feet. She shoved some toward Tyson who looked at her as though she was a crazy woman.

Lauren appeared at tree line. "Daddy?"

"In here, sugar," Tyson called, balancing the pinecones in the cradle of his arms. Dawn tossed a few more on the growing stack.

The girl stared quizzically at the prickly mass her father juggled. "Mom's waiting for you. She feels kinda weird about being here with people she doesn't know. What are y'all doing, anyway?"

Dawn would have answered, but her mind was trying to wrap around the fact Karen Hart was at the house. What the hell? It was bad enough they had to endure their disagreeable kids, but an ex? The unfailingly polite Nellie would invite her. The only thing worse was if Larry showed up.

A prickling of awareness rose on Dawn's neck.

Oh, God.

"Just picking up a few pinecones Dawn needs for... for—" Tyson stuttered.

"The centerpiece," she said, forcing a smile. Her heart dipped and swayed in her chest.

"But Daddy brought y'all a pot of mums for the table," Laurel said, her brilliant eyes narrowing as she took in Dawn's heated cheeks and her father's obvious nervousness.

"Bingo," Dawn said, lifting a few more pinecones off the ground. She had no idea what to do with the blasted things. But she'd manage.

She just had to hold it together.

TOM AND LILA DARBY BLEW into the house like a Santa Ana wind, lifting little Mae from Jack's arms and whisking her up for Mere and Popa kisses. Lila had brought her eight new outfits and Tom had purchased her a little white rocking chair with Grandfather's Princess written across the back. They'd shoved it all at Jack as they absorbed themselves in their newest grandbaby.

No one else existed but the two-month-old baby who cooed and smiled at her grandparents as if she'd rehearsed her response for weeks.

"Oh, she's beautiful!" Lila crowed. "She looks just like Jack when he was a baby. Oh, you little darling."

"Doesn't she, though?" Tom Darby finally looked up from the wriggling baby and noticed everyone else standing around the living room. "Well. I thought we were having dinner. Didn't know it was a danged party."

Nellie laughed. "Well, you were distracted."

Introductions were made, gifts were stowed and the turkey was retrieved from the smoker. Bubba Malone had arrived with something called turducken, which was a chicken in a duck in a turkey. As he carved it, Jack snuck slivers exclaiming it was the best thing he'd ever tasted. Dawn's stomach contracted at the smells wafting from the kitchen. Or maybe it was the fact Karen kept darting strange glances her way.

Nellie had just brought the turkey from the kitchen when the doorbell rang.

"I'll get it," Andrew said, springing up from the couch, where he'd sat all morning glued to the television set.

Dawn looked at Nellie who herself lifted a questioning eyebrow. No one else was expected. The prickling on Dawn's neck returned. Surely not.

When Andrew came back into the room, Dawn knew why her son had been so quick to get the door. Larry followed him, looking dapper as always in a corduroy jacket and designer jeans. His smile was pure California sunshine.

"Hey, everybody, sorry I'm a bit late. Andrew said he wasn't sure what time we were eating."

Larry didn't look at her, specifically. He allowed his smile to touch everyone in the room. The chameleon blended in quite nicely. Even brought a bottle of wine to soften the fact he was a Thanksgiving Dinner crasher. Just like Karen.

Nellie looked at Dawn. She could do nothing but shrug. She should have known something was up. Her son had been too agreeable, even volunteered to take out the garbage. Guilt did weird things to people.

"Well, Larry, we didn't know you were coming," Jack said, rising from his recliner. "But you're welcome to join us, of course."

Tom glowered at Larry, but Andrew looked genuinely happy his father was there, so Dawn decided she wouldn't shed any blood. Though it might be good to stay far away from the sharp knives.

She glanced at Tyson. His eyes said way more than the smile he gave her. He got it. They were stuck in this and would have to muddle through as best they could. Once again, she could feel his presence steady her.

So, she sighed and motioned Nellie to the kitchen. After she gulped down a glass of wine, she helped her sister-in-law set out the buffet. Because it was such a large group, they'd set up into separate tables. Unfortunately, they hadn't thought of place cards. It would have to be first come, first served seating. After Tom gave the blessing, everyone scattered with their laden plates.

Dawn found herself at the dining-room table in between Bubba Malone and Tyson. It was a tight fit between the two big guys, but she liked having Tyson's thigh next to hers.

Directly across from her sat Karen. And Tyson's ex wasn't dressed in blue jeans and a sweater from Target the way Dawn was. No, the North Carolina beauty wore mulberry wool trousers and a delicate cream blouse with flounces at the wrist that screamed designer. Her auburn hair fell to her shoulders, framing her face. A skilled hand had applied her makeup and Dawn could have sworn Karen had Botox injections because her forehead had a smooth, unmoving quality. Still, the woman looked amazing. And made Dawn feel like something found at a yard sale.

Which was probably why Larry the Snake plopped his plate down next to Karen. So much for spending time with his son.

"Hey, guys," Larry said, sliding into his chair. "This looks delicious, huh? That Nellie sure knows how to cook."

"It looks—" Karen looked down at the hearty traditional food on her plate "—filling."

Larry smiled, allowing his blue eyes to slide down

and take in Karen's form. "I don't think you'll have to worry about that."

Karen gave an affected laugh and rested her hand on Larry's arm. "You Southern men sure know how to make a girl feel good about herself."

Dawn wanted to make a gagging sound, but figured Bubba would slap her on the back. He'd done that once before and she'd nearly lost a lung. "He's not Southern."

"Oh," Karen said. "Where you from?"

Before Larry could answer, Bubba interrupted. "Southerners know when to let the vittles fill our mouth. Y'all get to eatin'. The Boys is comin' on in half an hour, and I got me a date with Jack's recliner."

"Hell, no, you don't," Jack called through the open door of the dining room. He and the rest of the group had settled at the large table in the kitchen.

Bubba laughed and a piece of turkey fell out of his mouth. "'Scuse me,"

Karen looked horrified. She stared with wary fascination at Bubba for a full minute before lowering her fork. "Who are *the Boys?*"

Larry laughed a slimy little laugh. "It's what all these Texas rednecks call the Dallas Cowboys."

Karen looked bemused. "The football team? As if they are neighborhood boys?"

Tyson took a drink of the sweet Texas tea. "People around here are a bit obsessed with the Cowboys. It's very personal."

Bubba, not the slightest bit offended by the redneck remark, leaned back and suppressed a belch. "Damn straight."

Karen smiled at Tyson. "But you grew up in North Carolina and you weren't obsessed with the Panthers."

Her voice was low, teasing and intimate. But Bubba got there before Tyson did. "It's 'cause they got that pansy-ass Delhomme boy. That's what you get when your quarterback comes from U of L. Ragin' Cajuns, my ass."

"I like Jake Delhomme," Karen said, stiffening her shoulders.

"I bet you do," Bubba said.

Tyson looked at Dawn, humor dancing in his eyes. He was having a good time, damn him. She could hardly enjoy the melt-in-your-mouth sweet potatoes. Her stomach felt tied up in knots.

Everyone at the table let sleeping dogs lie and got busy paying tribute to Nellie's delicious Thanksgiving meal.

Forks clattered, cheerful conversation floated out from the kitchen spurring Dawn to make appropriate conversation. About the weather.

Everyone joined in except Bubba who dedicated himself to finishing three plates of food before the clock hit one o'clock, aka game time.

Finally, he pushed back his chair. "Okay, folks, later."

He took his empty plate and vanished.

Karen observed his movements like a scientist would study a newly discovered species. "Well, he's certainly an interesting…person."

Dawn smiled. She loved Bubba. He was crass, slovenly and as country as a pot of turnip greens, but he was the kindest person she knew. He was also Nellie's dear friend. "He's quite a man."

"Well, a bit…"

"Unpolished?" Dawn offered.

"Um, yes." Karen shuffled her food around on her

plate. She'd hardly touched anything. She kept cutting glances at Tyson as he finished the last of his peas. The woman was hungry for something. It wasn't turkey or ambrosia.

With Bubba's departure, silence fell round them like an oppressive curtain. Dawn figured it had to be the oddest of situations. It felt like a scene from a romantic comedy. She half expected Vince Vaughn or Ben Stiller to walk in with a shaved cat. Or a vomiting baby.

Finally after a full five minutes of no conversation, Larry scooted his chair back. "Well, think I'll get me some of that chocolate pecan pie and join ol' Bubba in the den. You wanna come with me, pretty lady?"

His comment was addressed, of course, to Karen.

"No, I'm still working on my turkey," she said, tucking a strand of auburn hair behind her ear where a full carat diamond winked flirtatiously. She pulled her eyes from Larry's beachy good looks to Tyson. Her gaze warmed and caressed him. "Tyson, I'd like the chance to talk to you later, if you don't mind."

Tyson shrugged. "Sure, but I'm thinking we should get in the kitchen and get some pie before it's all gone. Or before Laurel ends up in Andrew's lap."

Karen laid down her fork. "Please. You know she's too young for him. He's in college."

"Yeah, I know that. You know that. But the question is, does Laurel understand that?" He stood and scooped up his plate.

Karen rose, too. "Of course she does. She just can't help it. You know the girls in my family can't resist handsome men."

Flirty words, evident intentions. Karen was throwing her hat into the ring with Tyson as the prize. And the woman was up for the fight. She had all the right equipment. She was beautiful, elegant and held the trump card—she was the mother of his child.

Tyson paused at the dining-room door. "You coming, Dawn?"

She tossed her fork onto her half-eaten plate. "Do I have to?"

"If you want pie," he said with a grin. She longed to run to him, bury her head in the warmth of his chest and have him wrap his arms around her. Because at that moment she was plain scared.

Scared she'd risked her heart for nothing.

Karen watched her as a hawk might watch a lizard beneath its talon.

"Dawn?" Tyson prodded. "Pie?"

"No," she said, "Think I'll finish my—" she looked down at her plate "—creamed corn."

"Okay, see you in the den."

He left. Dawn shoved her plate away and crossed her arms. Then she got mad at herself. She'd let Karen waltz out the dining-room door with her man. Okay, no one knew he was her man, but that didn't matter. He was. Wasn't he? She should have done something to stake her claim on him. But what? They'd decided to break the news to Laurel before openly admitting their relationship. And with Larry and Andrew pulling her one way and Laurel and Karen pulling Tyson the other, it all felt so hopeless.

How could the tender, new feelings in her heart survive this mess?

She stared at the table and sighed. So much for a cheerful Thanksgiving. Nothing could be worse.

CHAPTER SEVENTEEN

"OKAY, WE'RE GONNA run a reverse. Hand off to Dawn, she hands off to Marcie. Marcie, you haul butt down the left sideline. We need to score. Everyone got it?" Jack asked.

"Where's the left sideline?" Marcie asked, whisking her ponytail over her shoulder and studying the perimeter of their makeshift football field. Andrew's girlfriend had arrived right before half-time—in time for the flag football game.

"Just don't step outside the line of the silver-leaf maple."

Marcie nodded, but Dawn could tell she had no idea what he was talking about. Their team huddled together near the non-operational water well on a stretch of flat land. It was halftime for the Dallas Cowboys, and they had only five more minutes before Bubba abandoned their flag football game for the comfort of Jack's recliner and the second half.

"What do I do?" Larry asked.

"You block." Dawn almost smiled at Jack's exasperation. Larry loved to showboat any chance he got. Her ex wanted the ball so he could dazzle the few spectators on the sidelines. Jack wasn't going to give him the pleasure.

They clapped and broke the huddle. Dawn made sure the old tube socks were tucked in her jeans on either side of her hips. They could have gotten a flag football set, but Jack insisted on playing old school with old striped socks tucked in their waistbands. Darby tradition.

Dawn watched Tyson as he lined up to play defense. His demeanor was relaxed, but his eyes were intent. Like almost every man on the planet, Tyson loved a good contact sport. Field or bed. The man brought the heat.

"Down. Set. Hut. Hut," Jack yelled.

Dawn swung to the left and allowed Jack to tuck the football into her breadbasket. She immediately untucked it and handed it to Marcie, who came the other way. Faking the carry, she ran straight toward Tyson. He wasn't fooled, but he made no attempt to follow Marcie, who trucked it down the opposite sideline. He came right toward Dawn, reaching out for her socks.

"No ball," Dawn said wiggling her fingers and coming to a halt.

"I know." He gave her a sharky grin. "I just wanted to cop a cheap feel."

And so he did. His arms came around her, skipping the dangling tube socks, and settled on her butt. He gave it a squeeze. Laughter bubbled inside her, but she swiftly silenced it. People watched. In fact, Dawn risked a glance to where her mom and Karen sat in canvas camp chairs on the sidelines. Sure enough, Karen's eyes were on them. And they narrowed.

Tyson's arms stayed around her.

"Better stop," she said under her breath. "We've got spectators."

"To hell with 'em."

She tugged at his arms. "We tell Laurel first."

Tyson dropped his arms, and they both turned to

watch Marcie leap into the air and perform a touchdown dance. The girl had definitely been a cheerleader.

Dawn moved away from the warmth of Tyson. The chill of the afternoon stung her cheeks and made her long to snuggle beneath a throw on the couch with the man who took her breath away. She liked football, but she'd rather be playing footsies with Tyson.

"Hey! She stepped out of bounds!" Bubba cried, clomping toward Marcie, where she celebrated jubilantly. "She went past the maple. Anyone else see her?"

"You still get the ball back. Stop being a big baby," Jack hollered, trotting down the field and giving Marcie a high-five.

Andrew grinned at the sight of his girlfriend slapping hands with her team. His smile dimmed a bit when Larry slapped Marcie on the rear.

"Good, 'cause we got a little somethin' for you," Bubba said, gathering his team together. Andrew pulled Nellie from the sideline where she'd gone to kiss Mae's pink cheeks. The baby was wrapped in layers of faux fur sitting on her grandmother's lap. As the other team huddled together, Dawn noticed Andrew didn't put his arm around Tyson.

Jack motioned them to spread out. "Don't let anyone past you. We can't let them tie this one up."

Dawn lined up on Nellie while Larry covered Tyson. Marcie leered at Andrew, giving him the come on signal with her hands. Andrew waggled his eyebrows. Sheesh.

Bubba called for the ball and her dad hiked it to him. Jack started counting, "One Mississippi, two Mississippi."

Bubba took two steps back and veered to the right. He was going to throw it to Tyson. He never looked for any other receivers. Dawn pulled off her coverage on Nellie and ran toward Tyson. The ball arced through the air, a perfect spiral a bit too high.

Tyson leaped for the ball, as graceful as any wide receiver she'd seen. He snatched the ball from the air. And then he came down.

Right on Larry and his perfect upturned nose.

"Son of a bitch!" Larry screamed, dropping to his knees.

Tyson didn't seem to realize his elbow had just taken out the competition. He never stopped in his pursuit of the end zone. Dawn stopped right next to Larry.

"Shit!" Larry covered his nose, which spurted blood all over his no doubt expensive sweater. Dawn darted over to her mother and pulled a diaper cloth from her lap.

The game ground to a halt. Everyone stopped and stared at Larry as he muttered a few more colorful expletives. Jack loped over as Dawn bent to place the mostly clean cloth over Larry's nose.

"Here, Larry. Use this," she said, pulling away his bloodied hand and pressing the cloth to his injured face. She felt Tyson's presence even before he spoke.

"Hell, Larry. I'm sorry, man. I didn't realize—"

Larry held up a hand. "Ith okay."

The Elmer Fudd words had her wondering if Larry's nose was broken.

"The hell it is." Andrew's voice came from behind her.

Dawn held the cloth against Larry's nose and turned to look at her son. He stood indignant. Pissed. A posture that was starting to become too familiar.

"Look, I didn't do it on purpose," Tyson said, propping both hands on his hips. He opened his stance. She could feel the tension thicken, smell the confrontation.

"Bullshit. Just 'cause you're screwin' around with my mom doesn't give you the right to nearly take my dad's head off."

"Andrew James Taggart!" She rose and crossed her arms, hitting him with a glare designed to wither. Her smart-mouthed nineteen-year-old had no business airing her laundry in front of the world. "Who I date and who I don't date is none of your concern. Besides, that has nothing to do with this accident."

"Not an accident," her son said, shaking his head.

"Come on, Drew. You don't really think Tyson hit your dad on purpose?" Jack asked, stepping between Andrew and Tyson.

"She's dating my dad?" Laurel asked.

Dawn hadn't realized the girl had come outside. The last time they'd seen her she'd been sulking on the couch with her cell phone in hand. Marcie's arrival had squashed the tween's dreams of pass interference on Andrew. The girl now stared at Tyson. "You're dating *her?*"

Dawn blinked. What was she? Chopped liver?

Karen showed up right behind Laurel. "I wouldn't mind knowing the answer to that myself."

Tyson's eyes briefly met hers before shifting away. She read his look, though. It said, "Oh, hell."

"Now is not the time for this discussion. Larry needs to be the priority," Tyson said.

Everyone's eyes shifted back to the man still sitting on the ground, holding the cloth to his oozing nose. Dawn had momentarily forgotten her ex-husband.

Andrew glared at Tyson. Laurel started crying. Karen

glared at Dawn. Everyone else looked at Larry…or off into the woods.

She'd been wrong earlier when she'd thought things couldn't get worse. They had. Again, she had to survive.

"Here," she said, offering Larry her hand. He took it and she helped him stand. She heard his knees crack and he issued another moan. She concentrated on Larry because she didn't want to look at Tyson. A goose egg had lodged in her throat and her anger at Andrew had soured her stomach. "Here, Lar, let me see your nose."

Larry obediently removed the cloth. His nose bore resemblance to the famous reindeer—red and swollen. Blood still trickled from both nostrils. If it were broken, she couldn't tell.

"Ith it broken?" Larry asked, tipping his head back while keeping his blue eyes on her.

"I'm not sure," she said, spinning toward Jack. "You think we ought to get him to a doctor?"

Bubba ambled over and squinted at Larry's nose. "It ain't broke. Just gonna have two black eyes is all."

"You sure, Bubba?" her brother asked, cocking his head and looking at Larry's nose.

"See my nose?" Bubba asked, turning his head left and right so they could all get a good look at the bent appendage. "It's been broke twice. Never looked like his. Put some ice on it. Boys are back on."

With that Dr. Bubba lumbered up the porch steps and disappeared into the house, passing Nellie who came out holding a plastic bag of ice. She gave the bag to Dawn. "Try this and see if you can get the swelling down."

"Thanks," Dawn said, helping Larry apply the ice.

Jack waved everyone else away. They dispersed— Tom and Lila cooing to Mae, Laurel sheltered by her

mother and Marcie with a disclaimer about needing
something from her purse. Tyson slapped a hand on
Larry's shoulder. "Sorry again, Larry."

"No probwem," Larry muttered, wincing.

"Dad, you sure you gonna be okay?" Andrew asked,
still shooting daggers at Tyson. Larry wasn't nearly as
upset, even with a busted nose. He wouldn't care if Dawn
dated a serial killer. She had never really concerned him
much. Andrew grasped at straws if he thought anyone
could pin Larry down.

"I'm fine." Larry waved his son's concern away.
Andrew nodded then headed toward Marcie where she
leaned into her low-slung Mustang.

Dawn placed a hand on her ex-husband's back and
directed him toward the steps leading into the house.
She didn't want to be responsible for doctoring him, but
there was really no one else. Yet one more time she took
care of him. "Sit down, Larry. Once the bleeding stops,
you can go inside. Do you want to call a doctor?"

"Nah," he said shaking his head. "Thanksgiving. No
one will be avaiwable. I think I'm okay."

His words had her reeling. Larry not wanting person-
alized attention? Larry not wanting to disturb someone
else's holiday? Larry not having a plastic surgeon on
speed dial? What alien had taken over his body?

"Pwus, I have a buddy who does pwastic surgery.
He's the best in Houston. Don't want no wocal yokel
jacking me up."

Exactly. No aliens. Just Larry.

"Fine," she said, unable to stop herself from noticing
Tyson stopping Karen and Laurel on their way to the car.
He had a hand on Laurel's back. It was a tender scene.
One that ripped at her.

She could see Karen nod her head. Then Laurel.

What was going on? Dawn's emotions galloped full speed ahead, zooming past reason and speeding toward disillusionment.

There were facts she could not dispute. Karen and Laurel were Tyson's family. The divorce wasn't final. And Karen wanted him back. The woman might as well have lit a fire and grabbed a blanket with the signals she'd been sending out. Even sleep-deprived Nellie had cocked an eyebrow at Karen's innuendos earlier. If Karen wanted Tyson back, where did it leave Dawn?

After all, Karen had chosen to end the marriage. Not Tyson. Did he want a second chance with his family?

"Dawn?" Nellie popped her head out. "Andrew's in the guest room, packing his bag. He said he's taking his dad back to Houston."

"What?" Dawn's feet moved before her mind truly accepted the concept. Her son acted like a complete ass in front of everyone, accused Tyson of hurting Larry on purpose, then packed his bags like a spoiled brat and took off? Not likely, not if she had anything to say about it. Of course a small voice niggled in her subconscious, taunting her. Andrew acted this way because she'd always allowed him to. She'd always put his wants and needs first.

She tossed one last look at Tyson and Karen. They stood shoulder to shoulder looking at a cloud of dust disappearing on the winding drive to the blacktop. Grady and Laurel had taken their leave.

But Dawn couldn't worry about Karen or Tyson. She had a son to deal with. A son who should have been dealt with a long time ago.

Her chickens had come home to roost.

Was it too late to close the henhouse door?

"WHERE DO YOU THINK you're going?" Dawn said as she entered the guest bedroom in which Andrew had been staying the past few days. The warmth of the decor did little to dispel the chill radiating off Andrew. He silently shoved jeans and underwear into a large duffle. The boy had never even learned to fold his own clothes. She'd always done it for him.

"I'm taking Dad back to Houston. I'm not staying here while you...you do that with that dude." Andrew's hair flopped into his face, a face that still held the vestiges of boyhood. Though he shaved, his cheeks held firm to the sweet curve of youth. She wished he had not grown up so quickly. Maybe she hadn't done such a good job of raising him. Maybe she needed more time to teach him how to be a man.

"*Do that with that dude?* Seriously? That's what you have to say to me? Especially after you bring your dad here when I told him he wasn't invited." She crossed her arms and leaned against the doorjamb. She wasn't letting him out. He'd have to pick her up and move her.

"What do you want me to say? Dad came here to be with us. And what happens? Your boyfriend shows up to dinner. A *family* dinner. And then he hits my dad in the nose."

Dawn tried to stamp down the anger she felt bubbling inside her, but she couldn't. "I didn't ask your father to come to dinner. He came uninvited. And Tyson was invited. By Nellie."

He shrugged. A smart-ass shrug. She wanted to smack him on his bottom. The boy needed it.

"I guess you don't want Dad in our lives at all. But I think he belongs here more than your new boyfriend does. Who, by the way, obviously still has his own family to deal with. His daughter is out of control."

"Andrew, this isn't about Tyson or his issues. It's about your father. Your dad will always be part of our life, but he and I are over. I don't know how to get that into your head."

Andrew looked at her with wounded brown eyes. Her stomach dropped, but she wouldn't give in. This time he had to understand.

"What's so bad about Dad? I know he's not all uptight and organized like you, but he's a good guy. Lots of other women seem to appreciate him."

Dawn wanted to laugh. Boy, did she know that. "Exactly. And that's part of the problem. Look, you're old enough to admit what we've known all along."

"To admit what? What a bad father Dad is? I don't need to hear you bash him, Mom."

She rubbed her hands over her face. She needed patience for the task at hand. She let go of her anger and settled on compassion. "Give me a few minutes before you go storming off. Okay?"

Her son's jaw clenched, but he nodded.

Dawn shut the door. It was time to be totally honest with her son. For the first time.

"Sit on the bed."

She sank onto the soft quilt Nellie's grandmother had made and took her son's hand. He pulled it away, but lowered himself to the edge of the bed.

"You know how I started with your dad, right?"

"You got knocked up, but I was the best thing that ever happened to you."

Dawn managed a tiny smile. "Told you enough, didn't I?"

He gave a quasi-smile and nodded.

"But it's true. You're the best thing I've ever done. I'm so proud of you and wouldn't trade *getting knocked up* with you for anything," she said, trying to catch his eye so he could see how much she meant the words. But he wouldn't look at her.

"I've always protected you, Drew. Always made sure you weren't hurt by anyone. I started from the moment you were born and I never stopped. But I think I did you a disservice."

"Why?" he asked. "That's what parents do. Protect their kids."

"Sure, that's part of the job. But as I've gotten older, I've realized I protected you too much. You never saw what was right before you."

"What?" he asked, finally meeting her gaze. It was like looking into her own eyes.

"Your father had no choice but to marry me. Your Poppa Tom made sure of it. It wasn't a good situation for either of us. We really didn't know each other that well, and suddenly we were married, expecting a baby and moving to Texas. Your dad didn't really want me, Andrew. Do you understand?"

"That's not true. He cares about you."

She shook her head. "Not like I deserve to be cared about. He cares about me because I'm family to him. I took care of him as much as I took care of you."

Dawn stopped to gather her thoughts. How could she tell him what kind of man his father was? How she spent her nights alone in a strange house while he partied? How she nursed a sick baby while Larry slept, refusing to budge to fetch medicine or take a shift with the howling infant? How could she tell him his father missed his first word, his first steps and his first birthday?

"Okay, I know he cheated on you."

"Yes," she said, nodding. So her son knew more than she thought. "He cheated on me for many years. He didn't want only me. He didn't want to be a husband or a father. He wasn't able to be what we both needed."

Andrew flinched, then he nodded. "I guess there were times when he took me places then pretended I wasn't there."

A ping of hurt struck her heart. Larry truly was an asshole. "But that doesn't mean he doesn't love you. He does. And he's proud of you. But there were times when he wasn't available to either of us like he should have been. And I always covered that up."

"Not always."

"But most of the time. If he didn't show for your school play, I made up a business appointment he had to attend. If he didn't bother to meet us for dinner, I said he had car trouble. One Christmas he didn't come home until late and I told you he was helping Santa. Truth was I didn't know where he was or who he was with."

She could feel moisture gathering in her eyes. She had vowed to never shed another tear over Larry the Snake, but this time it wasn't about her feelings. It was about Andrew's.

Her son's hand found hers. "I'm sorry, Mom. I know it was hard on you."

She lifted her head. "No, I'm the one who's sorry. You deserved better. From him. And from me."

He shook his head. "But you were always there for me. Even when I was pissed at you for coming down on me, I knew I could count on you. Dad is Dad, you know? I know he's not the one who will help me fill out financial-aid papers or teach me how to iron a shirt. He's not the parent I depend on. He's just…Larry."

Dawn smiled. "True. But my point isn't to rehash how difficult it was or to bash your dad. My point is…I want to be happy. I deserve a chance to make a new life for myself."

Andrew put an arm around her. "I want you to be happy, too. That's why I thought if you got back with Dad, you wouldn't be alone. Y'all seemed to have fun that weekend. It was, like, normal again. Plus, you still have me. And Jack and Nellie. And Poppa Tom and Mere."

Dawn laughed. "Sure, but you're in school and who knows where you'll be next. And Jack and Nellie are raising a family. And Poppa Tom and Mere are world travelers now. I don't want to be alone. Not anymore."

Andrew ducked his head. "You think this guy, Tyson, can help you be happy then?"

Dawn wondered that herself. But deep down inside, she knew he could. What they'd shared over the past few weeks had given her hope for a future filled with something more than her day planner and a cup of coffee. She wasn't exactly sure what her future held. But she was pretty sure it would hold Tyson Hart.

If he still wanted her.

"I'm not sure, but I'm not going to run away from the opportunity. I've got to take a chance. Nothing ventured, nothing gained, right?"

She smiled at her beautiful son, who may, just may, have gotten the bigger picture about his mother. She'd like to think he saw her as something more than the woman who folded his underwear.

"I'm sorry, Mom. Sorry for making it so hard on you these past few weeks. And I think I owe Tyson an apology, too. I'll try hard to accept you're growing up."

She laughed. "Growing up, huh? More like growing old."

Andrew pulled her closer and kissed her cheek.

"You're still pretty hot for a mom. Better go find Tyson and pry his ex-wife off him. She looked pretty determined."

She laughed and pressed her finger in his dimple. "You're a pretty good kid, you know?"

"Yeah, you raised me that way."

CHAPTER EIGHTEEN

TYSON WANTED TO BE ANYWHERE but where he stood. Tears trickled down Karen's face, ruining her makeup and making him feel like something on the bottom of his boot.

Which was pretty dumb-ass of him. She was the one who had slept with his business partner. She was the one who filed for divorce. She was the one who plunked herself in the middle of his holiday and time with Laurel.

He shouldn't feel anything other than aggravation.

But, she had been his wife for almost fifteen years even if the swoop of a pen had changed everything. He'd signed and sent the papers to the attorney yesterday afternoon. It was truly over.

"Here, Karen, take this," he said, pulling a clean handkerchief from his pocket. It had a monogrammed *H* in one corner and had been a gift from his grandfather long ago. Grady still believed in carrying one, a sort of archaic wet wipe. He'd ingrained the habit in his grandson.

"Thank you," she sniffed, swiping her perfect nose with the clean linen. "You always have one of these."

And the tears fell all over again.

"I can't believe you've moved on to that woman. What am I going to do without you, Ty?" she asked, wiping dampness from her cheeks. "None of this would have happened if you hadn't gone to Iraq. We'd still be together, planning our Christmas holiday in Galveston or arguing over what kind of tree we want to buy this year. That damned war."

Tyson managed a chuckle. "I don't think it was started to inconvenience you, Karen."

"Well, I know that, but still…" She left off, staring out at the gray clouds on the Texas horizon. "You wouldn't have left."

"I think we can face we were over long before Iraq. Things were already unraveling."

She shook her head. "No. We weren't. I still loved you. I mean, I still do love you."

Tyson shook his head and motioned her to a section of the fence that slumped low enough to lean upon. The November wind chilled him as clouds swooped by overhead. Another front moved through the Texas countryside tasting of snow. In fact, a few flakes skated on the breeze. "I could see what was happening between you and Corbin before I left. It didn't surprise me when I came back and saw I'd been right."

His ex-wife shrugged. "You weren't there. I couldn't talk to you. I couldn't see you. The brakes on the Lexus would start slipping or Laurel would come home crying about her lost homework…and you weren't there. Corbin was. I didn't mean for it to happen. It just did."

Tyson swallowed because, even though the pain had faded, his pride was still a man's pride. Karen had betrayed him. So had Corbin, the man who'd been his roommate at the University of North Carolina, the man he'd brought to Texas to form a construction company.

Karen moved beside him. "I can't believe it's snowing."

Tyson nodded. "Doesn't happen often, does it? But

Mother Nature has been known to scatter some flakes on the Lone Star State."

Karen huddled in her wool coat and leaned her head against his shoulder. "Sorry, Tyson. I'm sorry I ruined our marriage."

Tyson didn't make a move to curl an arm around her the way he normally would. Funny, how birdlike she seemed against him, how fragile. That was her problem. She couldn't stand on her own. It was why she'd sought another guy while he wallowed in the grit and heat of the desert thousands of miles away. She couldn't be alone. She was the opposite of his Dawn, who'd fought the world by herself for too long.

"I accept your apology," he said, patting her shoulder and moving away from her. "And I don't regret our marriage. We had a lot of good times. A lot of laughter."

"We could try again. You could come home with me and Laurel. We could be a family again. I'll try so hard to make you happy," she said, regarding him with pleading eyes. "Say yes. Give us one more try."

"Why are you doing this now? Is it over between you and Corbin?"

She wouldn't look at him. She lifted one shoulder. "I don't know. Maybe."

Tyson shook his head. "Doesn't matter. It's too late for us, Karen."

"Why? Because of her?"

Dawn. Like a song in his heart or a blast of warm air to the dank caverns of his soul, Dawn gave him peace. He'd known it from the moment he watched her stride purposefully into the E.R. managing everything for her laboring sister-in-law. She would give him what he so longed for. She would give him a place to rest his head.

"No, Karen, not because of her. If Dawn hadn't come along, the results today would still be the same. You and I are finished."

He straightened, facing the wind, staring out at a horizon the color of wheat. Pine trees dotted the hills beyond the pasture, giving a Whistleresque landscape to East Texas. Here he felt at home, had always felt at home even as a boy staying only a random year here and there. Oak Stand was where he belonged. And Dawn was who he belonged with. The idea had settled in his bones long ago before he'd given a name to what they shared.

"But she's the reason," Karen insisted.

"I told you. It's over no matter what."

Karen stiffened. "But she's nothing close to the kind of woman you like."

"What? Faithful?"

Karen's blue eyes no longer looked pitiful. They crackled with ire. "That was low."

"You're right. It was."

Uncomfortable silence fell between them. He shouldn't have baited Karen. She was right. Dawn wasn't his usual type. She was subtle and competent. He didn't have to rescue her. The only similarity she held to any other woman he'd ever dated was that she was utterly beautiful and sexy.

"Look, Dawn is a good person. She's someone I want to rebuild my life with, though right now it's not looking too easy."

His ex-wife crumpled against the fence, crossing her arms over her brown cashmere coat. "I thought—" She silently regarded the landscape, seeming lost in thought. "It's really too late, isn't it? You really want her. And you want me out of your life."

Tyson thought about that. Karen would never be out of his life. She was Laurel's mother, and though she'd tumbled into his friend's bed too easily, she wasn't a horrible person. "No, you'll always be part of my life, Karen. I loved you and you are the mother of my child. I'm not saying it will always be a walk in the park, but it is what it is. We're big people and we've got to act like big people. Our marriage was over the day you went to Corbin's bed. I can't change that and neither can you."

She nodded. "I guess. I just…I just thought you loved me. That if I said I was sorry we could start over again. I didn't realize you didn't want me anymore."

Silence fell between them as snowflakes swirled around them.

She shrugged. "Stupid of me. Arrogant, really. I guess I thought I could just snap my fingers and erase what I've done."

She rose from the fence and stood in front of him. "I never meant to hurt you, Ty. I'm truly sorry. You do deserve to be happy, and if it takes Dawn to do that, then I'll do my best to swallow my pride and step aside. I don't really want to, but I will. And I'll talk to Laurel."

Karen's lower lip trembled. That same lower lip he'd kissed for fifteen years. Regret washed over him. For a moment, he, too, was sorry they had ended so badly. That Laurel would have a less than ideal family. That the future they'd planned had unwound like a cheap rope, fraying and shedding all over the present.

"Thank you," he said, gently chucking her on the chin. "I've already accepted your apology, so no more looking to the past. Let's look to the future. We still have a daughter to raise."

A lone tear slid down Karen's cheek. She nodded. "Thank you, Tyson. Thank you for loving me once."

He nodded, then pressed a soft farewell kiss against her forehead. It was brief and final. She wrapped her arms around his waist and gave him a squeeze.

And that's when he saw her. Standing as forlorn as a stranded calf, eyes wide, body trembling.

Dawn had witnessed the tender moment. And if her stormy eyes were any indication, he was screwed.

Dawn heard him call her name, but she didn't stop. Didn't even toss a look back at where Tyson stood with Karen in his arms.

Her heart felt like it had exploded in her chest and now lay in throbbing bits and pieces.

She was done.

It didn't matter how many king's horsemen or how many king's men showed up. Hell, the whole armed forces of the United States could show up and it wouldn't matter. Her heart would never be put back together again. Because Tyson had finished her.

Once and for all.

Her tennis shoes slapped the hard ground as the questions beat her conscience. Why had she done it? Why had she let him talk her into loving him? Hadn't she known he'd been hurt by his wife? That it hadn't been his choice to end the marriage? It was obvious. He was still in love with Karen.

Damn it. Hadn't she learned men weren't trustworthy? How many times did she have to put herself out there before she caught on that she was destined to be hurt?

She was stupid.

And Tyson was an ass.

"Dawn." His words pierced the wind. "Wait!"

But she wouldn't. He could go to hell. Or back with Karen. They'd probably be one and the same.

"Dawn, please, it wasn't what it looked like."

She snorted. Yeah. Right. He hadn't kissed Karen. He hadn't folded the brittle woman into his arms. Dawn had imagined it all. Because she was the idiot.

He grabbed her elbow and pulled her back to him.

"Damn it, Dawn. It wasn't what you think."

She spun around. "Leave me alone, you lying bastard."

"What?"

"If you were going back to that cheating bitch, I don't know why you bothered to wreck my life. So stay the hell away from me." Her heart no longer felt broken down. It beat strong and hard, thumping with anger, with righteous indignation.

"How dare you kiss her right in front of me? On my brother's ranch? How dare you kiss me with those same lips and make me think we had something. You're a liar. You son of a bitch!" All the rejection and hurt she'd felt over the past twenty years came boiling out, lurching loose and rampaging out of control.

He raised his head, his eyes reflecting shock. He really didn't get what he had done, how he'd hurt her. She didn't feel one fleeting moment of guilt. The man deserved to be horsewhipped. He was the worst because he'd given her hope then stole it away like the Grinch tiptoeing into Whoville in the dead of night. Even the smallest crumb of her dreams had been pocketed.

"It wasn't a real kiss. Just one on the—"

"Yeah? That's not how it looked from here."

She headed up the graveled road. Her eye caught Karen lurking in the background, slowly walking several yards behind, cautiously watching them.

"Dawn," he called. "At least give me a chance to explain. You owe me that much."

"I don't owe you a damn thing. Nothing," Dawn called over her shoulder. "I don't want your fabricated apology. Just go away. And take her with you."

"That's not fair."

She spun to face him. If her eyes had been laser beams, he'd be dead already. "I don't give a damn what you think is fair. You talked me into taking a chance with you then you kicked me aside for a woman who cheated on you. She *cheated* on you, Tyson!"

"But I'm not—"

"Just stop. I'm tired of being a doormat for men. You all suck."

"Fine. Go. Run. It's what you're good at. Jump to conclusions and run away. I just gave you a reason."

His words made her madder. "*Run away? Jump to conclusions?* You were holding her. It was obvious. My eyes work, Tyson."

"I know what I was doing. I also know why. You don't, yet you accuse me and storm off without giving me a chance to talk about what happened. It wasn't what you think." His eyes were as plaintive as a Labrador retriever's. She remembered he'd looked much the same when she'd first met him. Whiskey eyes, lovable grin and warm energy. And idiot that she was, she'd taken him home and scratched his belly. Four times.

"We don't need to talk. Eyes don't lie." She marched away.

"Fine. I'm tired of chasing you, Dawn. Don't expect me to come after you."

She wouldn't turn around. No matter what. "I don't expect you to. Nor do I want you to. Just leave me alone."

"No problem."

Emotion clogged her throat. She wouldn't cry. She wouldn't show weakness. He didn't deserve it.

She neared the house and saw Larry standing out front, cell phone to his ear. God, she didn't want to talk to him. But his eyes landed on her and he ended his conversation, pocketing his phone. His blue eyes didn't bother to note her obvious distress. Larry never saw what was right before him. His nose, however, looked to be near normal. Still a bit red and puffy, but the ice had worked.

"Hey, I was just coming to look for you. Would you mind giving me a ride back to the motel? I'm not sure I can drive and Andrew went to Marcie's."

"Why didn't you ask Jack?"

"I didn't think about it."

"Don't worry. Your nose is fine. You can drive," she said, not bothering to stop for the conversation. She needed to make it to her room. Had to get there before she lost it in front of everybody. Before everybody knew she'd lost again.

For the third time.

Before everybody gave her those sympathetic looks. Poor Dawn. Lost her man, lost her business, lost her mind. And she was so tired of playing that part. Yet she fell into it every time.

Tyson was supposed to be different.

He wasn't.

It was time to give up for good. Time to think about a future for herself. One that did not include a shadowy male figure lying beside her at night. One that focused on her and her goals and dreams. New goals and dreams. That had nothing to do with anyone but herself.

A future without Tyson.

She climbed the steps to the ranch house, dodging Dutch, who seemed to think his sleeping spot was in the direct path of any doorway. He lifted his head, yawned and regarded her with his Labrador retriever eyes. Whiskey. Just like Tyson's.

Dawn sighed, backtracked and bent to scratch Dutch's ears. The dog groaned with pleasure.

"Maybe I should have gotten a dog. A dead squirrel on my new boot was nothing compared to this."

A single tear fell onto Dutch's ebony coat.

The dog didn't seem to mind.

CHAPTER NINETEEN

TYSON ROLLED OVER AND a slat fell from the bottom of the bed. Hell. He hadn't had time to put together the sleigh bed he'd found in the back of an antiques store in Jefferson. It still sat in his grandfather's workshop, now a painful reminder of his torn relationship with Dawn.

He eased from the bed and made his way to the kitchen, where Gramps had a pot of coffee waiting.

"Morning," Gramps called from behind the *Oak Stand Gazette*. "Coffee's hot."

"Thanks," he mumbled, grabbing a mug and pouring himself a cup. "Is Laurel up?"

"Is the Pope Jewish?"

"A simple no would suffice," he grumbled, staring at the raw day outside the window. Everything looked gray. It matched the way he felt.

"And you call me grumpy?" Gramps said, licking his thumb and turning the page. "Does this have to do with your lady friend?"

Tyson shrugged. "Not my lady anymore. We're done."

"Is that right?" His grandfather peered over the paper at him. His bushy eyebrows lifted and his normally misty blue eyes looked very sharp. "You giving up on her just because Laurel and Karen don't approve? Sounds chicken shit to me."

Tyson slammed his mug against the counter. "*Chicken*

shit? I'm not giving up. She's the one who gave up. She doesn't trust me or any man, for that matter. I'm done with trying to convince her." He grabbed a paper towel and wiped up the coffee that had sloshed from his mug. "The whole thing is just not worth it. Too much stacked against us, and she won't listen to me, wouldn't even let me explain. I don't need another woman who gives up when the going gets a little tough. I barely survived the last one."

"I wouldn't compare Dawn to Karen. I've known Karen a long time, son, and I've never thought much of her." Gramps folded the paper and set it on the table. "She's always been a bitch."

Tyson looked hard at his grandfather. "So why didn't you tell me this before I married her? It would have saved me a lot of time and money."

His grandfather shrugged. "You were twenty-two. You weren't going to listen to some old coot like me. You had to learn for yourself. Painful lesson that it was."

Tyson looked out at the frost on the ground. His heart felt as cold, as though Dawn had stolen away the pilot light and left him without any heat. "Yeah, painful. Seems women bring a lot of it."

"They bring joy, too. You gotta figure out if this one, this Dawn, is worth it. I'm of a frame of mind that she is. Reminds me a lot of your grandmother. Stubborn mule she was. But I wouldn't have traded her for a passel of beauty queens. She was my Annie."

Gramps rose and clamped a hand on his shoulder. "If she's worth it, you better find you a plan to get her back. If not, dump your worries. No sense in totin' them around. They just bring you down and make you cranky."

Tyson covered his grandfather's thin-skinned hand with his own. Tyson didn't think there was much planning he could do but he still appreciated the support. "Thanks, Gramps. You've always been here when I needed you."

His grandfather gave a squeeze then toddled out to his workshop, where he'd putter around till lunch. Tyson took a sip of his coffee. Strong and black. He'd forgotten the sugar. And like his coffee, he could deal with the bitter if he had a little sugar to sweeten it. That's what Dawn had been in his life, a little sweetness to make the rest of it tolerable.

A knock sounded at the back door.

"Knock, knock?" Nellie's voice sounded before she popped her head in. "You decent?"

"Hey," he called. "Come in."

Nellie stepped into the kitchen and shrugged off a puffy pink ski jacket. She tucked her gloves in the pocket and rubbed her hands together. "*Brrr!* It's really cold outside."

He nodded to the coffeepot. "Help yourself."

Nellie shook her head. "Nursing, but thanks anyway."

She settled against the counter and crossed her arms. "We need to talk about Dawn."

He blew out a breath. He didn't want to talk about Dawn. He didn't want to talk about anything. He wanted to go out to the workshop with Gramps and find something to fix or build that would hush his thoughts. "What's there to talk about? She'll think what she pleases. I'm tired of chasing after her, trying to prove what we feel is strong enough to build on. She doesn't trust me and I can't work with that."

Nellie shook her head. "You don't get it. You don't

get Dawn. Words won't mean anything to her. She's had a lifetime of two-timing smooth talkers. You've got to show her."

Show her? Hadn't he already shown her? In the wee hours of the morning when he'd whispered sweet words in her delicious ear. Hadn't he brought her flowers? Helped out at the center when he was so dog-tired all he wanted was to go home? Hadn't he shown her she meant something more to him than the average short-lived affair? He wanted to commit to her. She was the one jumping to conclusions and guarding her heart so tightly it could masquerade as Fort Knox.

"Nellie, I don't think you should get involved. Dawn is a grown woman, and I can't make her feel something she doesn't feel. Neither can you."

"But she does feel. I heard her crying all night long. Hard sobbing crying. Her heart is broken because she thinks you still love Karen."

Tyson felt his own heart contract. He didn't want Dawn to hurt. But what could he do? He'd already tried to tell her that what she'd witnessed between him and Karen was merely a goodbye. Closure. But Dawn wouldn't have it. She had shut herself away from him. "What can I do? I'm tired of trying to prove myself to her, Nellie."

His friend remained silent for a moment. "Here's the deal. Dawn doesn't show what she feels to the world. Or at least, she doesn't think she does. But everybody can see she's in love with you. And, if I'm a betting woman, I think you love her, too."

He shrugged and drank the last of his coffee. "But I've got pride, Nellie. I'm not going to beg the woman to love me. I'm just not going to do it."

She sighed. "I'm not asking you to. But I think I have

a plan. All I needed was to make sure you thought Dawn worth fighting for before I put it into action."

He turned toward the window. He didn't want any part of a plan. He didn't really know what he wanted. Except Dawn. But he didn't know how to get to Point B from Point A. "I'm not fighting for her. I'm done."

Nellie shook her head. "No, it's not over. Not yet."

Her voice sounded prophetic. Certain.

He looked at her, at the stubborn tilt of her chin. He got a scared feeling in his gut. Nellie wasn't what she seemed. He'd seen that firsthand when he'd met her at camp. He was a counselor, she was his charge. There was steel in her spine though people often underestimated her. "Okay. So what kind of plan are you cooking up?"

"Oh, don't worry. You don't have to do a thing. I'm of the mindset if Oak Stand brought you together once, it can do it again."

He groaned. "Nellie, Oak Stand didn't bring us together any more than—"

Nellie held up a hand. "Fine. God. Fate. Whatever. But you and Dawn came here for a reason, and I think that reason is each other."

He shrugged.

She grabbed her jacket, slipped her arms into it and smiled at him. "I love Dawn and I love you. I'm going to give you both another shot at loving each other."

"I'm feeling a little sick."

She smiled. "Take some Pepto and get your butt over to Tucker House. Out of sight is out of mind, and I need you in full view, mister."

DAWN WATCHED GRACE TRY to balance as she walked across a tightrope between two buildings. Her forehead wrinkled in concentration as she focused on the rope. She was almost across. One more step and...

"Oh, yeah! Bite me!" she whooped, throwing her hands up in glee. The Wii avatar on the TV screen did much the same.

"My turn," Ester said, wrenching the control from Grace's grasp. "I'm gonna beat your score and be top dog around here."

Grace huffed but relinquished the control. "Go ahead. I've seen your balance. Kiss your chances goodbye."

"We'll see about that," Ester said, stepping onto the Wii control board.

Dawn shook her head and continued on her way to the kitchen. She needed to courier some papers to the state department of health then find where Ed Murray left the eyeglass kit. He'd lost a screw out of his trifocals again.

"Hey, Dawn," Ester called as she waved the Wii control at the TV.

"Yeah?"

"If I don't beat Grace's score, I'll likely try again," she said.

"Well, you should. I firmly expect you to make it to the other side," Dawn called as she stepped into the kitchen.

"I expect the same of you, honey," Ester called.

That had Dawn stopping in her tracks. Weird answer. She hoped Ester was feeling okay. Dawn had never even played the balancing games on the Wii Fit. She reversed her steps.

Ester stood on the board, doing her best to place one foot in front of the other. Her gray-headed avatar mimicked her movements.

"What do you mean? I don't play Wii," Dawn said.

Ester teetered. "I'm talking about second chances is all."

"It sounds like you're talking about more than the game you're playing," Dawn said, tucking her hands into her pockets. She wore her favorite angora sweater with a front pocket muffler. She needed all the comfort she could get. A broken heart wasn't an easy thing to deal with. She knew all the tricks of getting over a guy. Comfy clothes. Ice cream. Liquor.

"Just in general." Ester pressed her lips together. The game was reflected in her glasses so Dawn couldn't read her eyes to determine her intent. "Sometimes I've needed a do over. Maybe you need one, too."

She felt her aggravation rise. She didn't need advice from a smart-mouthed geriatric. "Maybe I need a lot of things. Maybe I need a new job."

Ester cackled. "Maybe you do. But *I* don't think so."

Then Ester reached up and turned her hearing aid off.

Dawn had been dismissed.

Dawn blew out a breath. Great. Everybody wanted to give her advice about Tyson. It had started with Nellie. Then Jack. Even Andrew suggested it was Karen who'd made the moves. Had Dawn jumped to conclusions? Maybe. But she didn't think so. She stood firm. The man had taken that woman in his arms and kissed her. Okay, it was on the forehead, but still. Didn't look like anything but a new beginning for them.

She'd been a fool.

Again.

She stomped toward the kitchen, determined to put the mistake she'd made from her mind.

"Hey, I found the eyeglasses kit. Mr. Murray had

left it out back. It was underneath the swing covered by leaves. Lucky my eyes are good. Hey, what's with you?" Margo asked.

"Just Ester. It's nothing."

She smiled and handed over the kit. "It's never nothing with Ester. The woman was born to irritate."

"Yeah, I'd argue with her, but she turned her hearing aid off. Maybe I should get one of those for when I want to tune the world out."

Margo laughed. "Well, hang around long enough and you'll likely get one."

Dawn shrugged on her jacket and wrapped the scarf Nellie had knit for her around her neck. "I'm heading to the package place. Need anything while I'm out?"

"We're out of coffee."

Emergency. If she needed anything other than tequila to get through a heartache, it was the warmth of a good brew. "I'll stop by the grocery."

Dawn headed out, dropped off the package and made it inside the Shop and Save with no problem. She was glad. Her eyes still looked puffy from crying and she didn't want to make small talk. Too bad, she ran into Betty Monk on the coffee aisle. The woman loved to gossip. And never could remember her name.

"Hey, there, Donna," Betty called. "Did you have a good Thanksgiving, darlin'?"

Dawn nodded. "It was fine. How about you?"

"Fantastic. Kitty Lou made the best dressing you've ever put in your mouth. She took that recipe right out of that South Carolina cooking woman's cookbook. You know the one with the big hair? And the bright blue eyes?"

Dawn wasn't sure if she meant Kitty Lou or Paula Deen. "Well, sounds like it was good."

"I heard your boyfriend's ex-wife had dinner with y'all and he broke your ex-husband's nose. That must have been fun." Betty blinked at her with eyes rimmed with too much eyeliner. Her painted-on eyebrows arched high.

"Um…you know, I really need to get going. Margo's waiting for me to bring her…toilet paper. It's an emergency."

"Well, darling, you're in the wrong aisle. But, hey, don't you go letting that ex-wife get the better of you, you hear? If a man's worth it, you gotta hold on to him, honey." Betty's words rang out. Dawn knew everyone from aisle four to seven likely heard. She wanted to slink out. But she needed that coffee in the worst way. And now toilet paper, too.

She picked up the items and got in the express line. Only two people were in front of her and she didn't know either one of them. Thank God.

"Well, hey, Dawn," Emma Long said, grabbing the coffee and sweeping it over the scanner. "You have a nice Thanksgiving?"

Dawn wanted to say something along the lines of "You know I didn't," but bit her tongue. Instead she smiled and nodded.

"Oh, good. We did, too. Avery fried a turkey. It was so good we don't have any leftovers for turkey salad. Oh, I like this kind of toilet paper. It's worth the price."

Emma scanned the toilet paper and punched a few buttons on the register. "Yeah, I had to go through a couple of kinds before I found the right one. Sometimes you just have to do that. Go through a lot of different ones. But when you find the right one, well, nothing else will do, will it?"

Dawn didn't really want to discuss toilet paper. She

didn't want to discuss anything. She wanted to drive out to Jack's ranch, pull on her ratty flannel pajamas and throw the quilts over her head. She didn't want to deal with life. She wanted to avoid it. Unfortunately, life wasn't going to wait on her to get over Tyson. The world kept turning. Buying toilet paper and making idle conversation.

Emma smiled. "That will be $12.78."

Dawn slid her debit card through the machine.

"Yep. Once you find the right one, you can't go back," Emma said, her eyes finding Dawn's. Finally, Dawn understood. Emma wasn't talking about toilet paper.

Dawn opened her mouth, but couldn't think of a thing to say.

Emma handed her the receipt and the bag. "Here you are. Have a good day, Dawn. And try to find it in your heart to give him a second chance."

Dawn couldn't reply. Emma had already turned to Betty Monk who grinned at her like an elderly Kewpie doll.

Dawn stood there for a moment, holding the bag of coffee and toilet paper, and wondered what in the hell had happened. People in Oak Stand must have gotten a hold of some bad turkey. Or they didn't have anything better to do than meddle in everyone else's business. What had happened between her and Tyson wasn't anybody else's business.

Last night, she'd chucked out her earlier reasons for staying in Oak Stand, deciding she needed to get back to Houston. She was a city girl. She had no business in Small Town, U.S.A.

But deep down, she didn't want to leave.

She liked her job.

She liked her life in the simple town.

And she loved Tyson.

Her heart crumbled as the doors swooshed open. Tyson walked in and Laurel trailed behind him.

No way.

Surprise registered on his face. Laurel looked up from tapping on her phone and stared. *Uncomfortable* wasn't even the word. There was no word for the moment.

Dawn ripped her gaze from his broad shoulders and hurt eyes. He'd made his bed. And now he could lie in Karen's. Because Dawn's bed was no longer available. Neither was her heart. It was closed. Not just temporarily, but in a condemned, no-one-else-is-going-in sort of way.

"Dawn." His voice was soft.

She ignored him and slipped out of the store before the tears could fall.

Broken hearts sucked.

CHAPTER TWENTY

HERMAN THE CHIHUAHUA SAT on the back porch, licking his dainty paws. He was the ugliest of dogs, so homely, in fact, people couldn't help but love him.

The Sandersons had outfitted him with a bright red Christmas collar. A note was attached.

Dawn pulled it loose as Tyson pulled his truck into the drive.

He climbed out of the truck, gave her a cursory glance, then headed around the front of the house, holding his tool kit. His dismissal said it all. Laurel slid from the passenger seat and followed behind him, as silent as a monk. She didn't even have her phone in hand.

Dawn sighed. Tyson was working. He had a job to do. Just like she did. No time for nursing wounded pride or overthinking bad decisions.

She glanced down at the note in her hand which said something about needing to go out on a limb to pick the fruit. Herman blinked up at her in expectation.

Great. Now the dog was giving her advice.

She knew why she shouldn't go out on a limb. Because the damn thing would break and she'd end up bruised and battered. Better to stick to admiring the fruit from afar and eating something from a package. Like a Snickers bar.

Dawn gave Herman a pat on the head and balled up the paper. Someone was up to something. The whole town couldn't be in on it. Or could it? Who would have rallied the troops?

Tyson?

No. She couldn't see him doing something so… strange. But she knew who would. Someone who knew this town. Nellie. But how had she accomplished it so quickly?

"Dawn? You out there?" Margo called from inside the center.

"Coming," Dawn responded. She pulled the bag holding her purchases from the patio chair and went inside.

Mass confusion met her. Ester had Christmas lights stretched across the parlor, and several of the elderly men held pruning shears which they used to lop off jutting branches on the tree sitting in front of the double windows of the parlor. Grady stood to one side, directing everyone while Rufus Stevens played carols on the piano.

"We're putting up the Christmas tree Tyson brought by earlier," Grace called as she tried to untangle a ball of ornament hooks.

"I see," Dawn said, rubbing her temples. She'd forgotten today kicked off the Christmas season. Funny, how having one's heart yanked from one's chest made everything else fade into white noise. Yep, blue Christmas on its way.

Laurel came through the front door, juggling boxes of what looked to be more Christmas lights. The girl's hair had been caught in a low ponytail, making her look much younger than she usually did. She flashed a smile at Ester. Her braces gleamed in the twinkle lights.

"Right here, honey. I'll check all those in a moment," Ester said, patting a spot right next to her on the settee.

Tyson's daughter sank down and started taking the cardboard lids off the boxes.

"My Grammy boxed these up years ago. Gramps hadn't gotten these decorations down from his attic in so long. I'm glad he's letting y'all use them. I think they're pretty," Laurel said, handing a strand of old-fashioned large bulb lights to Ester.

"Not as pretty as you are, though, honey." The older woman patted Laurel's cheek and the girl beamed.

Tyson's daughter looked different.

Something warmed inside Dawn to see the young teenager so pleased to be involved. It was the way Tyson had envisioned his daughter many times—a young girl with a tendril of joy wrapped around her. For once, genuineness shone on Laurel's face.

"Why, they *are* pretty! Look at these," Grace said, holding up several crocheted angels. "I think Annie must have made them."

Dawn moved into the room. Laurel caught sight of her and her smile faltered. Dawn took an angel from Grace, fingering the intricate crocheted lace. "Yes, handmade and exquisite. Thank you for letting us borrow them, Grady."

"Weren't doing a bit of good up in the attic sitting underneath that old moose head," Grady said. "Laurel suggested we bring them here."

Dawn looked at Tyson's daughter. "Thank you, Laurel."

The girl's cheeks pinkened slightly as she ducked her head. "You're welcome."

The glow that had started inside Dawn spread, filling her with warmth. For the first time since she'd spied Tyson with Karen, she smiled.

"Dawn, you'll help us, won't you?" Ester asked as

she picked through a box of extra bulbs. "Margo went to make hot chocolate, and we need someone to start wrapping these lights around the tree."

Dawn gave Ester a salute. She should let the woman run the center. She ordered everyone around anyway.

"I'll help you," Laurel said, grabbing a strand from Ester and meeting Dawn at the tree. "I'll stand on this side and hand them to you."

"Thanks," Dawn said, taking the extension cord Grady stuck in her hand. She couldn't figure out what had come over Laurel. The girl looked eager to please. Like a magic wand had been waved.

Several minutes passed as Rufus continued to pound out the carols. Several of the ladies sang along, their shaky sopranos a bit off-key. Margo emerged with a tray of hot chocolate and handed the steaming cups to participants while Laurel and Dawn silently wrapped the lights about the large tree.

"I'm sorry," Laurel murmured passing the strand to Dawn.

"No problem. I'll catch that spot on the next pass."

The girl held the lights and looked at Dawn. "No, I mean, I'm sorry for acting like…I don't know…a butt-hole this whole time."

Dawn stopped positioning the lights and looked at Laurel. "Oh."

The girl's cheeks were definitely pink. "I mean, I shouldn't have acted so—" she lowered her voice and leaned closer "—bitchy."

Dawn pressed her lips together to prevent the smile trying to emerge. Laurel pulled back and studied a way-ward branch.

"I was unfriendly to you for no good reason. I just—"

Laurel sighed "—I just don't know how things are supposed to go anymore in my life. You know?"

"I know. Life can hit you over the head sometimes."

Cheating ex-husbands, failed business ventures and broken hearts. Life could definitely rough a person up. But Dawn had sworn she would not be defeated. She'd even dared to hope again. Hope that Tyson would be different. Her third time's the charm guy.

Laurel's gaze finally met hers. "It's been crazy for me. Like everything got turned upside down. My dad being gone. Mom and Corbin. Dad moving away. It's got me—"

"Spinning?" Dawn finished for her. "Yeah, you know, things have got me spinning here lately, too."

Dawn continued tugging the string of lights through the inner branches of the fragrant pine. Sap glimmered on the trunk, ensuring a sweet fragrance though she knew she'd have to mind the ornaments didn't get ruined.

"I've made things harder for my dad. He and I talked about stuff last night. First time in a long time."

Dawn was proud of Tyson for meeting the problems with his daughter head-on. Yesterday must have been a catalyst for both of them.

"He's had it hard. I mean, what my mom did wasn't cool. I knew it back then, but I didn't know what to say. I was just a little kid."

Dawn stifled another smile, but didn't say anything. Laurel was still just a kid. In so many ways.

"I felt bad for Daddy when he came home from Iraq. I think he knew my mom had done something wrong. I didn't know what to do to make him feel better. I tried, but I was so mad at him. Like he could change everything to how it had been before he left, but he didn't want to."

Dawn finally spoke. "Well, you were in a bad situation. None of it your doing."

"Yeah, I know. But still, I haven't been acting too nice. My therapist told Mom it was, like, normal. I guess I just allowed my anger to make me sorta out of control."

"I think it's very mature of you to recognize it."

Laurel nodded. "Yeah, I've been thinking about a lot of things here lately. Mostly about Dad. He's been unhappy for a while, but when I got here, I could tell something was different."

Dawn felt her heart leap at the girl's words. Like an inflatable raft with the first puff of air, life stirred, unsticking the collapsed parts. She could feel tears in the back of her throat.

"He was happy again. And I could see the way he looked at you. You know, that look the guy gets in the movie when he stares at the girl he just saved. Right before they kiss and stuff." Laurel paused and fingered one of the bright Christmas bulbs. "This place makes him happy."

Dawn cleared her throat. "It's a special town."

Laurel nodded. "Yeah. When I was little, we visited all the time. I rode horses and went fishing and stuff. I like it here."

"I do, too." Dawn glanced back at the clients of her center. They smiled and sang along with the carols, feeling purpose, feeling alive. Nellie had done a good thing with the center. And at that moment, Dawn knew Tucker House was exactly where she belonged. Something bad had brought her to Oak Stand, but something good kept her here. She'd stay here. Build her future here.

"My dad's miserable, Mrs. Taggart." Laurel's blue eyes, so like her mother's, were plaintive. "Maybe you could talk to him."

Dawn looked hard at Tyson's daughter, so pretty, young and intent on making amends. And that's when she felt the dam of emotions break, flooding her with the sweetest, most intense sense of rightness.

Of conviction.

She loved Tyson.

And that was all she needed to know at that moment.

"My dad's upstairs, staining the bookcases," Laurel said, giving her an encouraging smile.

Dawn smiled. "Maybe I should go see if he wants some hot chocolate."

"Yeah." Laurel's smile stretched into a grin.

Grady appeared at her elbow as if summoned. "Let me help this grandbaby finish up the tree. I haven't strung lights in twenty years."

Dawn handed him the bundle of lights. "Then I better let you get back into practice. Laurel seems the kind of girl who expects things to be decorated in her life."

"Yep, she's a real ballbuster like her grandmother."

"Grady!" Dawn sputtered.

Laurel and Grady started laughing. Dawn shook her head and turned toward the stairs.

Time to talk to Tyson.

TYSON SLID THE BRUSH along the wood in even strokes, taking special care not to come in contact with the freshly painted baseboard. He'd have to do a few touch-ups, but he wanted to minimize the amount of time he'd spend cleaning up his mistakes.

He needed to finish this job on time. If only because of Dawn.

He sighed as he dipped the paintbrush into the golden oak stain. How would he survive the censure in her eyes every time he looked her way? How could he stand seeing her each day as she smiled warmly and stopped to assist a client at the center? How would he endure her scent in the air, the curve of her backside, the plumpness of her lips?

He couldn't fathom it.

The monotony of the painting calmed him. He'd given his workers the day off, so the room was quiet. Perfect for thinking. Which was likely not a good thing.

Music filtered up the stairs along with the chatter of the elderly clients. He heard Margo announce hot chocolate was ready then he heard his grandfather and Laurel laugh.

His heart swelled to hear his daughter's laughter. Laurel. Something had happened with her over the course of the past twenty-four hours. He figured she and Karen had had a little heart-to-heart. It had made his daughter lighter, more accepting. She'd even left her cell phone in the truck. And she'd actually agreed with him when he said they should buy a huge blow-up Christmas Snoopy for the front lawn. He'd nearly fallen over in the middle of the Shop and Save.

He set the brush on a piece of cardboard so he could stretch his stiff shoulder then realized he wasn't alone.

Dawn stood in the open doorway with a steaming mug.

"Hey," she said, her voice as soft as the expression in her eyes. She looked different. No censure. No stubborn tilt. No radiating ire.

"Hi."

"It's looking really good in here." She stepped into the room and glanced around.

He took her in like a dying man takes in water. She wore a fuzzy dark pink sweater that was worn at the elbows. Her hair spilled about her shoulders and she had circles under her eyes. Still, she was the prettiest thing he'd seen this side of the Mississippi.

"Getting there," he said, walking toward the kitchen to where the granite countertops had just been installed. He ran a hand over the surface, sweeping away construction dust. "Do you like the counters?"

Dawn strolled toward him. She glanced at the surface beneath his hand. "They're beautiful."

"And the windows? I think the window company did a nice job preserving the original look." He watched as her eyes flitted toward the beveled walnut windows. She licked her lips and he felt himself stir. Damn. He had to control himself. He couldn't get hard every time Dawn ran her tongue over her delicious mouth. He saw many cold showers in his future.

"They're lovely," she said. Her fingers slid through her hair, pushing it behind her ears. He knew what that meant. She was nervous. "Hot chocolate?"

He took the mug but didn't take a sip. "So the bookcases will be dry by tomorrow. I'll come put another coat on them so we can install the hardware on Monday."

"I should have listened to you."

Something lurched in his chest before he could tell himself she likely spoke about the construction of the room. "About what?"

"Yesterday. I should have listened to you. Let you explain what happened."

He wiped the dust from his fingertips as relief

flooded him. Maybe they could salvage the disaster of Thanksgiving. "Yeah, you should have."

She had the decency to turn the color of her sweater. "Yeah, wasn't my best moment. All I can say is that I was really angry."

"Out of control," he said, hooking his thumbs in his pocket and leaning against the island in the middle of the kitchen.

"You do that to me. Make me feel out of control. Schedules, intentions, reason all fly out the door when you are around. I can't believe I'm admitting this," she said, shaking her head. Her smile quivered when she turned it on him.

"That's not necessarily bad," he said.

She shrugged. "Sometimes it's not. Sometimes I like to be out of control. Just not in that way."

He'd seen her out of control. He'd enjoyed those ministrations a whole lot. "So…"

"So, I'm sorry I didn't listen to you. That I didn't allow you to explain. I thought with my head, not my heart." Moisture trembled on her lashes.

"I've been trying to get you to listen to your heart all along." He smiled. "I'll forgive you if you'll forgive me for being an idiot to begin with."

A small furrow appeared between her eyes.

"I shouldn't have kissed Karen even if it was only on the forehead. I don't know how to explain why I did it. I'd just sent the papers. The divorce is final. But it hadn't sunk in for her. She thought she could say she was sorry and she wanted me back and everything would be the way it was. But she was wrong. It was a strange moment. It was the end. What you witnessed was nothing but a farewell."

Dawn pressed her lips together. "It didn't look like

nothing. It looked so tender. Like a beginning, not an end."

"But it was the end. Karen and I have to remain friends. Laurel is too important to both of us. I loved Karen once, but I don't love her anymore."

"Still, it knocked me back on my heels. I felt so torn apart. So vulnerable." Dawn's eyes were pools of pain and his heart literally clutched for this woman he'd hurt, this woman he'd fallen in love with.

"I hate feeling that way," she said, wrapping her arms about herself. "I've felt that way too much."

"But you forget that I've felt that way, too. I was on the receiving end of being betrayed. I get what you feel, but I can't take what happened back. I wish I could because I never wanted to hurt you, Dawn."

For a moment they stood gathered in their thoughts. Tyson wanted to be careful with his words, make her understand how much she meant to him, but he couldn't think of the right way to explain everything that had occurred between them. How could he tell her she was his destiny? That he knew this as surely as he knew the sun would set in a matter of hours. Especially when she was so damned scared. "I'm in love with you, Dawn."

At his words, her shoulders sagged and the tears fell. "How can you say something so... I feel so—" She stopped. Something passed between. Something so sweet and simple. Something that no words could ever capture. It was like the ribbon of healing that had been wrapped around them had come unwound, revealing a new and perfect love.

She wiped her cheeks. "I'm afraid."

He stepped toward her and tilted her chin up so her pretty brown eyes met his. "Everyone's afraid, baby."

"I do love you, Tyson. You make me feel strong. And good. And new."

He lowered his head and pressed a soft kiss to her lips. She met his kiss, pushing herself against him, wrapping her arms about his neck. His hands found her waist and tugged her whole body to his, fitting her against him. As she was meant to fit.

He deepened the kiss, allowing his tongue to invade the heat of her mouth. She tasted so good. So like Dawn. Sweet and damned tempting.

He broke the kiss and smiled at her. "See? That's a beginning."

Her eyes glowed in the waning light of the day. "So that's what a beginning feels like?"

"Yep. And just wait till you get to the middle. It's going to be even better."

"Juggling our family, this town and our jobs—"

"We'll do it together. A united team."

She arched an eyebrow. "You sound sure about that."

"I am. As certain as I can be." He tucked a strand of hair behind her ear. "Taking a chance can be hard for everyone. I know you've been hurt, but lots of people have been hurt and they go on, putting one foot in front of the other. They don't ignore love or avoid it."

"I wasn't trying to avoid— Okay, I *was* trying to avoid love. I wanted to make my world a little more stable. Even though I know I love you, it still feels like I'm climbing into a roller coaster. It feels—"

"Like love should," he finished for her.

Dawn smiled. "I do like roller coasters."

"See? I'm already learning new things about you. So buckle up and get ready to scream," he said, dropping little kisses on her forehead, nose, mouth.

"I'm guessing y'all don't need this?"

They both turned their heads to where Laurel stood in the doorway. She waved a pathetic piece of mistletoe in one hand.

Tyson bent his head and gave Dawn a peck. "Nope."

Laurel rolled her eyes. "Jeez. Don't go grossing me out, Dad."

He dropped his arms from Dawn. "I don't need that for Dawn, but I might need that mistletoe for you."

He leaped toward Laurel who shrieked, threw the parasitic sprig at him, and flew down the hallway toward the stairs. Tyson thundered after her making kissing noises.

The girl's laughter was the icing on Dawn's cake. The big cake she'd made for herself in her head. The one that said Happy Ever After.

She couldn't believe it. Yesterday, her world had crashed around her. Today, it had been resurrected with three little words.

Tyson loved her.

Dawn reveled in the glow. She'd finally found her place in the world. In Oak Stand, Texas. In the arms of the man she loved.

She wasn't going to overthink it. She was just going to do it.

She mentally clicked that safety belt in place. She was ready for the ride.

EPILOGUE

DAWN KNOTTED THE TIES on the last of the trash bags and sank onto the settee in the parlor. She and Tyson were the last people left at the center after the Tucker House Holiday Extravaganza. Her toes ached in the new boots she'd bought and her voice was scratchy from singing karaoke with Ester. The woman did a mean Elvis Presley impersonation.

The King was likely rolling in his grave. Or on that private island he'd escaped to. Whichever.

But Dawn had never been happier.

Tyson turned off the parlor light so only the glow from the Christmas tree lit the room. He sank onto the settee beside Dawn, wrapping one arm around her and pulling her close so she rested against him. "Whew, you throw quite a party, lady."

"It was fun. They loved it, didn't they?"

"Who knew they were such karaoke fans? Poor Rufus pulled a muscle on his tribute to show tunes. I had to get him a heat pack."

She laughed as she snuggled closer into his warmth. Tyson was like a constant well-tended fire, always warming her, lighting her fire, physically and emotionally.

"Did you like the gift?"

She chuckled. Tyson had given her a beautiful red leather daily planner. "It's totally appropriate."

"You're not disappointed?"

She shook her head. How could she be disappointed? Tyson was as he'd always been. The steadfast guy. The one she'd always needed. No fancy lingerie or flashy jewelry would ever be beneath her Christmas tree. Only well-thought-out gifts that suited her nature and needs. "No way. I need a new one of those."

"I guess you didn't look through it?"

She shook her head as a niggling of something popped into her mind. What had he put in her planner?

She sprang from his arms and crossed the room to where she'd set the bag containing her gift. She pulled the planner from the depths and returned to Tyson.

"Did you schedule something for me?" she asked, wriggling into her original position. She fit perfectly beneath his arm.

"I don't know. You'd better look," he said. She could hear the smile in his voice. She fingered the gilded "D" on the front cover before leafing through the pages. She thumbed through January, February and March with no sign of anything unusual. "I don't see anything."

"Check out May."

She turned to May and started through the weeks. At the end of the month she found something that made her swallow.

Hard.

"I know how you like to plan everything. I hope you don't find it too presumptuous, but that was Grady and Annie's wedding day."

Dawn turned her eyes on him. "Wedding day?"

He shifted and pulled a box from the depths of his pants pocket. "It's a little early. Not yet Christmas. But I bought this in Jefferson. I don't think I can wait any longer."

He opened the box and a square emerald winked at

her in the festive light of the tree. "Dawn Claire, I love you more than I ever thought I could love a woman. Will you marry me?"

The emotion swirling within her nearly choked her. She could feel the tears coming, the sob lingering at the back of her throat. Her heart contracted so hard in her chest that she pressed a trembling hand to it.

Tyson wanted to marry her.

"I—I—it's too fast. I don't want to—"

He pressed a finger against her lips. "No more, Dawn. No more being scared. We're in this together."

She swallowed again and looked into his whiskey eyes. They were so warm, so certain.

"Look at the ring."

She did. It was gorgeous. Square-cut emerald flanked by two rounded diamonds. It was obviously an antique, set in white gold with small etchings.

"I saw it in a window and knew it belonged on your finger. No traditional diamond for my Dawn. You are unique. And I saw the promise in the stone. It's green, like life. A symbol of what you have given back to me."

The tears trembling on her lashes fell. This man got her. This man was the right one. So worth the risk. Finally.

"Yes," she croaked. "Yes, I'll marry you."

His lips brushed hers as he removed the ring from the box and slid it onto her left hand. No cold metal, only warmth from the ring. It felt as if it had always belonged there.

And she knew that she belonged in Tyson's arms.

And on May 28 she'd make it official. She'd stay in his arms forever.

She had to. It was already scheduled in her planner.

* * * * *

HARLEQUIN® *Super Romance*®

COMING NEXT MONTH

Available January 11, 2011

REQUEST YOUR FREE BOOKS!

2 FREE NOVELS PLUS 2 FREE GIFTS!

HARLEQUIN®

Super Romance®

Exciting, emotional, unexpected!

YES! Please send me 2 FREE Harlequin® Superromance® novels and my 2 FREE gifts (gifts are worth about $10). After receiving them, if I don't wish to receive any more books, I can return the shipping statement marked "cancel." If I don't cancel, I will receive 6 brand-new novels every month and be billed just $4.69 per book in the U.S. or $5.24 per book in Canada. That's a saving of at least 15% off the cover price! It's quite a bargain! Shipping and handling is just 50¢ per book.* I understand that accepting the 2 free books and gifts places me under no obligation to buy anything. I can always return a shipment and cancel at any time. Even if I never buy another book from Harlequin, the two free books and gifts are mine to keep forever.

135/336 HDN E5P4

Name	(PLEASE PRINT)	
Address		Apt. #
City	State/Prov.	Zip/Postal Code

Signature (if under 18, a parent or guardian must sign)

Mail to the **Harlequin Reader Service:**
IN U.S.A.: P.O. Box 1867, Buffalo, NY 14240-1867
IN CANADA: P.O. Box 609, Fort Erie, Ontario L2A 5X3

Not valid for current subscribers to Harlequin Superromance books.
**Are you a current subscriber to Harlequin Superromance books
and want to receive the larger-print edition?
Call 1-800-873-8635 today!**

* Terms and prices subject to change without notice. Prices do not include applicable taxes. N.Y. residents add applicable sales tax. Canadian residents will be charged applicable provincial taxes and GST. Offer not valid in Quebec. This offer is limited to one order per household. All orders subject to approval. Credit or debit balances in a customer's account(s) may be offset by any other outstanding balance owed by or to the customer. Please allow 4 to 6 weeks for delivery. Offer available while quantities last.

Your Privacy: Harlequin Books is committed to protecting your privacy. Our Privacy Policy is available online at www.eHarlequin.com or upon request from the Reader Service. From time to time we make our lists of customers available to reputable third parties who may have a product or service of interest to you. If you would prefer we not share your name and address, please check here. ☐

Help us get it right—We strive for accurate, respectful and relevant communications. To clarify or modify your communication preferences, visit us at www.ReaderService.com/consumerschoice.

HSR10R

HARLEQUIN®

A Romance

FOR EVERY MOOD™

Spotlight on

Classic

Quintessential, modern love stories
that are romance at its finest.

See the next page
to enjoy a sneak peek from
the Harlequin Presents® series.

*Harlequin Presents® is thrilled
to introduce the first installment of
an epic tale of passion and drama by*
**USA TODAY Bestselling Author
Penny Jordan***!*

*When buttoned-up Giselle first meets
the devastatingly handsome Saul Parenti,
the heat between them is explosive....*

"LET ME GET THIS STRAIGHT. Are you actually suggesting
that I would stoop to that kind of game playing?"

Saul came out from behind his desk and walked toward
her. Giselle could smell his hot male scent and it was making
her dizzy, igniting a low, dull, pulsing ache that was taking
over her whole body.

Giselle defended her suspicions. "You don't want me here."

"No," Saul agreed, "I don't."

And then he did what he had sworn he would not do,
cursing himself beneath his breath as he reached for her,
pulling her fiercely into his arms and kissing her with all
the pent-up fury she had aroused in him from the moment
he had first seen her.

Giselle certainly *wanted* to resist him. But the hand she
raised to push him away developed a will of its own and
was sliding along his bare arm beneath the sleeve of his
shirt, and the body that should have been arching away
from him was instead melting into him.

Beneath the pressure of his kiss he could feel and taste
her gasp of undeniable response to him. He wanted to
devour her, take her and drive them both until they were
equally satiated—even whilst the anger within him that
she should make him feel that way roared and burned its

resentment of his need.

She was helpless, Giselle recognized, totally unable to withstand the storm lashing at her, able only to cling to the man who was the cause of it and pray that she would survive.

Somewhere else in the building a door banged. The sound exploded into the sensual tension that had enclosed them, driving them apart. Saul's chest was rising and falling as he fought for control; Giselle's whole body was trembling.

Without a word she turned and ran.

Find out what happens when Saul and Giselle succumb to their irresistible desire in

THE RELUCTANT SURRENDER

Available January 2011 from Harlequin Presents®

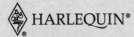

HARLEQUIN®

American ★ Romance®

C.C. COBURN
Colorado Cowboy

American Romance's
Men of the West

It had been fifteen years since Luke O'Malley,
divorced father of three, last saw his high school
sweetheart, Megan Montgomery. Luke is shocked to
discover they have a son, Cody, a rebellious teen on his
way to juvenile detention. The last thing either of them
expected was nuptials. Will these strangers rekindle
their love or is the past too far behind them?

**Available January
wherever books are sold.**

"LOVE, HOME & HAPPINESS"

www.eHarlequin.com

har75341

Love Inspired®

Bestselling author

JILLIAN HART

brings readers another heartwarming story
from

the
GRANGER
FAMILY
RANCH

To fulfill a sick boy's wish, rodeo star Tucker Granger surprises
little Owen in the hospital. And no one is more surprised than
single mother Sierra Baker. But somehow Tucker ropes her heart
and fills it with hope. Hope that this country girl and her son
can lasso the roaming bronc rider into their family forever.

Look for

His Country Girl

*Available January
wherever books are sold.*

www.SteepleHill.com

Steeple
Hill®

LI87643